INTO THE BLACK

ALSO BY BETH BARANY

HENRIETTA THE DRAGON SLAYER SERIES

Henrietta The Dragon Slayer

Henrietta and The Dragon Stone

Henrietta and the Battle of the Horse Mesa

TOUCHSTONE OF LOVE SERIES

Touchstone of Love

A Christmas Fling

Parisian Amour

A Labyrinth of Love and Roses

A Cupcake Christmas

WRITER'S FUN ZONE SERIES

Plan Your Novel Like A Pro: And Have Fun Doing It!

Twitter for Authors: Social Media Book Marketing Strategies for Shy Writers

The Writer's Adventure Guide: 12 Stages to Writing Your Book

Overcome Writer's Block: A Self-Guided Creative Writing Class to Get You Writing Again

ALSO BY WRITER'S FUN ZONE PUBLISHING

Mastering Deep Point of View: Simple Steps to Make Your Stories Irresistible to Your Readers by Alice Gaines, *USA Today* Bestselling Author

INTO THE BLACK

A JANEY MCCALLISTER MYSTERY, BOOK 1

BETH BARANY

FIREWOLF
BOOKS

FIREWOLF BOOKS
771 Kingston Ave., #108
Piedmont, California, 94611
www.firewolfbooks.com

SIGN UP HERE FOR NEW RELEASE NEWS:
http://bethb.net/itbfr

COVER DESIGN by Nada Orlic
BOOK DESIGN by Beth Barany

ISBN: 978-1-944841-27-0 (ebook)
ISBN: 978-1-944841-30-0 (print)

For all the star dreamers and way bringers.

ONE

FROM HER ELEVATED VANTAGE POINT ON THE stairs, Janey McCallister, lead investigator of L'Étoile's security team, scanned the crowd of gamblers for the elusive pickpocket—the thief who'd been striking every night for the last few weeks. She didn't see him, but he was down there somewhere, hunting for his next mark. She had to find him before he stole from another guest and cost the casino more business.

And before she was fired.

She was facing a three-strikes-and-you're-out scenario.

What the stardust!

She wasn't a green recruit anymore, but she'd already messed up twice since she arrived on the L'Étoile space station twenty-five days ago—and on her first job as a lead investigator.

Tonight, she'd make an arrest that would stick and get her back in the good graces of the chief.

On the floor below her, the immense viewscreen window flickered to life, and a deafening cheer went up.

On the casino floor, three hundred bejeweled men and women attired in tailored tuxes and evening gowns whistled and hooted at the show broadcast on the viewscreen. The heady smell of expensive alcohol and perfumes permeated the football field-sized area.

Out in space, beyond the energy shield that protected the station from cosmic rays and other hazards of space, crazy acrobats twirled for their nightly gravity-defying act. Their fantastic contortions a literally out-of-this-world spectacle. They danced with no tethers, using only jetpacks on their sleek, sparkly space suits to control their precise movements. One of the many reasons people flocked to the hotel-casino space station, L'Étoile. *The Star.*

"Sections, check in, please," Janey said in a low voice into her wrist communicator and scanned the crowd. Their attention was on the show.

"Section Two, ten-twenty-six," Security Agent Meilani Shawhan said, her tone cool. The all-clear. Section Two was off to Janey's right, near the slot machines and the exit. Security Agent Shawhan's sparkly black pantsuit and fabricated diamond necklace made her hard to pick out from the rest of the revelers.

Janey glanced again at the daring acrobats flying through space out there beyond the floor-to-ceiling viewscreen window. Itchy pain stabbed through her solar plexus like a thousand bees swarming. Panic flooded her limbs, urging her to run. She shouldn't have looked. Her damn zero-g-force phobia was back—the one she battled during space walk training at Space Wing Basic. There really was no reason for it; she loved everything else about space.

The job. *Breathe.* She could do this. She thought she had arrested the culprit—two different times, two different men. But both times, the chief had said there was not enough evidence for them to be the nightly thief, and he wrote her up, putting her back on probation. They may not have been the nightly pickpocket, but she'd certainly caught thieves. Someone must be putting pressure on the chief to release the suspects, but when she'd confronted him, the chief had merely given her a beady stare from behind his archaic eyeglasses. Who wore eyeglasses anymore?

For all her hustle, she'd landed two demerits on her work record and the enmity of her new team. And that fracking warning. One more wrong arrest and she was out, the chief warned her.

She couldn't believe it. She'd never done so poorly in a job, and she'd no idea this one would be so rigorous. She'd been expecting a low-key job—and she needed this one. For Mom. She probably would have stayed in Space Wing Command working as an MP Criminal Investigator if Mom's illness had responded to standard treatment.

No, that wasn't true. Her contract was up with Space Wing, and she'd been hungry for something new.

"Section Three, ten-twenty-six." Security Agent Antonia Lane's iridescent mermaid gown fit right in among the high roller tables in Section Three, to Janey's left. "You need to stay off the comms and let us do our job... ma'am."

"Lane—*Enough.*" Janey snapped. Then she softened her tone. "Roger that. We're all in this together." She tended to be too clipped, too military. That's what the chief had said, anyway.

Lane muttered something that sounded like, "Yah, right," but Janey let it go—for now. She'd speak to the agent later. The op came first. If this had been Space

3

Wing, Lane would have earned herself a formal warning for her backtalk.

Janey caught another glimpse of the acrobats gyrating in space. A high-pitched whine vibrated in her head—no more than a half-second—and made her ocular implant screen flicker with grey lines and white dots. Then the sound stopped, and the screen flipped back to normal.

Thank the stars, but what in Venus hell was going on? What was glitching her system?

It had to be something hardcore because her world-class implant was supposed to be unhackable. Yet, she'd had another glitch her first night on L'Étoile. She'd searched for the source in the security logs but hadn't been able to find any breaches or anomalies—not that her hacking skills were anything but average. Venus hells—the glitch was messing with her focus.

In her previous attempts to catch the thief, she'd left her team behind and gone undercover, after learning that no one had tried working the case covertly. But flying solo hadn't worked either. So, she'd brought in the rest of the team. Tonight, either she'd catch one of the previous men in the act or apprehend someone new, with enough evidence to convince the chief to approve the arrest.

"Kou?" Janey prompted.

"Oh, yes, ma'am. Section Four, ten-twenty-six also." Security Agent Eduard Kou cleared his throat. He was above them, in the overwatch position on the mezzanine.

"Is there anything else, Kou?" Janey asked.

"No, ma'am."

Kou hadn't given her a hard time about messing up the first two arrests. He'd rather be relaxing with his buddies than working, though he did his job competently enough from what she'd seen these past few weeks. In his tux with a shimmery bright green cummerbund and matching bow tie, he looked like someone's favorite uncle or big brother, with a kindly smile for everyone.

The full-immersion pop music accelerated, thumping through the floors and walls of the cavernous casino. Another cheer went up.

Janey admired the acrobats' courage and athleticism, but after the first night aboard, she couldn't watch the show anymore. As it had the previous nights, her heart rate jumped, and her breathing picked up at the thought of whirling weightless in the void, no connection to anything solid.

No up or down. No control. No answers.

You're not thirteen anymore, Janey, and flat on your back, blind in the hospital in Spaceport Las Cruces. You're thirty-two years old and a former Lieutenant Commander of Space Wing Command Orbital Criminal Investigative Unit.

It was 2130, dammit.

Work, here and now. *Breathe and blink,* she commanded herself.

A waiter rushed past, a tray full of highballs of caffeinated fizzy vodka, its pungent fruity aroma in his wake. The lights dimmed, and the viewscreen brightened as the music rumbled louder. She'd worked during the show enough since arriving about a month ago to know that she had twenty minutes until its end. Time enough to catch a pickpocket in the act. If they felt invisible as they moved through the riveted crowd, they might be less careful.

"Nineteen minutes left," Janey said through the comm, though she didn't really need to remind them.

From her periphery, she spotted a flash of red and black—a movement out of place. Perhaps someone was shoving their way through the crowd.

With a mental command, Janey focused her ocular implant to scan, but there was no one in red and black, no further movement out of place. First, the glitches, and now this. Never in all the nearly twenty years since she'd had her state-of-the-art artificial right eye had anything like this happened. Minor, but troubling. It had to be more than space dust. She'd run another diagnostic as soon as she got off duty.

More oohing and aahing by the crowd. The show was winding down. Guests in their dazzling silks and classic black tuxes, wrapped in twinkling jewels and real furs, sipped drinks and whispered in excitement to each other. Still no conspicuous movement.

As the guests turned their heads in profile to chat, their hotel records flashed in the corner of Janey's ocular screen. All looked normal, except one—a Ms. Eliza Jamon, listed as a hotel guest, not as a staff member.

Eliza had introduced herself as Beliza Ramon and had traveled via StarEl, the staff space elevator, along with Janey and thirty other hotel-casino staff members and asteroid miners a month ago. Now under a false name, Beliza was mingling with guests as if she were one herself, in an iridescent, sleeveless black gown fringed in a sparkly green fringe.

Beliza chatted and giggled with the women around her. As she watched the show, her posture relaxed. Beliza most likely wasn't her pickpocket, but maybe she was up to something else. And what had she been doing for the last three-plus weeks?

Starting at Earth Port in the central Pacific Ocean and during the five-day trip up in StarEl, they'd chatted several times about their exciting new jobs. Beliza had mentioned starting her new job as a supplies project manager in the hotel-casino's engineering department, then diverted the conversation to the beloved dishes she'd learned to cook at the feet of her abuelas—her *grandmothers*. Yet on Janey's ocular screen, the hotel records showed Beliza had registered as a guest under her false name the day she arrived on a business trip for a metamaterials conglomerate. No staff record matched Beliza's face.

A discrepancy? Her gut fluttered. Janey hated discrepancies. How could she do her job if the hotel records weren't accurate—or was this a security breach? Why hadn't engineering noticed that one of their staff hadn't shown up for duty? She flagged Beliza's record for the security office manager to review in the morning. No need to bother nightshift security about it. Best stay focused on the current case.

Fourteen minutes to the end of the show, when the crowd would disperse, and the pickpocket could slip away.

Janey released a breath slowly, straightening her midnight-blue silk gown, a slit down one leg. If only she could adjust the laser-sighted pistol strapped to the inside of her thigh unnoticed—to calm her nerves.

The side of her head tingled. Was someone watching her? She turned. A dark-haired man was indeed gazing at her, mesmerized, as if he knew her and had been studying her, instead of the show. After a long moment, he broke eye contact and shifted his cool gaze to the crowd, as if removed from the frivolity and the devil-may-care attitude that people sauntered around with here. He acted like he was casing the place.

He sported a black tux with a candy-cane-red silk pocket square and thin red tie to match. He was probably the one she'd noticed in her weak peripheral vision earlier, and he looked familiar.

Very familiar. Oh, yes, she distinctly remembered his strong clean-shaven jaw, those expressive lips, that very cute dimple when he'd smiled during their poker game the night she arrived on the station. She'd admired him while playing poker undercover on her first assignment—an initiation of sorts—dressed in her red cocktail dress and short brown-haired wig. From over his poker cards, his brown eyes sparkled with mischief and delight. He made her laugh, smile, relax—even as he was losing a hand and she winning it. She hadn't felt that playful in a long while. Like anything could happen, and it would be fun—an adventure.

The brown-eyed man had invited her to his room. She'd been tempted—his genteel manner, his smarts, and his humor were qualities she appreciated. If only she wasn't staff. But she was, even though she wasn't properly logged into the hotel registry yet. The chief had wanted to test her with no net.

If only guests weren't off-limits per employee regulations. She was on probation and couldn't afford to bend those regulations.

For an instant, when she was laughing and flirting with him, she'd felt carefree, light, full of hope, and full of the wish: If only this wasn't her life.

But it was her life, and love was not in the cards for her. She'd looked him up anyway in the hotel registry when she'd gotten back to her quarters—the fantasy of another life swirling in her.

He was Roberto Gonzalez. Her room's digital assistant had narrated his short hotel guest profile: a salesman in the asteroid metals business, on a three-night stay, traveling solo.

But tonight, his profile didn't pop up in the hotel registry on her implant screen. How had he managed that? Had he breached security to scrub his name? Who was this guy?

The fantasy was definitely dead.

Her chest tightened. She told her implant to take footage of him—and to scan him for any transmitters, body enhancements, or any other physical anomalies. Maybe he was working with a partner. She needed to catch him in the act.

Seven minutes left of the show.

On her screen, his heart rate and respiration displayed as normal for a man of his estimated age of thirty-five. He looked trim and healthy, so no obvious signs of subterfuge. He had one hand in his pants pocket, and his weight heavier on one foot than the other—a casual stance. But he could be trained to regulate his body. Maybe a paranoid thought, but that was the job. He didn't look ready to bolt. He gazed at the viewscreen, still and relaxed, but didn't sway or smile. He didn't seem to be caught up with the spectacle. Maybe he was thinking about a business deal. Many people combined business and pleasure on L'Étoile. He certainly looked the part of the wealthy metals industrialist his profile had described.

The music crescendoed—an even-faster beat that had the crowd cheering in anticipation of the show's finale outside the enormous window. She wouldn't, couldn't watch. Janey's heart pounded.

Yet nothing was out of place. So far. Maybe the wrist baubles thief wouldn't strike tonight.

Over a dozen hotel guests had filed reports about thefts in the previous few weeks—petty cash to them, but still, it was the principle of the thing to them. Items stolen included a Louis Vuitton multi-planetary time zone watch, several diamond wrist-phone bracelets, a women's emerald-studded band containing her engineering patents, and even a few rare pearl necklace heirlooms embedded with several generations of family records—always lifted in the crowded close quarters during the acrobats' nightly show, but only discovered and reported missing the next morning.

The thief had to be smooth, flawless in his or her ability to lift such intimate objects while blending into this crowd.

Could Gonzalez, or whatever his name was, be the pickpocket?

Three minutes left of the show.

He turned his back on her and leaned in close to speak to a tall brunette, adorned in a rainbow-sequined gown. He snaked one hand around her waist, snuggled close. The woman giggled, a half-filled flute of bubbly sloshing in one hand. An irrational flash of jealousy burst through Janey's chest but quickly vanished. Oh, for star's sake.

Janey turned her attention back to the crowd, scanning for anything out of place. A woman yawned in boredom, and the man beside her swayed, spaced-out on some mind-altering substance—indicated by how his heart rate and respiration were slow and level, as if he were sleeping.

Her implant flagged a quick movement in the crowd. Out of place, a shadow shifted. She clicked on her video. She'd get irrefutable evidence this time. Hope and determination fluttered in her chest.

A short, grey-haired man wove his way through the crowd, shoulders hunched, barely jostling people. Her implant flashed an ID: Mortimer Xang. His hotel record showed he'd arrived via space jet a week ago, and he had a room in the mid-priced level. No others in his party. He was leaving on the next transport Earthside in a few hours. Payee: Xang Enterprises.

One minute left.

He looked innocent enough, except for how one corner of his mouth quirked up in a faint smirk even though his gaze was downcast. His arms seemed pasted to the side of his body, and he took tiny steps as if to make himself even smaller.

Classic moves of a thief. Suspicious, though not evidence.

Her vid was recording, but all the other thefts had happened under the casino cameras and had not been detected.

She'd always trusted her intuition and her ability to read body cues before. But since she'd come to the station, she'd gotten it wrong twice. Should she wait for another sign that Xang was guilty? No, her gut told her he was up to something. She trusted that.

If she waited for the pickpocket to strike tonight, they could be here all night and still come up empty. She had to act now.

But if her instincts were wrong again, she'd be looking for a new job tomorrow.

"Got a possible," Janey said to her team. "Shawhan, guard the exit. Lane, converge on my position. Kou, take our six."

The team acknowledged. In her sturdy, strappy high heels, Janey glided down the stairs, wove around the poker, blackjack, and pai gow tables, and slipped through the crowd.

Head down, the salt-and-pepper-haired old man glanced sideways, not seeing Janey until she was right in front of him, blocking his path. Maybe he wasn't the thief she was hunting, maybe he was. Either way, he was hiding something. Time to find out what.

She bent down and spoke loudly into his ear. "Excuse me, sir. I need you to come with me." She caught a whiff of a faint perfume that reminded her of someone.

His gaze snapped to her, and he jolted back a step, but not before Janey noticed a slight skin color difference where his grey-white sideburns met his ears. She zoomed in with her ocular implant. His aged pale skin was mottled at the edges and clashed with his darker scalp and microscopic black hair follicles. A disguise. It was a very good prosthetic job, but most people couldn't see what she could.

She spoke again, with more force this time. "Come with me. Don't make a fuss."

He squinted up at her as if confused and spoke, his voice warbled with age. "I don't know you, do I, young lady?"

He sounded innocent and confused. Befuddled, her mother would say. But his rapid breathing, sped-up heart rate, and pupil dilation revealed something else—fear perhaps or shock. It was virtually impossible to hide the body's reaction to these emotions as they were part of the primal flight-fight-freeze responses. And he smelled odd. She still couldn't put her finger on where she'd smelled it before. There was a definite mismatch between this bent old man and the lingering sweet, fruity feminine perfume.

Then she remembered. It was the same perfume—a rare and expensive blend of pepper, ylang-ylang, vanilla, and orange accents—that had been worn by a woman she'd had in holding last week, long enough to get a good whiff and have the perfume analyzed by the in-room sensors.

"I believe you do know me," Janey said with force. "The craps table. You were dressed as a woman from New Hong Kong by way of Moscow Prime, Stephanie Lee. If that's even your real name. I banned you from the casino for card counting. Let's go."

"Who? I'm Mortimer Xang, financier." He frowned up at her. His voice shook with confusion, but his eyes narrowed for a fraction of a second, as if calculating odds of escape. Janey's ocular implant caught it. "You're talking nonsense."

"I'm not." Janey took his upper arm, but he jerked free, glared at her, and stepped back. The back of her hand brushed against his jacket and something hard under the fine black silk. That was probable cause for a search. People carried all they needed in their identity bracelets or necklaces. No one carried items in their pockets anymore.

"Stop." Janey glared. She scanned for his identity bracelet but didn't see it peeking out of his jacket cuffs.

Lane slipped in behind Xang, blocking that escape route. Xang glanced over his shoulder, gulped.

"Got your six," Kou said from behind her.

"Nowhere to go," Janey motioned ahead. "Except with us."

Boxed in, Xang stuffed his hands into pants pockets and headed for the casino exit, Lane leading the way, Janey a step behind.

Janey came alongside Xang, and using the x-ray band of her implant, she scanned the side of his body. She could only handle a millisecond scan since the x-ray frequency was dangerous and tiring, and it worked only short-range and over a small area—but it was enough.

There *was* something under his coat. Three bracelet shapes showed up on her mental screen as distinct grey outlines. She could even make out the watch face of one of them. *Yes!* She wanted to shoot a fist into the air and do a happy dance. Thank the stars. Her job was safe.

"Gotcha," she said softly, and to her team. "Shawhan, we're heading your way. You'll be back up. I'm taking in a suspect. Lane, Kou, keep working the floor."

Lane nodded and turned to watch the casino, and Kou headed deeper into the crowd.

The crowd cheered at the end of the acrobats-in-space show.

"Where are you taking me?" the thief said, his warble pitched loud over the noise. "You have no cause—"

"I do have just cause to search you." Janey leaned in and slid a hand into his inside coat pocket. She pulled out two diamond fitness tracking bracelets and a platinum-banded multi-planetary watch. *Yahtzee.* "These for me?"

"Those aren't mine!" The thief blinked rapidly, acting surprised. Maybe it wasn't an act. It seemed unlikely that someone planted them on Xang, and for Xang not know or not object if he did know.

"Then I'll take them." Janey smiled. "You're under arrest." Janey recited the rights warning. "Do you understand these rights as I've recited them to you?"

Xang grunted, glared at her, and stopped beside a poker table. Nobody paid them any attention.

"Say yes for the record." Janey lifted her wrist comm to his mouth and gripped his arm tighter than an air lock hatch. If he was going to rabbit, well, he couldn't.

"Yes," he said, his gaze shuttered. Janey led him without further fuss past the busyness at the poker tables, SkyBar, and the clanging slot machines, out into the wide lobby, thankfully less crowded. The quiet was a balm to the nerves.

Shawhan was leaning against the front desk chatting with one of the staff. When she saw Janey and the suspect, she came to attention. "Investigator McCallister."

"Shawhan, we talked about that," Janey said in a warning tone. The newest security recruit knew better than to use official titles in the public areas.

Luckily, no guests were around. The hotel owner wanted security issues handled discreetly, so his guests would feel relaxed in his peerless "Jewel of the Sky," which meant security staff had to blend in.

Janey handed the junior agent the jewelry. "Log these, and check to get a clear ID. His ident bracelet may be counterfeit. Then search his suite."

"On it." Shawhan waved her standard-issue one-inch-wide wrist comm over the suspect's identity bracelet—a thin platinum band tight around his wrist. She studied her wrist comm screen. "Mortimer Xang, double-verified, ma'am," Shawhan announced.

Jane nodded, and Shawhan hurried to the staff elevator.

"Let's go, Mr. Xang," Janey said.

"This is an outrage!" Xang exclaimed and struggled unsuccessfully to free himself of Janey's grip. "I can get you fired. I have connections to the Russian Underground." Xang glanced about the near-empty lobby, as if he expected his connections to be strolling across the Mediterranean marble floor.

Why would the resistance against the Russian dictatorship care about a fleet-fingered jewel thief?

"That's nice." Her sarcastic remark didn't seem to dent Xang as he straightened and stood tall, no longer looking like a hunched-over old man.

"Frederick Schoeneman, L'Étoile's owner, is a friend of mine," Xang said.

She knew who Schoeneman was.

"Why is it whenever I catch a guest in a lie, they bring up how chummy they are with the hotel-casino owner?" Janey said.

"Not going to help me this time, is it?" Xang sighed and stared at the blue-green swirls in the marble. Xang seemed to give up the fight. That was quick.

"Doubt it. We have evidence of items stolen over the past few weeks. And probably more evidence in your suite." Janey glared at Xang. "Meeting a buyer, were you? Who?" Scuttlebutt was that illegal trade was happening in the hotel, but so far Janey hadn't seen any evidence of it, nor any old cases on such matters.

Xang didn't answer, he only sighed, slipped off the grey wig to reveal a skullcap, and peeled away a prosthetic nose. He *was* really a she. And Janey was right, it was Lee—her facial image matched Lee's hotel record. "I need to contact my lawyer." The voice was now higher.

"Sure, once we book and hold you for the requisite twenty-four hours." Janey headed across the lobby, toward the security wing.

"You can't... I'm due on the next transport. I will complain to Schoeneman about this. I pay good money—"

"Who do you pay good money to?"

Lee firmed her mouth, as if she wanted to spill but wouldn't.

"Let's go." Janey led Lee down a side corridor and took the curve toward the center ring of the space station. All the corridors curved as the hotel was built in a circle. The guest rooms and amenities were on the outer ring, and the hotel administration offices, the security center, and all the mechanics that ran the hotel and station lived in the inner ring. The hangar and other operations took up the entire bottom level.

Was the hotel owner corrupt? Was the chief of security as corrupt as her former commander back at Space Wing? Her career had almost been ruined by the commander. Details about her first two failed arrests ran through her mind—how they got released with only a warning by the chief; how their high-powered lawyers dropped Schoeneman's name in defense of their clients. Both facts seemed suspicious.

Her stomach dropped, as if she'd taken a too-fast elevator. Not again.

How could she do her job if the hotel owner and the chief were involved in something illegal?

She had no evidence, only a hunch. No sense jumping to conclusions, not when her livelihood was at stake.

And she needed this job for both Mom's sake and her sanity. If she walked away, she'd need to find a job all over again. This position had taken a month to secure. If she lost this job, she wouldn't have enough cash reserves to pay for Mom's med treatment next month.

Once again, she had Lee in holding—a small plain room with two chairs and a table.

Lee frowned at Janey. "You can't keep me here."

Janey had to get ahead of this. She couldn't be outmaneuvered by the suspect or the chief. She had to do her job in the best interest of L'Étoile's security. Then an idea came to her. She'd have to hustle. "I don't plan to keep you here."

"What?" Lee froze.

"As soon as I get your arrest logged, I'm walking you to the transport myself. Sol Space Authority cops will pick you up Earthside." Hopefully, her former co-worker at Spaceport Las Cruces would accept her call.

Sol Space Authority was a military unit of the Sol Unified Planets government, like Space Wing was. The Sol UP government governed all peoples, Grantons, and corporate entities spread out across much of the solar system.

Lee gaped like a fish and flopped in the chair. "You have no idea what's going on here," she said with no oomph, her voice flat.

"Why don't you tell me?"

Lee fished a packet from her pants pocket, tugged out a dainty square, and wiped the greyish-white makeup from her face. "Why don't I not?"

"Doesn't matter. I have all the evidence I need. Sol Authority can handle it from here." *Hopefully*.

Lee sucked in a breath at that but continued her grooming, as if it didn't matter. But it did. Sol Authority wouldn't let this thief squirm away.

What exactly was going on here at L'Étoile?

TWO

THE NEXT MORNING, IN HER TINY BATHROOM, Janey brushed her teeth and read on her mirror-screen Shawhan's report of Stephanie Lee's theft, arrest, and removal from the station. Hopefully, this time, the removal order would stick.

Lee's comments about Janey not knowing what was going on at L'Étoile implied something other than gambling, nightly entertainment, and the best-in-Sol cuisine. If it threatened the security of the station, Janey really should know about any off-book activities.

Maybe the thief was spouting nonsense to try to distract her—but from what? She'd caught Lee with merchandise; the woman didn't deny she was the thief. But still, Janey should look further into the security archives—like when, though? Her hands were full of getting up to speed on the new job.

At this point, it made most sense keeping an eye out for anything else unusual. Janey spat into the sink and dictated her summary remarks for the report to the mirror-screen. She reread her comments, fixed a typo, and was about to command the report to send when the screen comm beeped the chief's signal. At zero seven twenty? He never called this early. She didn't have to be on duty for another forty minutes. What could be so urgent?

In her bathrobe, she answered in audio-only mode while pulling her damp blonde hair into a ponytail. "Good morning, sir."

"McCallister, I need you in my office, pronto," Chief Milano said, his voice loud and abrupt.

"Is something wrong?" Did he want to see her about her probation? She brushed muffin crumbs off her bathrobe, heart rate quickening with stress.

"Just get in here. Velocemente." *Quickly.* Milano sprinkled in Italian, his native tongue, at odd moments, especially when he was stressed.

"Yes, sir. I was about to send you the theft report from last night." Janey switched on the voice comm on her wrist communicator, turned off the mirror screen, and moved into the main room the size of most hotel room closets—the extent of her quarters. "I escorted the suspect personally to the jet. At arrivals in Las Cruces Spaceport, Sol Security took her into custody without a hitch."

Milano didn't reply right away.

Venus hells. Should she be worried?

Wait to worry, Mom always said. Janey fiddled with her pearl choker necklace Mom had given her and swiped the muffin crumbs off the table into the recycler.

"Thanks. Send it." He clicked off the comm without waiting for her reply or telling her what this was about. His voice sounded tight.

Janey sent the report. She then dressed in classy cobalt blue slacks, a long, flowing matching silk duster jacket, and a cream top. She kept the pearl choker on. It went perfectly with the cream camisole's crew neckline.

She opened a channel on her room mirror.

"Hi, kiddo!" Mom said, smiling at the screen. "Guys, it's Janey."

The four aunties yelled hi and waved their cards. They played Pinochle every day.

"Calling early, aren't you?" Mom flushed and fanned herself with her hand of cards—a side effect of the new meds. "How the model of Saturn Station coming I gave you? Do you like it?"

"Love it, Mom. I'll show you later," Janey said. "I have an early meeting, so I don't know if I'll be back in time for our call." They connected daily at 8 a.m. station time —lunchtime the previous day for her mom, as L'Étoile was on coordinated universal time plus fourteen hours and therefore ahead of the rest of the planet.

"You look gorgeous, dear. Going on a date after work?"

"No, Mom, it's for work."

Mom scrutinized her. "Are you eating enough space veggies, sweetie?"

The aunties giggled.

"Mom!" Janey couldn't help it that she sounded eight again. "Gotta go! Love you to the stars and back."

"And around the galaxy." Mom finished their standard send-off, then coughed. She closed the comm before Janey could say something about how her cough sounded worse than last night and how she looked too thin, still.

If the expensive experimental drugs didn't work, what would their options be? She'd cross that yawning precipice when they got there.

Janey hurried to the chief's office down the curving corridor.

What could Milano be uptight about? It was too early for guests to report lost items; they usually did that later in the day, after a long night of gambling and partying.

Maybe something intriguing and challenging was finally happening.

Where had that thought come from? Calm was fine. Handling petty thefts, public squabbles, card counters, and filing minor accident reports—all fine.

What more could you want, McCallister?

Mom's current experimental medicine would be covered as long as she kept her job. That was all that mattered.

Her four-year contract would fly by, and her mother would be healthy again. Fingers crossed. She swallowed past the lump in her throat.

Sure, the hotel-casino cases weren't jetting her to one of the dozen military or civilian space stations around the planet every few days, handling high stakes cases with Sol-wide importance. That was fine. That part of her life was over. It was her turn to take care of the family. After all Mom had done for her. Her mother needed her now, and that was that.

Five minutes later, she stopped at Chief Milano's door. When it didn't slide open with the characteristic whoosh, she rapped her knuckles in a one-two knock and announced herself to the door camera. She refrained from lifting an eyebrow or sticking her tongue out. Silly was not part of her job description, so she maintained her serious "I am competent" expression. But silly would relieve some of the restlessness stirring in her chest.

She'd expected the lead investigator job to be exciting and glamorous—the setting, the stars, the customers—after four years in the rigorous stressful grind of Sol Space Wing Command Military Intelligence

Corps. Yet she did about the same amount of filing reports as she had in her last investigative job for the Space Wing, except now she was extremely well-remunerated.

Why was she feeling the blahs? Perhaps the post-case blues. She'd finally caught the pickpocket plaguing the casino floor. She blew out a breath and squared her shoulders.

She had a job to do and would do it to the best of her abilities.

Finally, the door snicked open. Janey entered the chief's office and stood at attention in front of the large grey desk that dominated the room. The room was a ten-by-ten-foot box. Milano had covered the grey walls with screens showing silent, moving landscapes of Mediterranean mountain and sea views. She recognized the Rock of Gibraltar and the Qrendi Temple on Malta. Milano's office was on an inner ring, much like her quarters and the rest of the security team's offices.

Station Security Chief Daniel Milano didn't look up at her but glared at his work screen from behind his antique glasses and mumbled. He was in a navy-blue suit with a crisp cream shirt.

"Sir?" Janey said after a minute.

Finally, Milano glanced up at her. "Ah, McCallister, nice work last night. Good initiative with the team. You'll be happy to know that we've lifted your probation."

"Thank you, sir. It was a repeat offender—in disguise this time. She got back on board using a very good fake ident, down to a robust financial credit check."

"Mr. Schoeneman's head office screens all guests." Milano glanced at his translucent screen, distracted.

"I'll send him a memo to watch for fake idents. You'd

think their screening processes were updated regularly," Janey said.

"Don't send memos to Mr. Schoeneman. That's my job, McCallister. I thought I made that clear on Day One."

"You did, sir, but—"

"No, buts. Don't do it." He picked up a data crystal, the size of her pinkie, and handed it to her. "I called you here early because I have a case for you. I want you to handle it with care." He glanced up at her and pursed his lips as if judging her.

"Yes, sir." She always handled her cases with care. What made this case special?

He waved the data crystal but didn't pass it to her. "You're different from my normal recruits, McCallister."

"I am?" This was the longest non-case related conversation that she'd had with Milano since she'd arrived.

"Yes, the agents Schoeneman usually sends me are younger, greener, but I see you've had some life experience under your belt."

"Yes, sir." She reached for the data crystal, but he pulled it out of her way. "The case?"

"Yes, yes, in a minute." He gestured toward her with the damn crystal but was studying his screen.

Maybe the case required something from her background—perhaps her special touch of astute observation, military expertise, and take-charge attitude.

Milano continued. "You left a cushy life as a high school science teacher in Granton San Francisco to enlist in Space Wing Command for four years and then jumped from the public sector to the commercial civil service with us."

"Is that a question?" She wasn't sure where this was

going. He'd had her file for a month now. He was fishing for something.

"Why did you come to work for L'Étoile when everything you could ever want was back in your San Francisco free income zone? The SF Granton." He said that last bit rolling the R Italian style. He also added a hint of disdain to his tone.

Ah, the million-credit question.

The Granton was much more than that—a place where every adult received a sufficient basic income to live on and could supplement it with work, which most did. Everyone needed a purpose, and work fulfilled that for most people. In the San Francisco Granton, like all Sol Grantons, health care and housing were provided to all, and crime was almost non-existent. She'd applied at eight and finally gotten in at eighteen, just in time for college.

Life had been great…until it wasn't.

"It's in my application, sir." She waved at the screen in front of him.

"I want to hear what's not in the application," Milano said.

Why now?

"Can I speak off the record?"

"Of course." Milano folded his hands on his rotund belly and leaned back in the chair. "But make it quick. You have a case to investigate."

"Of course. Then another time, sir."

"McCallister, I want to know what you so skillfully left out of the application interviews and screening process. Schoeneman didn't make any note of it."

Why did he think something had been left out?

Janey adjusted her jacket.

"I do my homework, McCallister. I want to know my people."

He hardly left his desk, but fine.

"My mother has a rare neuromuscular degenerative illness and wants to stay in her home, near her friends. So, I'm covering all her care, experimental medicine, and expenses with this job."

She didn't need to mention that this was the third experimental trial her mother had been in—and by far the most expensive for the Myasthenia Gravis the doctors took years to diagnose correctly. The first two trials had wiped out what little savings her mother had. To afford the third trial of the new and still-experimental drug, Janey had taken this job. She had to stick it out for four years, and then they'd be set up for a good while. Janey could save at least half of what she made and still cover her mother's expensive treatments.

"She's not a Granton citizen I take it, like you."

"No. That was my path. She never wanted to leave her hometown, like I did."

"Very well then. I see you're well motivated to stick around, unlike Drake."

Scuttlebutt was Drake Zerhouni, the previous lead investigator, had left without notice to marry one of the rich industrialists who'd frequented L'Étoile.

Milano pursed his lips and read from his light screen. Without preamble, he read. "Dima Bakaj in Suite 52 reported a theft of his property at 7:15 a.m. when room service brought his breakfast. Mai Chen in Foodservice reported the theft to the Security Office at 7:16, who reported it to me a minute later at 7:17." He paused and adjusted one of his belly dancing figurines that lined the edge of his desk.

Janey waited.

Without looking up, Milano resumed. "Security Chief Milano delivered orders to investigate at 7:30 to Lead Investigator Security Agent Janey McCallister, former Lieutenant First-Class."

Now he did peer up at her, his eyes a bit blurry behind the defunct, old-fashioned eyeglasses, and finally handed her the data crystal. "Report read and received?"

She took the crystal, tapped it on her wrist comm to transfer the data, called up her holo screen, and read to herself silently what Milano had just read aloud. "Read and received, sir."

She added her thumbprint to the readout and then turned to go, but Milano cleared his throat. She turned back toward him. "Sir?"

"Mr. Bakaj is one of Mr. Schoeneman's friends. Handle this case with care." He slipped off his glasses and rubbed the bridge of his nose. He didn't make eye contact with her. Her ocular readout screen showed his heart rate was elevated, and there was a ten percent perspiration increase, centered under his arms. Something was making him nervous. What was he hiding, and was it case-related? Or related to previous cases? Or something else entirely.

"Understood, sir." She cleared her throat. "Are you all right, sir?"

"Fine, McCallister." He waved her off and turned back to his work.

Yeah, right. However, now wasn't the time to confront him and find out what wasn't fine. She had a theft to investigate.

THREE

Janey palmed the door of Suite 52. A booming male voice called out to enter, and the door slid open. An older man reached out a hand to greet her with a strong grip and tipped his head in old-world gentility. He wore a black linen shirt with a choker collar and an intricately embroidered red vest, black linen slacks, and black felt boots.

Though Dima's hotel record stated his age as ninety years old, he had only a few wrinkles around his eyes and mouth. The ultra-wealthy had access to all kinds of treatments and enhancements to extend their health. He could easily be mistaken for fifty, maybe sixty years old, except for the weariness in his gaze, as if he'd lived many lifetimes and seen all that life had to offer—the beautiful and the ugly, the ecstasy and the torture.

His hotel record stated he'd arrived three days previous and had paid for his mid-range two-room suite via Krasivi Enterprises, a holding company based in Odessa, Russia.

"Investigator, thank you for coming. I'm Dima Bakaj."

She barely had the time to glance about the neat two-room suite done in warm brown and beige tones with royal blue accents when the door chimed. Dima boomed out to enter before Janey could stop him.

At the threshold was Gonzalez or whatever-his-real-name-was from last night. That dimple—a faint smile on his lips. In a smoky grey tailored suit, a pink pocket square and matching pink slim tie, he towered over the hotel guest, but he was only a few inches over Janey's five feet eight inches.

What was he doing here?

"Hello, Mr. Dima Bakaj?"

"Yes?" Dima squinted up at him.

"I'm Orlando Valdez with Silverstein Insurance, and I heard about the theft. I'm here to take your statement. It won't take but a few minutes."

"Enter then," Dima said, a slight frown his only sign of displeasure. "Won't you sit down? Tea? It's cold, but I can order more." A silver tea set, toast on a porcelain platter, jams, and clotted cream were arrayed on the oval wooden table—real mahogany probably. The kitchenette beyond them looked untouched, and the food crafter was unused.

"Thank you, but no thanks on the tea." He marched in and held out a hand to Janey and smiled broadly, acting like he was meeting her for the first time. "Well, hello. Orlando Valdez, Silverstein Insurance investigator." The Spanish accent he had when she'd first met him weeks ago was now gone. His English was Middle America perfect. Which was his real accent?

"I see. And you happened to be in the area, Mr. Valdez?"

He shrugged, but his pupils were dilated and his nostrils flared. "Yes."

He was attracted to her. She wouldn't let herself be drawn in. She couldn't afford the distraction.

"You're not Roberto Gonzalez?" Or he could be in fight-flight mode.

"I was working a case when we last met." He seemed to stand taller and puffed his chest a little.

"Checking." She made a show of waving over her wrist comm and typing into the holo screen. "I see." This time there was an entry for him, as Orlando Valdez, but no hotel room listed. Arrival date logged at twenty-four hours ago from Spaceport Las Cruces. Why the subterfuge? She'd have to keep an eye on this man. A big something didn't add up. When she ran his face through the database last night nothing showed; now this new alias did? Right.

"And you're not Liz, are you?" He lifted an eyebrow.

"I was working undercover when we first met too. And last night." She kept her voice cool and shook his outstretched hand. "Janey McCallister, Bijoux de L'Étoile's Security Investigator."

"I guessed that when I saw you during the show." His grip was firm, his palm callused. He was very much a warm-blooded male.

Her gaze shot to that dimple. Her heart rate sped up at his touch. She was staring. Her flirting with him that first night was definitely a mistake.

"Pleasure is all mine." He was all smooth charm, knowing full well the effect he had on her, probably on lots of people. "I needed to stop by—see that this case was handled in person. Mr. Bakaj is one of my premium clients."

"Ours as well. I'm the lead on this case, Mr. Valdez," she said firmly. "In fact, please take your statement and go."

"This won't take long. Call me Orlando." Well, he seemed pleased with himself—the cat that ate the canary and all that. She had to shut that down.

"I'd rather we kept it professional, Mr. Valdez." She gave him her cold glare, the one her Space Wing mates dubbed The Ice Queen Glare because it usually froze an unsuspecting interview subject in place. "You do what you need to do and go."

How he showed up so quickly was suspicious. Insurance usually took twenty-four hours to show up.

"I have the right to be here as much as you do. But, of course, Investigator McCallister, once I get a statement from Mr. Bakaj, I'll be on the next flight," He smoothed his tie and straightened what didn't need straightening.

"So, Mr. Valdez, how did you hear about the theft?" Janey asked.

She'd throw him out if she were still in the military, though that was uncalled for in this case and wouldn't do at all while she worked in the commercial civilian side. She had to play nice with private insurance. A jurisdictional pissing match wouldn't be a smart move.

"I was notified by my office when the theft was reported to your office. Protocol," he said and turned to Mr. Bakaj. "Tell me what happened."

Evasive as cosmic rays.

Dima wrung his hands and darted a glance at his closed bedroom door. "When I woke up, it was gone."

"The early report only said it was property. What was it specifically?" Janey followed his gaze and ran a cursory sweep of the sitting room. It contained a brown real-leather couch, accented with plush royal blue cushions, two matching easy chairs, and a glass coffee table. The space was tidy, no personal items strewn about. Dima had chosen a suite without windows to the stars. Above the ornate chest of drawers, he'd set the wallscreens to abstract art holograms in bold reds, greens, and blues that undulated at irregular intervals that evoked improvisational jazz.

Instead of answering her, Dima headed to the bedroom, strength in his gait. They followed, her and the interloping insurance agent—if he was even that. She'd ask for his credentials if they weren't in the middle of the first interview with the victim—always a sensitive time.

Dima's movements radiated youthful energy. He stopped beside a sloppily made bed and pointed to the bedside console table. "I always keep it—kept it—beside me or on my person. It was here when I went to sleep last night. My room was locked. Double locking security and all that technical mumbo jumbo." He said that last bit in anger. His heart rate spiked, and his blood pressure increased by fifteen percent.

"Was anyone else in the suite, Mr. Bakaj?" Janey asked.

"No, I tell you. I was alone."

"Did you hear or see anything during the night?" Valdez asked, his tone all business.

"I heard nothing, slept like a babe. No one entered my suite last night, as far as I can tell. And when I awoke, as I already said, it was gone."

"I am really sorry about that, sir." She softened her tone. "So, what exactly was taken?"

Dima eyed her, anger and defiance in his gaze, though a touch of sadness and regret too. "A rare gem of incalculable value."

"Describe it to me."

He sank to the bed, as if the gravity of his sadness pulled him down. He sighed, stared at the floor. "It's a rare one-of-a-kind gem of tremendous value. 2,585 carats, and about the size of a small egg. Oval in shape and translucent, like a diamond. Priceless really." He cupped his hands as if he held the small precious gem.

Valdez whistled, impressed.

Dima dropped his hands and glared at Valdez.

"Sorry, sir," Valdez said, contrite. "That was rude of me. I'll need a holo of it for the report."

He did seem sorry, with downcast gaze and slightly hunched shoulders—behavior that seemed so at odds with his bold, flirty manner. Who was this man, and how many masks did he wear?

"Indeed, it was, young man, but I entirely understand your reaction." Dima rubbed his red embroidered vest between his thumb and forefinger, a gesture that seemed to soothe him. "I'm afraid I don't have a holo of it."

Janey glared at the rude insurance investigator. "Do you have all you need?"

"I'd like to stay and gather any trace evidence that may have been left behind." He swept the room with a gesture, but he only gazed at her.

"I'll do the gathering. You may observe—for your report." Insurance agents had to do their jobs, after all.

"That's acceptable." The way he looked at her—as if she was the only one that mattered.

She smoothed down her long, flowing coat. "Mr. Valdez, I need a moment alone with Mr. Bakaj. Please, would you mind ordering up some more hot tea for him?"

Valdez raised an eyebrow at her but finally nodded his assent and left the bedroom without objection.

Dima rubbed still at the bottom corner of his vest, hunched over on his bed. He was caressing a monogrammed B.

Janey put a hand on his arm. "Sir, we'll do everything we can to recover your gem."

"You and Mr. Valdez?" He patted her hand, as if he was reassuring her.

"Possibly." After she reported him to Milano and double-checked his ident through the system.

"...looks at you." He spoke so softly Janey missed most of it.

"What's that, sir?"

"I see how he looks at you." Dima stood, a faraway look in his gaze. "That's a man smitten."

"I don't think so," Janey said and cleared her throat. He wasn't relevant, and he was an incorrigible flirt. "I have to ask you this, sir, so please forgive me in advance. Why did you bring such a priceless object on board? Why not, at least, keep it in the room safe?"

Dima stared past her as if lost in thought. Then he spoke softly, "Ours not to reason why, ours but to do and die." He blinked, his heart rate slowing. After a moment, he focused on her and smiled sadly. "How about some tea?" As if he hadn't heard Janey's request. He returned to the sitting room where Valdez waited.

Before Janey could ask him what he meant by the melancholy sounding poetry, Dima sat and poured himself a cup of tea and picked it up, then set his teacup down with a clatter without drinking it. He shoved himself out of his chair and rushed to a holo wall painting of a van Gogh sunflower. The painting undulated as if in a summer breeze. He touched the upper left-hand corner of the frame and the painting swung away to reveal the safe embedded in the wall.

He spun a wheel-spin lock. Then he input an eight-digit code on a keyboard. Finally, he pressed his palm for two seconds on a biometric pad. Triple-locking safes came as standard with all guests' hotel suites. Apparently, Dima had taken advantage of his for all but his most precious gem.

Janey joined him at the wall safe. So did Valdez.

Dima tugged the door open. The top shelf held one item, a black book that nearly disappeared into the shadows, its cover a dull, worn patina. The bottom shelf held a three-inch-thick stack of gold-edged paper that sparkled in the light.

Valdez whistled again and spoke with disbelief. "You travel with untraceable Signal Bearer Bonds? That's a risky move." Signal was one of the most secretive corporations in the Sol.

Janey glared at Valdez. Such poor taste toward a man who'd lost something precious.

"Something for the thieves to steal." Dima shrugged, as if unaffected by Valdez's tone. He could probably afford to lose that much. People in her hometown could live a whole year on what his hotel reservation cost. That stack of bearer bonds could probably support her whole neighborhood for a year if not more.

"Mr. Bakaj, why not keep the gem in the safe?" she asked. Perhaps Dima orchestrated this theft, an insurance scam to collect the money.

She glanced at Valdez, who seemed as puzzled as she was.

"It's precious to me." Dima patted his vest pocket. "I keep it–kept it—always close." He gazed up at her, clear-eyed, yet sad. No heart rate elevation, no gaze shifting everywhere. He was sincere.

Janey pointed to the little black book sitting by itself on the top shelf. "And that?"

"Old-fashioned I know." He reached for the book to lift it out.

"Wait, please, sir," she said. "We need the techs to check for fingerprints and other biomatter."

"Can't you do that? Please," Dima asked. "I don't want any more people in my room. I am a private man." He rubbed the monogram on his vest and looked inward. "I'd much rather it be only you. And Mr. Valdez."

"I can. Mr. Valdez can observe." She slipped on gloves she'd stashed in her pockets and adjusted the settings on her ocular implant screen to take footage of her evidence gathering.

Dima sat back down and sipped his tea, absently, not looking at anything and continuing to rub his vest.

She lifted the little black book and waved her wrist holo over it, scanning for fingerprints, DNA, biomatter, and any other anomalies, all the while also taking readings with her implant. Such an old-fashioned object. Most people recorded items in their wrist holos or secure wallscreen datahubs.

Janey returned the book to the safe shelf, though she itched to see what he kept in there, and ran the same scans on the bonds, then the exterior of the system's locks, and finally, all four sides of the van Gogh holo painting. Data ran across her implant screen, too fast to process consciously.

"Running a spectral analysis?" Valdez asked, waving notes into his wide holo screen that elevated from his wrist band.

"Among other things, yes." She glanced over her shoulder. "And you?"

Her scan ran through the entire electromagnetic spectrum on low power. An insurance investigator would probably know as much as she did about the standard light wavelength detection tests of the trade.

"Filling out the report." His wrist holo screen hovered in front of his face, the screen opalescent.

Even with her ocular on the highest magnification, she was unable to see the data on the screen. Valdez had state-of-the-art tech. And yes, she was a snoop. Came with the job.

He turned away from her and lowered the screen so she couldn't see it. "Let me know what I can do to help."

"Observation only. Until I clear you with my boss." She couldn't think of anything she wanted to delegate to him.

"Fair enough." He studied her—no smile, no dimple, only that deep gaze. He set her on edge.

She moved to the center of the sitting room and let out a breath when her comm vibrated against her wrist to signal it was done gathering data from the safe. Results scrolled across her internal screen.

"No one's prints on these items or the safe except yours, Mr. Bakaj." She frowned. There were a few chemical traces of biomatter she didn't recognize. Left by the thief? All suites were bio-cleaned between uses, so it couldn't be from the previous occupant.

"What is it?" Dima asked.

"I'm not sure. You can close the safe now. I'd like to scan the rest of your suite, if that's all right."

"Please do." Mr. Bakaj clicked shut the safe door, hit the reset button, and spun the locking wheel. He pushed the painting back into place. Since the bearer bonds and the little black book weren't evidence, it was best they stayed in the safe.

"Mr. Bakaj, do you have a holo of your gem?" Valdez asked, again. "That would really help us."

"As I said, no." Dima sat at the table, heavily.

Janey set her wrist comm to scan the rest of the room, then sat at the table too. "Why not?"

"What?" Bakaj looked up from staring in his near-empty cold tea.

"Why don't you have a holo of your gem?"

"For my eyes only."

"What was in your gem?" Janey asked. "What made it so precious beyond its value as a gem?"

"In the gem?"

Perhaps his age was catching up to him with the tragedy. He was repeating everything she said.

"Most people embed all kinds of data in jewels and jewelry these days." Janey touched the pearl choker at her throat. Mom had given it to her as a high school graduation gift, packed with photos and holos of her childhood.

Dima noticed her choker and nodded in understanding. "Nostalgia—it's a powerful driver. Pictures, mostly, of the grandkids and great-grandkids. The images are replaceable. It's the memories that aren't. It may be silly, but this gem is my memories."

"Do you have any enemies?" Valdez asked. He'd sat at the table too and fiddled with a teaspoon.

"A man in my position always has business rivals, but enemies, no." Dima clasped his hands around the teacup, sipped, then stood. "If you're done here, I have some business meetings... You will keep me updated on your progress, yes? I need the gem recovered quickly. I depart tomorrow."

"Understood, Mr. Bakaj. Just a few more questions. Did you see anyone suspicious by your room or following you?"

"No, ma'am."

"Did anyone act nervous around you?"

"Nobody pays any attention to an old man past his prime."

"Were there any glitches with your room service?"

"No, the service has been impeccable."

"Was there anything unusual or at all different from the other days?"

"None, whatsoever. This has been a smooth trip, full of pleasant meetings and wonderful meals."

"Thank you, Mr. Bakaj. I'd like to make one more sweep of your bedroom." Janey stood.

"No, thank *you*, Investigator." Dima waved his manicured hand in the direction of his bedroom door. "Anything that can help you find my gem."

"I'll do my absolute best."

"I expect no less. You seem like a capable investigator."

Janey nodded her thanks and headed for the bedroom.

Dima spoke to Valdez. "Mr. Valdez, I am still a bit confused. I didn't call you or the insurance company, though you are very kind to come."

"We were notified when the theft was reported. Speed of light communication," Valdez said. "Here to help,"

The door chimed.

"That must be the tea," Dima said. "Since you're here, Mr. Valdez, be a dear and get that, will you?"

Janey moved into the master bedroom, shut the door, and called the chief.

FOUR

"Did you find the gem?" Chief Milano asked, clipped, impatient.

"No, not yet. Just started the investigation."

"Then what is it?"

"I have an insurance investigator here. Arrived moments after I did. Bakaj says he didn't call him."

"What's his name? I'll check."

"Orlando Valdez, Silverstein Insurance. And, sir?"

"What is it, McCallister?" He huffed.

"I saw him casing the crowd at the show last night. He's got no hotel record, though he'd been here before under a different name." She'd flirted with him at the poker tables weeks ago. Had Chief Milano noticed? He'd been playing cards at her table too.

"We're not the only ones undercover on the station."

"Yes, sir, but shouldn't we be notified if other investigators come aboard?" Her wrist comm vibrated against her skin. Another call was coming in. What if it was Mom? Her gut clenched. Were Mom's new meds giving her more painful side effects? She glanced at the message on her holo screen. Her gut relaxed. Mom was messaging her about the latest discovery from Saturn station all about Saturn's moon, Titan. Fun. She'd wave back a reply as soon as she finished with Milano.

Milano grunted. Was that agreement or not?

"Sir?"

"What, McCallister?"

"Please let me know what you find. Something doesn't sit right about Valdez's—or Gonzalez's—story."

"Any evidence for that?"

She heard his monitor beeping with incoming data.

"No, sir. Only a gut feeling."

"Why? Because you're attracted to him?"

"I really don't see—not relevant—no one's business," Janey sputtered. Inappropriate much? So the chief had seen her flirt with Valdez. Or was it Gonzalez?

Milano chuckled at her unease. Then his voice softened. "Nothing wrong with a little fun, McCallister. Life is long and hard enough."

Janey sighed. "I know, sir, but still uncalled for. What do you have on him?"

Milano was unlike any boss she ever had, the way he effortlessly mixed the personal with the professional. That wasn't so easy for her.

"You're right. I'm sorry." Milano sighed and mumbled something like, "Getting too old." He didn't seem old to her. Milano spoke again. "He seems fine. Is who he says he is. Finish the scans and get back to the office. And bring Valdez with you. I want to have a little chat with him." His voice was back to clipped, now with confidence.

"What have you found out?" Janey straightened.

"Just bring him, and don't share your findings with him until I hear them first. Understood?"

"Understood." She signed off, replied to Mom that she had read up on the latest discovery on Titan, and got to work.

Twenty minutes later, Janey had completed her scans of the bedroom, main sitting area, and kitchenette, aware the whole time of Valdez making small talk with Dima. She'd picked up the same chemical irregularities in each area that'd she picked up on the safe. The lab would determine what it was. She didn't recognize their configuration, and they weren't listed in her standard chemical database.

She returned to the elegant sitting room. "Mr. Bakaj, who have you entertained in your suite? Anyone?"

"No one," he said seated at the dining table. "I prefer the conviviality of SkyBar or the exquisite class of The Phoenix restaurant. Why?"

"Often thefts of this type are done by people the victim knows and have invited into their private quarters," Valdez said.

Dima frowned. "No one has been in my suite except for me and the young Mai Chen. Very nice person. And now you two."

Mai had brought Dima breakfast this morning and notified security for him about his missing gem.

"Since the gem is insured to the tune of—" Janey eyed Valdez.

"More than adequately," Valdez said.

Dima sighed. "You suspect I orchestrated this theft, perhaps hiring a premiere cat burglar to thwart the state-of-the-art security protocols on L'Étoile." His shoulders drooped.. "I am an old man. One who has had a very fortunate life. Why would I do such a thing? I have more than enough—"

"For your heirs?" Janey said.

"They are amply provided for. No, Investigator. This —this theft greatly saddens me. I didn't orchestrate it." Dima rubbed the handle of his teacup, staring off to the middle distance. Shoulders hunched. It was hard to believe he was anything but distressed.

"Besides the value of the gem, was there anything else about it or you that would make you a target?" Janey asked.

Valdez shifted beside her. She ignored him.

"Its beauty." Dima sipped from his tea, a faraway look in his eyes.

"Translucent like a diamond, you said."

Dima nodded.

"Did anyone on the station know you had the gem? Or someone you traveled with?" Janey asked.

"No one knows." Dima shook his head. "I came direct from Odessa. Only passenger."

"On your own jet?" Janey asked. Private space jets weren't allowed to berth in the space station hangar, except for the hotel space station owner's jets.

"Frederick lent me his jet."

Of course, Dima was on a first-name basis with the station's owner.

"So, why did you bring it on board?"

"I can't bear to part with it, even though that is foolhardy. Some people bring jewelry, bonds, watches." He eyed his bedroom. "What is precious we like to keep close."

Sadness bent his shoulders forward and caved in his chest. He took small, short breaths.

This was the hard part of the job—dealing with people's grief.

Across the table, he gripped his hands around hers. "Investigator McCallister, please find my gem. It's very important to me that it's recovered as soon as possible. *Very* important to me." He released her hands and sat back, clenching his hands together in his lap.

She relaxed her spine to align with his, to lend support, show empathy, and connect. "Yes, I will. Do you need to call a family member? Is there someone I can contact for you for companionship? You're on the station alone, correct? What about your wife?" A quick scan in her mental screen revealed he'd been married for sixty years and had a large extended family of children, grand-children, and great-grandchildren.

"I had some business meetings to attend, and the wife didn't want to come. 'Seen one casino, seen them all,' she said. But there's nothing like Bijoux de L'Étoile." Dima shrugged as if it didn't matter that his wife wasn't with him, but the skin around his eyes and mouth pulled tight. Displeasure. Janey didn't know if it was for the meetings or the wife.

"Perhaps I can get a colleague to stay with you then?" Janey asked.

"No need, dear. I'll be fine. I'll get some lunch at The Phoenix and take a stroll on the SkyDeck. Then there's always the spa and a massage and my meetings."

"I see. Who have you been meeting with while you're here?"

"The Grande Chef, Gina Gutierrez, of The Red Phoenix. One of the best chefs in the world, if not *the* best. We've been discussing investment. I'm not sure why. She owns and runs one of the premiere restaurants in the Sol. How much more elevated can she go?"

"I've heard she's a fabulous chef," Janey said.

"The best. You really ought to try her signature dish. It's a delight—octopus with alpine nuts in a Scottish Highlands clotted cream sauce. The best of all the world's depths and heights. Delightful. Perfect for Frederick's Jewel of the Sky, don't you think?" Dima sighed again.

Janey nodded politely. She wasn't about to spend her hard-earned credits on painstakingly hand-crafted food at the expensive restaurant when crew and staff had their own commissary in sub-level two. She saved her credits to send home. But she would need to talk to the chef and confirm Bakaj's movements.

"I'll do my best not to interrupt your meetings, but we will need to follow up at some point soon."

"I understand. Now, go do your sleuthing." Dima peered up at her intently. "I have these old man bones to indulge. Life must go on, after all."

"If I may be so bold to say, sir," Valdez said, his voice full of warmth and humor, "you don't look a day over fifty."

Up until now, Valdez had watched their exchange with no movement, except for that one shift. No word, no indications of worry or agitation, his vitals flat. But now his vitals modulated into the warm zone of truth. Hard to tell if that warmth was an act too.

"That's fine, young man. You don't look a day over twenty-one," Dima said.

"Thank you for that, sir." Valdez smoothed his fine grey silk jacket. "But I was still growing into this coat at that age."

Janey's comm beeped—chief's tone. "Yes, sir."

"Where the hell are you, McCallister?" Milano shouted.

"Finishing up the initial interview, sir," Janey said, her voice calm. "We're on our way shortly."

"Five minutes," Milano said.

To Dima, she said, "I will need to access your records,

but I need your express permission for that. May I have it? Please state your assent and name for the record." She swiveled her holo screen toward him so he could see it was ready for video and audio recording.

Dima held her gaze a moment before speaking. He sighed. "You may have it but keep whatever you discover confidential—for the hotel corporate and the insurance. No others. That's it. Do give me your assurance."

"That's mandatory. I assure you," Janey said for the recording, "you have my promise that whatever we find will be kept confidential and used only for this investigation."

"Mr. Valdez, I need your assurance too," Dima said.

"Of course," Valdez said gravely.

"Fine," Dima said. "Dima Bakaj."

"Thank you." Janey turned to Valdez. "I need you to witness this assent."

"Witnessed," Valdez said clipped, professional.

"State your name for the recording," Janey added.

"Orlando Indigo Valdez." He buttoned his jacket and tugged it straight. His vitals scrolling on her ocular implant screen showed normal fluctuations—the most genuine they'd been since she arrived in the room. He most likely wasn't lying when he spoke his full name, but his gestures indicated something else. Discomfort perhaps. Or maybe he was hiding something else.

Janey nodded her good-byes to Dima and left his suite, Valdez behind her. Dima's door whooshed shut. She examined the security panel lock on the wall with her ocular implant. No visual signs of tampering.

"Studying the door panel." Valdez stood close, his body radiating heat. Her body wanted to lean into his. Damn distracting. She resisted.

"Thank you for stating the obvious. Back up, please."

She scanned the panel and tightened her jaw. No strange chemical traces or biomatter, only Dima's fingerprints.

With that last piece of evidence gathering completed, she waved her hand over her holo screen to send the preliminary report to the chief and the lab tech.

Left out of the report was the key question: How did the thief break into Dima's suite? Also left out were her speculations: Even though Dima denied it, maybe the thief was invited in.

The camera in the corridor would show more. She'd also check the door logs for any tampering.

Upon entry to the station, all guests and staff had entrance permissions and restrictions programmed into their identity bands. All entries were logged and flagged by the security system. While guests could only open their own suites and reserved meeting rooms, anybody in housekeeping or room service had access to all the suites, as did the entire security staff.

She needed a picture of the gem. She needed to meet the lab tech and have him double-check her work, and she needed to ignore the buzz in her body every time Valdez was near. Yet, she couldn't deny that he intrigued her. A man hadn't intrigued her in a long time. She'd shut down that part of her life years ago when she left her longtime boyfriend and abandoned her perfectly safe career as a high school science teacher back in the San Francisco Granton.

These days work always came first.

She had to dig into the facts. Too many missing pieces. Could this be more than the simple theft of a priceless gem?

FIVE

Janey strode down the hotel corridor, which was done up in soft cream with cerulean blue accents. Soft pan flute music piped in from the wall speakers, following them as they walked. Not her favorite, but she found her shoulders relaxing a smidge anyway, the tension unfurling a little. The man beside her awakened all kinds of things inside, not only the physical but the emotional too. Her body tingled with a heightened awareness of him. He matched her stride for stride and radiated a heat all his own. Orlando Valdez didn't need to speak to ooze sex appeal and charm.

Where had he come from? When she'd met him that first night, he'd seemed fun, imaginative, a risk-taker. A whisper of a promise that life could be so much more than work and worrying about her mom.

Now here he was an insurance investigator, and the one true thing she knew about him for sure was his name.

He was quite the distraction—and a complication to her case with too many loose threads. Seriously, how did the communication get to Earthside so fast? Her office wouldn't have placed that call for another twenty-four hours. He was an enigma wrapped in a puzzle, and he wasn't helping.

"You know," Janey said as they waited for the next lift at the staff elevator bank, "I don't need you every step of the way. I have a team. I'll let you know what I find."

"You can't brush me off that fast, Investigator McCallister." He gazed at her with a half-smile. The elevator arrived and he stepped in ahead of her. She gave the command for the security level, and the elevator began its smooth descent.

The music had been replaced by the soft sounds of waves lapping on the beach. That was more like it. She found herself taking a deep breath, shoulders relaxing even more.

After a few minutes, he said in a harsh whisper, "So estúpido."

"What's that?"

Valdez eyed the eggshell-colored recyclo flooring, designed to be antimicrobial and stain-resistant. "Oh, nothing."

"I'm sure. I still want to know."

When he glanced at her, it was with an intensity that had her sucking in a breath. Dark brown eyes gazed at her as if she was his lifeline. What the regolith?

"The job. It gets to you sometimes, you know." His Spanish accent was back—his real accent?—and he sounded sad, as if he were held down by something heavier than the weight of the universe. What was weighing him down so much? Was she getting a peek at the real Orlando?

"I do." Whatever prompted his comment, she could

relate. For a moment, she could be just a person relating to another person. What was the harm in that?

Why she hadn't been flattened by the weight of all her ghosts and phobias and worries, she didn't know. Something kept her going, one foot in front of the other. The Earth kept spinning and she along with it.

But she had to ask. She really wanted to know what was inside this intriguing, mysterious man.

"What is stupid?"

But then the elevator door opened. He gazed at her, gave a helpless shrug as if that ship had sailed, and motioned her ahead of him into the reality of the moment. She led them along the staff corridor, its walls a cool pale beige dotted by grey-green air plants and wall ferns. No music followed them on the staff side.

Janey pushed aside the past, which was done with, and her mom's health, which she couldn't do anything about in this moment, and counted her steps. A great centering tool. She assessed her vitals via her implant screen—all green— set aside their moment, and mentally cataloged all she knew of Dima's case, which was not much.

Dima's door lock contained his own handprint and DNA, along with Mai Chen's, and her own. As expected, the room contained Dima's DNA, his fingerprints and biomatter, her biomatter and that of Mai Chen's, who'd delivered Dima's breakfast, and maybe Valdez's. She still needed his DNA to cross-check and eliminate him as a suspect.

Then there was that odd chemical trace the lab would need to analyze that wasn't DNA or biomatter. It would probably take the lab tech some time to analyze that.

"I'll need a full bio-scan workup from you," she told

Valdez as they passed the security staff conference room. She was acutely aware of every breath he took.

"To rule me out." He waved a command into his wrist holo. "Here."

"Thanks." Janey punched in the relevant commands on her light screen to analyze his data and match his DNA with the evidence collected at the crime scene. As expected, she found trace amounts of his DNA in the evidence she'd collected. She stared at the results. No anomalies. What was she expecting?

"Find anything interesting?" Valdez chuckled.

"What's so funny?" Janey glanced at him. His eyes sparkled at her.

"You're checking up on me."

"Of course, I am. You'd do the same if you were in my shoes."

"I would."

You show up unannounced at my crime scene. You're lucky I didn't throw you out. If it hadn't been for Mr. Bakaj—"

"You didn't throw me out because you like me, think I'm a good guy, and need me on this case."

"I do not need you on this case." Maybe she did like him, sort of. As to whether or not he was a good guy, she wasn't sure. *You intrigue me*, she almost blurted. A puzzle, a challenge. Refreshing. Distracting.

Then they arrived at Milano's office, and she had no more time to ruminate. She waved at the door lock, and the door whooshed open.

"Enter." Milano was bent over his keyboard, the black-rimmed glasses perched on top of his head.

Janey stepped into the small box of an office and Valdez followed.

She straightened her hair in its hairband.

A young man sat in front of Milano's desk, bent over his large light screen, but he stood as soon as they entered. He was a tall Nordic blond with hazel eyes and a spiky haircut, except for his long bangs falling into his eyes, one strip a blue sparkly shade, the latest fashion. Janey had seen him sitting at the poker tables. Undercover, he'd been dressed in a dealer's white shirt, black vest, and bow tie, with his hair slicked back and that stripe covered by a cap. Today he was in a black jumpsuit, with a toolkit around his waist full of sensor wands.

"Soren Stinson, right?" Janey said. "Science Tech Level Five? Nice to finally meet you."

"Ma'am, hello, Investigator McCallister." Soren Stinson shook her hand, a big grin on his face. "Likewise. I'm studying your report. That chem trace—most unusual. Need to run some tests, then I'll have an answer for you. Hopefully. If the stars align."

"If the stars align," Janey replied with her favorite Star Church blessing.

"Your verbal report, Investigator, now," Milano said in a dry voice.

"Yes, sir," Janey said. "As you can see from the prelim I sent, I did a complete chemical and electrical scan, and I have found no trace of any intruder. No fingerprints, nothing broken, nothing else taken, including the contents of Mr. Dima's safe. There is that odd unidentified chemical trace. Soren will get into it."

"On it," Soren said. "I'll wave you as soon as I get the results. No telling though. Why there was this one time—"

"See that you do." Milano cut him off, rubbing the bridge of his nose. "Back to work, Stinson. Vai, ora." Go, now.

Soren left with a cheery wave to Janey and a quizzical look to Valdez.

"Sit down, Investigator McCallister, Mr. Valdez," Milano boomed.

There was only one chair in front of Milano's desk and another against the wall. Valdez grabbed that one, pulled it to square in front of Milano's desk, and waved to Janey to sit. He sat beside her, not touching but close enough that he could.

Antique glasses firmly in place over his noise, Milano squinted at Valdez. "The insurance claim approval came through, along with the ident verification confirming that you are who you say you are, but that still doesn't explain how you knew to arrive at the scene. Who notified you of the theft?"

Milano adjusted one of his veiled dancing figurines. She resembled a companion he gambled with, who had also been dressed in veils and bells, like a belly dancer from the Ottoman Empire.

Valdez held up his hands in a placating gesture. "I'll explain. It's simple, really." He took a data crystal from his pants pocket, tapped it once on his wrist holo to port the data over, and handed it to Milano. "The gem's proximity sensor is connected to Dima. When the distance between the two exceeds one hundred fifty meters the office is notified. I was on the station for other business when the office notified me."

"What other business?" Janey asked. Maybe he'd reveal an answer she could verify. Maybe he'd sidestep this question, like he had the others.

Milano inserted Valdez's crystal beside his keyboard, then removed it and handed it to Janey. She tapped the crystal to scoop the data, then scanned the information on her holo screen.

"On another case—confidential and unrelated," Valdez said without looking at her. His vitals showed no unusual spikes, though. It appeared he was not lying.

Yet he was definitely skirting the issue, holding something back. As much as she wanted to like him, she didn't trust him. What if whatever he was holding back had a bearing on this case? What was he playing at? His caginess had her grinding her teeth and holding back the impulse to snap at him.

Inside she was fuming, but she kept her tone neutral, curious. "This only indicates that there was a proximity breach. Not where the gem was located before it was stolen. How did you know where Mr. Bakaj's room was?"

"Silverstein Insurance had records of his visit here." He held out his hand for his crystal, his tone neutral.

Janey tapped the data crystal against her palm. "I need to know what's going on, so we don't get in each other's way. For professional courtesy."

"I'm not at liberty to discuss an ongoing investigation."

"You sound like a cop, not a private insurance investigator."

"I can neither confirm nor deny." He gave her a steady look that gave nothing away. His vitals stayed steady. He even looked a little bored.

"Really," she said dryly and handed the crystal to him, even though she itched to dig into his data and figure out what he was hiding. All his secrets. Even the ones he kept from himself.

He slid the crystal into his inside coat pocket, flashing a red silk pocket square like the one he wore last night. Maybe he worked for an intelligence wing for some big corporate state, or even for the Sol Unified Planets special investigations unit. She'd met other "neither-confirm-nor-deny" types when she docked at other space stations around Earth while working for Space Wing Command. Those types were great at revealing nothing important unless they wanted to. Yet Valdez seemed too flashy to be a spy. Red pocket square. Really... The intelligence types she'd met had been ordinary, boring, easy to overlook. Valdez wasn't at all easy to overlook.

"Your red pocket square—you were wearing it last night. Why were you casing the crowd?"

"Work and work," he said, making a show of straightening the silk square. "That other case I mentioned."

"Of which you said zero," Janey said.

Valdez examined his cuticles, then peered up at Milano when he spoke.

"Mr. Valdez, you can assist on this case," Milano said. "But under our jurisdiction, and under Investigator McCallister's command. By Sol provision, this is a commercial city under space station law, and our arrest power supersedes private insurance companies. Understood?"

"Understood, sir." Valdez looked contrite by the way he nodded his head, but Janey wasn't buying it. A rogue agent if ever there was one.

"I must object, sir," Janey said.

"On what grounds?" Milano asked.

"I need to work alone on this one," Janey said. "You insisted that I handle this personally—even Mr. Bakaj asked that only *I* sweep for evidence—and *Mr.* Valdez hasn't been read in on station security regulations."

"Nonsense." Milano waved away Janey's concerns. "Mr. Valdez is the insurance investigator for this item. Read him in."

"He hasn't given a good explanation as to how he was able to be on scene so quickly." Janey crossed her arms.

She was not about to give up her case. "How do you know Mr. Valdez is who he says he is? Idents can be faked. It all seems too coincidental, him happening to have a room at L'Étoile and not being in the hotel registry until this morning. And his story about his proximity sensor with little data. How did he know he'd need to have that switched on? Is it on for all his clients or only this one?"

Janey glanced at Valdez, who nodded as if she was putting forth decent arguments. His vitals still seemed too low for an honest person. Liars and card sharks tended to have low, calm vitals. But those vitals, while fascinating, were only clues that he was holding something back, not that he was actually lying.

"Plus." Janey turned back to Milano and leaned forward. "Dima did not know Mr. Valdez before this morning."

"That's not a reason," Milano said.

"Agreed. I was assigned the case. Really, Investigator," Valdez said finally, his tone one of mild indignation.

Milano gave him a stern look, and Valdez held up his hands in a surrender gesture. Milano turned to Janey. "I assure you, Valdez checked out. We don't have time for twenty questions. We need to wrap this case up as soon as possible. Mr. Schoeneman wants no trouble on his station. Someone breaking into the suite of an important guest and stealing a high-value item. Trinkets and baubles worn in public are one thing"—he shook his head—"but this... bad for business."

Janey opened her mouth to voice another objection, but Milano held up a hand. "Work together. That way I can be assured you will wrap up this case by end of day. Understood?" He peered over his ridiculous glasses. His heart rate had increased, and the blood vessels in his face dilated, turning his cheeks ruddy.

"Understood, sir." Something else was going on that Milano wasn't sharing. Janey clamped down on her irritation. Whatever was fishy she had to dig up on her own.

"You received permission to open the victim's records?" Milano asked, switching gears.

"I did."

"Good." Milano went back to typing furiously and eyeing his screen. "Vai, ora."

Janey stood to leave, and Valdez followed suit. The chief's console beeped. He scanned the screen. "Wait. One more question, Mr. Valdez. You know Johnson in the New York office?"

Milano was running the "one-more-question-before-you-go" routine to catch Valdez off guard, perhaps to trip him up in a lie to reveal a greater truth. Janey had to stay and watch and possibly learn something.

"You worked at Silverstein too?" Valdez asked.

"Back in the day." Milano chuckled. "You know him?"

"I don't. I'm an independent contractor—you know how that is. Big company."

Milano made a noncommittal noise, testing Valdez. Sneaky and well-done.

"But I know Susanna in HR," Valdez added. "You're welcome to check in with her or her assistant to verify my legitimacy to be here."

"Her assistant is Ms. Nakahira, right? How is she? As infatuated by her Hermes scarves as ever?" Milano asked.

"Well, one would never say that to her face." Valdez chuckled. " But old-fashioned Hermes? No, they're Arjek scarves."

Milano smiled and leaned back in his chair, hands on his rotund belly. Relaxed. Valdez had passed his test, it seemed. Idents could be faked, and deep covers could be built, but they required a lot of resources. What could Valdez possibly be doing on L'Étoile that would justify all the trouble of his multiple identities?

She left Milano's office and went straight to the conference room across the hall, and Valdez followed. She liked to work here, even though she had a tiny office in the security office bullpen down the hall. The cramped space didn't suit her needs. A larger office was being built for her and should be done by the end of the week. She hadn't minded the delay until now.

Her wrist comm buzzed against her skin. Preliminary results were in from Soren. He wanted to do a verbal report. She typed on the holo screen to meet them in the conference room.

Even though it was on the inner ring of the station, the conference room had a wide viewscreen piping in full view of the sun. Since it was morning, the sun had risen and sparkled off the chrome and marbled glass accents in the room, warming it up. The tiny air plants scattered artfully on the walls seemed to turn toward the morning light, appreciating the sun as much as she did. Sharing its orbit with weather, spy satellites, and the space junk robo collectors, the hotel-casino space station perched above Earth, connected to it by StarEl, and turned as the planet turned.

Ignoring Valdez who sat at the far end of the table and got to work on his holo, Janey drew a timeline on the large wallscreen with the crime timeline and stared at it. Hopefully, Soren's results would help her identify a lead because so far, they had no suspects on the board. What was even on the gem that was worth stealing? Its value alone couldn't be the draw. If guests could afford to come to L'Étoile, they could likely afford a gem as valuable as Dima's.

According to Dima, the gem had been on his bedside table when he went to sleep around midnight and was gone when he woke up at 6:00 a.m. Six-plus hours in which somebody had executed a robbery. She was dealing with a professional. This was no crime of opportunity like the casino floor thefts but a carefully orchestrated theft. Someone would have had to plan it, have special equipment, and training.

She logged into the biotag network. It showed Dima in his bedroom the whole night and other guests returning to their rooms and staying put.

But what about Valdez? She had nothing to track him by. Sure, she had his DNA from the scene but not his unique identifier connected to his wrist comm.

Valdez waved at his holo screen, sending commands and who knew what else, ignoring the view. She didn't recognize many of his gestures. His large screen was set two feet wide and hovered above the table. He read and typed away as if she weren't there. That was fine with her.

Janey puttered over to the coffee maker, part of the kitchenette that took up a wall, perfect for all their break room needs. Coffee had always been her time of connecting with her mom, ever since she was thirteen and after the eye accident. Despite their professional differences, she and Valdez were both investigators on a job. That spoke to a certain kind of kinship. And to kin, she was used to sharing food and being generous.

"Want a cup?" she asked Valdez.

"No thanks. Appreciate the offer, though." He spoke in a clipped, professional manner and didn't look up or pause in his rapid typing.

She poured herself a cup and sighed. Her first big case on the station and she was stalling.

All she needed was a bit of carbs. As they were every morning, the pastries were gloriously displayed in a covered case. She lifted the lid and inhaled the sugary, doughy scent of freshly baked sweetness. As good as her mom's recipe: cream-filled donuts with a powdered sugar dusting. Mai Chen did a great job making the lightly sweetened, airy donuts, the center filled with a tart mixture of goat cheese and cream cheese.

"I have to go," Valdez announced, behind her.

Janey spun, wiped her lips, and managed to speak around a mouthful of creamy sweetness. "Okay."

Go? Go where? But that didn't matter. She'd get more done without him.

Valdez chuckled and pointed at her lips. "You have some right there."

She wiped her mouth and finished her bite with an uncomfortable gulp. Her body heated, too hot.

She eyed his lips, that dimple... made for—*no,* McCallister.

She stepped back, hitting the counter. The coffee maker hissed and bubbled softly, kicking up a blast of pungent aroma. She spun to pour herself another cup of black heaven and then scurried to put the table between them—that and her scalding cup of joe a shield.

Valdez strode to the door, his expression hidden from her, but his heart rate had shot up too.

Jupiter's balls. She found her words and set the cup down a little too hard. Hot coffee sloshed on her hand, and she swore. What did it matter that she wanted him close to keep an eye on him?

"That's fine. I work better alone," she called out.

He shrugged without turning around to face her.

"The head office needs my vid report before they close for the night." He sounded almost apologetic. Then he exited without a backward glance. Though only 8 a.m. on L'Étoile, it was 2 p.m. the previous afternoon in New York.

She was left alone with her body yearning, her heart sinking, and her mind scolding. She needed to keep her focus on her job and not on his fine backside.

Get yourself together, McCallister. No time for a crush.

She rushed after him. She needed his biotag and his comm channel. She had neither.

SIX

THE CORRIDOR WAS EMPTY. A WALL FERN
waved, possibly due to the circulated air perfumed by a
touch of moss and peat, though the movement could also
be marking Valdez's rapid exit. Maybe he went back to
his room. She accessed the hotel registry through her
implant screen. Valdez's room number was listed, plain
as Sol. And it was one floor down from Dima's. Quick
access.

Security agents Meilani Shawhan and Antonia Lane
were entering the bullpen to start their shifts.

"Did you see someone pass by?" Janey asked them.

"No, boss," Shawhan said.

"You're up early, boss," Lane said. "Checking in
on us?"

"No, Antonia. Great job, last night, by the way."

"Oh, thanks," Lane said and smiled, surprised. "You
caught a new case?"

"Yes," Janey said. "A tall man, grey suit, brown hair,
brown eyes. You sure you didn't see him?"

"No, no one. Only us. Ed's coming soon. Can I help,

boss?" Shawhan said. "I was going to catalog the inventory from last night's case."

"I was going to help," Lane said. "Until the daily briefing."

Janey glanced in the opposite direction that led to the hotel lobby. "No briefing today. Milano has me working a solo case. Wrap up the Lee case files and the backlog."

"Yes, boss," Shawhan said. "But we'll be done by lunch. What else you got?"

Milano didn't say she couldn't work with her team on the Dima case, only that she be the only one to speak to him.

"Review the cameras on Level 5 from twenty-three hundred—"

Both Shawhan and Lane gave her confused looks. Right. Military time. They didn't have the same background she had. She needed to transition back to civilian time. As a private corporate city, L'Étoile used civilian timekeeping.

"I mean from 11 p.m. station local time to 7 a.m. this morning. And get me a list of all who passed by or went into Suite 52."

"Yes, boss," Shawhan said, "on it," and entered the security office. Lane followed. "So, the arrest took this time. I think I like McCallister... she's gutsy," Lane said with approval to Shawhan, and the door snicked softly behind them.

"Yes, it took," Janey called out as she passed the closed door and headed the hotel lobby. She was glad Lane was finally warming up to her.

In the hotel lobby, a few guests spoke to the front desk clerks, but there was no Valdez.

She commed Valdez's room but no answer. His hotel record didn't list a private comm link or biotag. All guests had to approve the monitoring of their bio-signals or biotags—both their life signs and whereabouts—so they could be tracked in case of emergency. Valdez had circumvented that protocol too. Slippery. Dangerous. So much for collaboration.

Twenty minutes later, she was back in the conference room. Valdez hadn't been in his suite, and she didn't have time to scrub the vids to see where he'd gone. Without a biotag, it'd take a long time to find him—time she didn't have. Milano wanted this case solved by end of station day. She'd work this case without Valdez.

She grabbed another cream-filled donut and cup of coffee and turned on the wall work screen to review her readings and notes from the Bakaj case.

Her comm vibrated—another message from Mom. It was a short vid of Saturn station and Mom's recorded voice asking her how the model was coming along. "Fine," Janey typed. "I'll send you a vid later. Feeling okay, I hope." Mom was probably settling into lunch with the aunties.

Back to the case.

Hopefully Soren would have the results of the unidentified bio-matter in Dima's suite soon. With no forced entry and nothing else taken, it was the only real evidence she had.

There'd been no forced entry and nothing else taken. A meticulous crime.

Maybe it was an inside job. Maybe Dima had hired Valdez to steal the gem to recoup the insurance money—which would be a huge fortune. Enough to buy a few asteroid mining conglomerates and maybe even one of the smaller moons of Saturn.

Stephanie Lee had been on a space jet headed for Las Cruces, so she couldn't have been the culprit. Anyway, she'd even confessed to stealing for the thrill of it, not for the cold hard credits only.

Who would have the motive to steal when everyone who visited L'Étoile could probably already afford one of Saturn's moons? Was there another thrill-seeking thief on board? Highly unlikely, but she couldn't rule it out.

Dima could probably buy his own planetoid, so maybe he was the thrill seeker. She opened a tab on Dima and set the station system to gather all his personal banking files. The data sweep would take a while. She let it run in the background while she turned her attention to the theft timeline.

"Got your list." Shawhan's face appeared on the wallscreen.

"Great. Anything stand out as odd?"

"No. Only Dima Bakaj entered 52 last night. Then Mai Chen arrived with breakfast at 7:15 a.m."

"That matches Dima's statement. Good job," Janey said.

"We trimmed the vid so you can see only the good bit." Lane's face came on screen. "You can see for yourself. I know how you like to do that."

"I do, thanks. Good job."

"Anything else, boss?" Shawhan asked.

Janey found herself rubbing her pearl choker necklace. She did that when she was thinking or needed comfort. Maybe Dima was like that too. Maybe he was careless and had taken the gem out of his vest pocket in the public areas when he thought no one was looking.

"No," Janey said. "Not now."

"We'll get back to the Lee case then," Shawhan said, disappointed, and she closed the vid channel.

She needed to give them more to do, including more

hands-on training. She had some ideas, but acting on them was an activity for another time.

She commed Lane and asked her to invite Mai Chen in for an interview for as soon as the sous chef could get away from the kitchen.

Where was Soren? She commed him and he picked up right away.

"Thought you were on your way."

"Sorry, Janey. I got involved in digging into that weird reading—nothing definitive yet."

"Need a second pair of eyes? Two heads are better than one." She cleaned up her crumbs and cup.

"Really? That'd be great. Wow. The previous lead investigator never came down to my cave."

"On my way." Labs used to be her second home —years ago.

"Awesome stars," Soren said. "Then you can meet Doc. She keeps to herself. I think you'll like her."

She hadn't met Doc because thankfully there'd been no need to. Doc was the station coroner and rumored to rarely leave her quarters or morgue, though what was keeping her busy Janey couldn't fathom.

Janey closed the comm and double-checked the station map on her implant screen for the lab's location. Not every room was shown. No one had updated the staff station map in a while, she guessed, as changes were happening all the time. She exited the conference room, took the staff elevator down one level, and swiped her wristband at an unmarked door.

The door swooshed open, and a forest of beeping and blinking machines greeted her. She had to be in the right place. She exhaled in relief and entered a room twice the size of the conference room. Lab equipment covered every counter and table—some she recognized and some she didn't. She smiled. Oh, the hundreds and hundreds of hours she used to spend in labs like this one.

Soren peeked out of an alcove and grinned. "Great, isn't it?"

She sighed. *"Reminds me of the good ol'."* The first phrase of the Granton University fight song spilled out of her.

" *'When we were young and stupid,'* " Soren jumped in right on cue, and they sang the next line of the marching band song together.

" *'And the world was ours for the making. And the shaping.'* " He pumped his fist in the air and grinned.

She grinned back at the unexpected kindred spirit.

"You went to Granton U, too?" Soren asked. "Which one?"

"San Francisco. You?"

"Stockholm." Soren breathed in awe. "Ah, San Francisco. I hear its Bay has been restored to its pre-colonial days even with all the seawalls, and that Golden Gate cleaned and polished."

"Yes. It's glorious." Janey gulped at the dull pain in her chest for her previous life. "I miss it." She paused in front of a silver-blue domed machine the size of a coffee maker. "You have the triple-quad mass spectrometer 9500? Make much use of it?"

"Not much, but Schoeneman wants only the best." He patted the silver-blue machine. "It's the premiere blood, gas, and chemical analyzer."

"I thought violent crimes were virtually non-existent on the station." Milano had her knee-deep in petty theft for the last three weeks and hadn't said anything about violent cases.

He grimaced. "We get more than Schoeneman lets

the PR hacks share. You'd be surprised. Take your theft case, for example."

"It's not violent, but it is the first high-value case reported since I've been here," Janey said. "I'm a little surprised B&E room theft hasn't happened sooner, but still, I was told this would be a cushy job."

"It is. Mostly. I like it."

"You have something to share—your odd results— you need help with?"

"Great, yes. Come meet Doc." Soren waved to a shadowed corner and lowered his voice in a tone of awe. "There she is."

A woman in a white lab coat typed in staccato at a standing console, with only the bright blue light of the screen to illuminate her high cheekbones. Her black hair was done up in an ornate bun, a long silver and turquoise necklace draped down her front.

"The master at work," Soren whispered. Then he cleared his throat. "Doc? Sorry to interrupt. The new investigator is here to discuss the results of the chemical test we did."

"The test you did, Soren. Do not sell yourself short on my account. I'm only acting as your second pair of eyes on this one." The statuesque woman's voice was rich and textured, captivating. She held out a hand. She was at least as tall as Janey's five foot eight inches. "I'm Doctor Wellesley Running Feather, forensic pathologist and resident medical examiner, but you can call me Doc. Everyone here does."

"Pleased to meet you, Doc. I'm—"

"Janey McCallister. I know. I read your file." She hustled to the mass spec. "According to this baby"—she rubbed the side of the silver-blue machine affectionately —"that trace of chemical you found was a synthetic bio-mimetic compound, like the kind secreted by sala-manders."

"Bio-mimetic? Meaning 'similar or the same as'?" Janey asked.

Doc nodded approvingly.

"To mimic what?"

"Regrow limbs."

"Where's it from?" Janey said.

"I can't tell where this specific synthetic compound is from."

"But it's based on a salamander compound from somewhere, right?

"Yes, the island of New Guinea," Doc said.

"Can that help us track it?"

"No."

Darn, that was too bad.

"Why not?"

She'd think a master like Doc could do anything, discover anything.

"All lab-made compounds should have nanomarkers. This chemical trace has none."

"I take it that's unusual," Janey said.

"Very." Doc frowned. "Hard to trace."

"Crap," Janey said.

"That means a black-market laboratory," Soren said, in an awed tone. "Whoa."

"So if someone took this or had it injected—how is it administered?" Janey asked.

"What you scanned looks like skin cells, so it could have been added as a cream," Soren said.

"That's possible," Doc said. "Or an injection that the body then secretes on the skin."

"This synthetic compound is designed to act exactly like the compound secreted by the salamanders to grow something," Janey said. "Like what? What could people use such a bio-mimetic compound for?"

"Redifferentiation enhancements," Doc said.

"I heard a lecture on that… Stem cells in the body becoming anything they were programmed to do, like grow a sick organ. That research was outlawed years ago by the Sol Unified Planets Science Council," Janey said.

"Right," Soren said. "Too many people who tried it died from cancer, due to mistakes in the bio-programming. Perhaps your victim is involved in such things."

"Why would Dima Bakaj use such a compound?" Janey wondered.

"You'd be surprised at the things the very rich do." Doc shook her head and hit some buttons on the mass spec. Seemed like she wanted to say more there but stopped herself.

"Perhaps," Janey said.

She had no definitive suspects and only persons of interest on the fringes—according to the vid feed of the hallway passing by Dima's suite. The feed had captured staff and a few guests passing during the theft window.

"Maybe someone who came into contact with the objects in the safe is part salamander. Like the thief." Soren chuckled.

"Don't laugh," Doc said.

"I know, sorry," Soren said soberly.

"Still, maybe this compound is unrelated to my case," Janey said.

"I doubt it," Soren said.

"Why?"

"For any bio-matter to be left in a suite between guests is unthinkable."

"So when one guest checks out and before another one takes the room, what happens?" Janey asked.

"Our state-of-the-art UV cleaners and scrubbers, that's what," Soren said proudly. "One of my improvements—enhancing the efficiency of that system."

"After the housekeeping staff have manually gone through the rooms. Walk me through it," Janey said.

"Yes, they run a light cleaning scan remotely," Soren said. "Ultraviolet LED, UV light-emitting diodes, have been built into every structure of the room. So when they hit the green button, a specific electric field is turned on and kills every single bacteria or microbe or other biomatter that shouldn't be there."

"I get it. So the odd salamander-like trace had to have been left after Bakaj arrived."

"You got it," Soren said.

"Which black market labs could have created it?" Janey asked.

"Outside my scope," Doc said.

"I don't have such a list," Soren said. "But I could ask one of my Granton buddies. He's out on Titan Station. SOL oversight is weaker out there."

Titan Station was one of the pure science space stations in orbit around Saturn.

"Please, but discreetly." Janey suppressed a sigh. When she'd been twelve, and before she lost her eye, it'd been her dream to work on Titan Station. "Black market is no joke."

"You crossed laser guns with them in your work with Space Wing?" Soren asked, excitement in his wide eyes.

Stardust and sunspots. And way before that.

"Yes, in a manner of speaking." Janey kept her tone light. She switched back to the case before Soren could ask for more. "Anything else you can tell me about this compound or any of the other bio-matter I found?" Janey asked.

"No, I'm afraid not," Soren said.

"Janey, I sent you the bio-mimetic results," Doc said.

"Thanks." Janey opened her wrist holo screen and stared at the chemical formula she didn't understand.

"I don't envy you your job." Doc shivered. "Talking to people."

"I know how you feel."

"You seem well adjusted socially," Doc said, kindly.

"Thank you. Things have changed. My favorite place used to be my lab workshop, even after my accident."

"What changed? If you don't mind me asking," Doc said.

"Life." Tragedy. Her best friend murdered in the prime of life. Janey sighed.

Doc nodded, sympathy in her gaze.

"I'd love to stay and chat, but—"

"The chief is breathing down your neck because Schoeneman breathes down his."

"I was going to say, 'Duty calls,' but essentially yes. Par for the course since I got here."

Doc shrugged. "Frederick D. Schoeneman, industrialist, philanthropist, explorer, inventor, doesn't want a whiff of crime to mar his perfect gem of a casino, yet he is not so perfect himself."

"Nobody is."

"True." Doc stepped closer to Janey. "Watch yourself around him. He's a slippery one."

"He didn't seem that way to me, but I only met him on vid," Janey said.

Doc stared at her as if examining her soul and seeing things even Janey couldn't see. Then she nodded, understanding something. "How long?"

"How long what?"

"How long have you had your Model X52 ocular implant?"

Soren said, "Wow! I didn't spot."

Janey ignored Soren and held Doc's gaze, heat creeping up her cheeks. Most people couldn't spot her eye implant. Doc wasn't most people, clearly.

"An accident?" Doc asked sympathetically.

Janey nodded. "Since I was thirteen." She didn't normally confide in people she just met, but Soren and Doc seemed like good people.

Doc squinted, scanning her face. "You have someone to service it?"

She wanted to step back from Doc's cool clinical gaze, yet it was so familiar to be looked at that way—all those doctors over the years, gazing at her as if she was a puzzle to be solved. "I was going to use Medical. It has been acting up since—" She shrugged.

"Since when?"

"Since I got here, off and on. Something's wrong with the periphery sensors."

"Come back tonight. I'll check that out," Doc said.

Janey rubbed the spot above her right ear where a tiny, one-nanometer computer embedded under her skull allowed her to see with her ocular implant.

"She's our resident enhancement expert," Soren said proudly.

"Don't worry. I'm meticulous, careful, and discreet," Doc said.

"Thanks." Janey let herself relax. "Please do keep this knowledge to yourselves."

"Of course," Doc said. "People have their prejudices and don't understand all the privacy protections around implants." Her eyes got hard as marble.

"And the security clearances," Janey said and firmed

her lips. At thirteen, she'd had to sign a massive amount of digital documents and a mountain of paper ones to swear she'd never use her ocular implant for anything illegal, or she'd be thrown into Luna's deepest and darkest penal cell forever.

Soren mimed zipping his lips shut and nodded solemnly.

Janey left the lab and returned to the conference room, where Eduard Kou was grabbing coffee with fellow security guard Mandlenkosi Dube and gossiping about the latest asteroid space jet races. She waved hello to them and made for the wallscreen with the theft case timeline splayed across it. She really needed her own office.

Her only lead was a bio-mimetic compound akin to that of a salamander. One more mystery in addition to the sketchy appearance of Valdez. And still no suspects. What was she going to do? Put out an APB on a salamander?

SEVEN

Since her colleagues had left and she was alone in the conference room and wouldn't disturb anyone, Janey voice-requested Mai Chen's file from the station's employee database. She needed to prepare for the upcoming interview. Instead of the straightforward personnel file she was expecting, a red error message flashed on the wallscreen.

What? Weird. Perhaps the voice synch was acting up, so she punched in the request manually on the wallscreen. Again, the annoying error message blinked the stupid word Error over and over, an unrelenting mockery. It was always too early in the day for tech issues when there were bigger problems to solve.

Kou and Dube had left the conference room, so she couldn't get their help to troubleshoot. They'd been around the security office years longer than her and were probably familiar with all the common glitches and their fixes.

She left the room and strode to the security office several doors down. One of her team should be able to help her troubleshoot. She was about to enter the bullpen, the warren of cubes where the security agents worked, but was stopped by the ever efficient and bubbly security office manager, Kim Iona.

"Investigator McCallister, nice to see you in here today, finally," Kim said, looking up from her desk. She smiled, open and toothy. Soft blond-pink ringlets framed her heart-shaped face. A real and gorgeous hothouse hibiscus, a bright pink-orange, was tucked into her bun, perched high on her head.

Janey stopped the curt response that wanted to fly out of her mouth. Instead, she took a breath and gave a weak smile. "Kim, hi, I know I missed—"

Kim gave her a stern look and brushed a curl from her cheek. "—our daily briefing today. Did you want to go over that now?"

"I forgot to send you a cancellation. Milano didn't tell you?"

"Tell me what?"

"The theft in 52?"

"Right. Yes, I saw the call came in before my shift." Kim fiddled with the hibiscus in her bun, even though it looked fine to Janey. "But we still could have met."

"I'm sorry. I needed to—"

"Do the hustle? I get it," Kim said. "What do you need?"

"I'm trying to get into the file for Mai Chen, one of the new cooks on Chef Gina's team, but all I get is an annoying red error message and a note to come see you."

"She's a wonderful baker," Kim said. "Let me see it."

Janey called up her holo screen on her wrist comm.

"May I?" Kim asked.

"Sure."

Kim waved a hand in front of Janey's screen, no

doubt waving in commands Janey couldn't see and didn't know, then frowned. "Did you use the updated data crystal I gave you last week to upload the most recent changes to the station database?"

"Yes," Janey said and paused.

"But?" Kim raised an eyebrow.

"You seem to know me so well."

Kim tapped a pink fingernail against her desk.

"I tinkered and rearranged some files—research." Janey shrugged.

"No, no, no. Don't. You probably tripped something in the base code."

"I don't think so."

"No matter. I'll get you a reconfigured data crystal. One sec. Don't move. And no more tinkering."

"Thanks," Janey said. "But don't you think it's weird? I've been able to access employee files fine up to now. My tinkering was weeks ago."

Kim wiggled a foot in her retro bright pink pumps with orange accents as she waved a handful of commands in front of her flat translucent keyboard. Her screen was several feet wide and nearly as high, also translucent. The thin silver edges were barely visible.

"How do you see on that?" Janey asked.

"Come around to my side," Kim said.

Janey stepped around to Kim's side of the desk. Kim waved up a calendar, full of color and acronyms. The screen was opaque from the data side.

"Gorgeous. I mean the screen, not your psychedelic calendar," Janey said. "While you're getting my new crystal ready, can you port me Mai Chen's personnel files?"

"Sure. Done." Kim's fingers flew across her keyboard

and chuckled. "Now about getting one of these screens for you—"

"For my office."

"That's right. The engineers are building it."

"Still? It's been weeks. I haven't minded 'til now, but..."

"For this lovely screen, you'll need to fill out Requisition Form number 372. Then file it with the shop. You know they make everything down there, and I mean *everything*."

Officially called Engineering, the machine shop filled nearly a whole level near the bottom of the station.

"I thought I'd requisitioned everything I needed for my new office. What's taking so long if the shop can make everything?"

"They're redoing some of the mezzanine level suites again. Fred wanted them updated in advance of—"

"Boss, Mai Chen is on her way over." Lane came over, and Kim busied herself with her large screen.

"Thanks, Lane," Janey said and glanced at Kim. "My office?"

"They're almost done. I'll let you know the minute they are."

"Thanks."

Back in the conference room, Janey had enough time to fill up her coffee cup, scan Mai's files from Kim's data port, and organize her approach.

Mai Chen chimed the conference room door.

"Enter." Janey stood to greet the woman who, from their five-day ride together to the station in StarEl, already felt like the sister she never had. Mai was in a neat outfit of black slacks, black tunic, and sturdy black shoes. "Thanks for coming, Mai."

"Is everything all right? You need me for the theft

case?" Mai Chen entered and glanced around. "Did you want more pastries? Different teas? I hope you like the coffee, it's the absolute best." Mai busied herself at the sink and wiped down the counter, even though that wasn't her job.

"Mai, yes, about the theft this morning. Please sit. I have a few questions for you. Then you can get back to work."

Mai Chen wiped her hands on a white towel tucked into her black sash belt and sat, a towel bunched between her hands. "I don't know how I can help you. I brought Mr. Bakaj his breakfast as he'd ordered up the night before. Housekeeping told me he always has the same thing."

"And what is that?"

"Freshly squeezed orange juice, two kinds of arugula —both from Terra and from the station solar gardens— a soft-boiled egg, and spelt toast with whole burnt butter. Plus, thick Turkish coffee and a glass of hot water."

Janey's stomach rumbled.

Mai hid a smile behind her hand.

"Breakfast was at…"

"Did you even have a proper breakfast?"

"Yes. What time did you deliver Mr. Bakaj's breakfast?"

"The delivery was requested to arrive by 7 a.m. I was right on time. I'm sure I wasn't late." Mai eyed the floor. "Did I do something wrong? Am I a suspect in some crime?"

"Mai, we're covering all our bases," Janey said. A non-answer would have to do for now.

"I can't afford to lose my job. I need it." Mai hugged herself.

Janey softened her voice. "Why would you lose your job?"

"Like I told Investigator Valdez, Chef Gutierrez is a strict taskmaster. She tolerates zero tardiness. I had to clock out for this interview."

"You're not salaried?"

What was Valdez doing conducting interviews without her and without her approval?

"No, I am. It's that she counts all the time to ensure that our time is maximized at the highest efficiency possible." Mai Chen crinkled up her nose in distaste. "I knew it going in…living it is another thing entirely. She's so strict."

Being so strict was maybe not so odd for the world-class chef, but Janey hadn't met her yet to form her own opinion.

"You said you already spoke to Investigator Valdez. Orlando Valdez? When was that?" Her voice harder than she intended.

"On my way here. I ran into him on the service turbo." Mai squirmed in her chair. "Was I not supposed to talk to him? He said he was looking into the theft for Mr. Bakaj. He was so sweet and easy to talk to."

Of course, he was. Damn him. She itched to demand that he get his butt back here, but she didn't even have his direct link. All the stars.

"Mai." She blew out a breath and tried a smile to shift her mood. It usually did wonders, but not today. She let go of the smile. "When you delivered Mr. Bakaj his breakfast, did you happen to see anyone else in the hallways or corridors? Anything unusual?"

Mai considered the table, scrubbing at a spot with her cloth. "I don't think so. There were a few other servers out at that hour delivering food or drink on different floors."

Janey waited her out. An empty moment was often worth gold. Her instructors had taught her just that, and she'd seen first-hand how people would rush to fill the silence with a revelation or a telling detail that broke open a case. She needed something to break open this case.

"Oh, right," Mai said. "I did see Paula at the T-junction before the guest wing."

Janey nodded. "Paula who?" She knew who Mai meant but needed to be thorough.

"Paula Redstone. She's in charge of Hospitality Services along with her brother, Peter Redstone. You met her. Remember? She greeted all of us when we got off StarEl when we arrived."

"Yes, of course. And what was she doing?"

"I'm not sure. She was standing there, reading her holo screen."

"Anybody with her?"

"No."

"Was that normal? Is her presence unusual at that time and place?"

"No, I don't think so. I don't know." Mai looked up and to the left, likely reviewing what she'd observed of Paula this morning. All of Mai Chen's vitals read at normal levels. She squinted at Janey and crossed her arms over her body. "Are you reading me?"

Janey shrugged. "It's my job."

"I know. It's weird." Mai stared at her right eye.

Janey nodded and said nothing. Mai knew not to talk about her eye implant with anyone. Everyone had secrets for a reason.

Mai jumped out of her chair. "Mind if I get a coffee?

We stock you with the strongest blend we carry. Kim loves it. I've been wanting to taste it."

"Help yourself."

Mai served herself a cup of coffee and leaned against the counter. "Want a cup?"

"No, thanks. Tell me more about what Paula was doing this morning."

"Well, Paula was overseeing the serving staff, no doubt in coordination with Chef Gina and Jorge, her assistant."

"Was everyone working as they should be? For example, were there any staff substitutions? Any glitches with service? Anything at all that was different from other days. Did anyone act nervous?"

"No." Mai stared out the window, lost in some thought.

Janey leaned on the counter beside Mai, careful to not touch her and jar her musing. She was also careful to set her body to the same level as Mai's, her shoulders parallel and spine aligned.

"Sometimes I get an itchy feeling between my shoulder blades that's hard to reach and won't go away without a vigorous scratch." Janey rolled her shoulders to demonstrate. "Like a feeling that something is off. You know what I mean? Maybe there was some odd detail that stood out without you knowing why."

Mai Chen took another sip. "Well..." Her gaze remained defocused.

The more Mai relaxed and the more she sensed Janey was similar to her, the more her subconscious would bring to the surface whatever she was musing on. The body-mind remembered everything, and every little bit helped. The smallest detail could take on the biggest importance in a case, and she needed all the details she could get.

After a few minutes, Mai shifted her stance and turned to face Janey.

"I forgot until you asked... Samira was supposed to take the breakfast shift, but at 6:30 a.m., Chef assigned her to some special prep instead and gave me the job." She cocked her head to one side. "Does that help?"

"I'm not sure, but I'll make a note of it for our timeline," Janey said. "And I'll ask Chef Gutierrez not to dock you for talking to me."

"Please don't do that." Mai's heart raced as she squeezed Janey's hand. "That might make things worse."

Janey placed a hand on Mai's shoulder. "Okay, I won't."

Mai's heart rate slowed back toward normal.

"Good. I need to get back." Mai headed for the door.

"I may have more questions for you but will try to reserve them for your off-hours. Want to meet in the bar at seventeen-thirty?"

"If you mean 5:30 p.m., then sure." Mai arched a black eyebrow." Then you can tell me about the new investigator."

"Who?" Janey's cheeks heated as if on cue. She knew who.

"Investigator Valdez. Weren't you playing cards with him our first night here? Was he undercover too?"

"I don't know," Janey said. "What did he ask you about?"

"What I did this morning—just like you did."

"What did you tell him?"

"Just what I told you." Mai threw up her hands, as if exasperated with her. "That I served Mr. Bakaj breakfast and called the security office for him about his stolen item. He didn't say what it was, and I didn't ask. Poor sweet old man."

"Why do you say that?"

"He looked so forlorn," Mai said. "Like he'd lost his prize goat. Whatever he lost must be worth a bundle. Isn't he the CEO of some company?

"Did Investigator Valdez ask you anything else?"

"No, but he's hot." Mai brushed her short black hair behind one ear, revealing four rainbow-themed crystalline studs pierced up her earlobe. "All Latin dark, those chiseled cheekbones, and that jawline, how his tux molded his—You didn't notice?"

"Not at all." Janey blew out a breath, her cheeks still hot.

"Right. Did I get him in trouble?"

"No. He did that all by himself."

Why was Valdez mucking up her investigation? What was his game?

EIGHT

As soon as Mai left, Janey strode to the window and stared at the swirls and switchbacks of the shaded corona rays for a long moment. Then she commed Lane. "For my next interview, page Paula Redstone, and let her know I'll be stopping by her office."

Maybe Paula had noticed something that would help them.

"She's in charge of Housekeeping," Lane said.

"Yes, I know she is."

"She hates being interrupted while on shift," Lane said. "Sorry, boss."

"Nothing to be sorry about. She's got to take a break sometime."

"I never see her in the staff break room," Lane said, "but I'll track her down and let her know you're coming."

"Thanks." Janey was about to close the comm channel when Lane spoke softly, too softly, as if she was talking to someone else.

"What's that?" Janey prompted.

"Sorry, Kim was asking for you to stop by before you head out."

"She wants to do a once-over of my wardrobe before I meet with Paula, right?" Kim was such a fashionista.

"She's like that," Lane said, disapproval in her voice.

"Tell her I'll be right there." Janey washed out her cup and returned to the security staff room and Kim. It was zero nine hundred, and she was no closer to finding Dima's thief.

She strode into the staff room. Kim had a headset on, nodding at her wide holo screen, and she lifted a finger to indicate for her to wait. Janey turned toward the bullpen to check in on Lane and Shawhan's progress logging the cache of stolen jewelry in Lee's suite.

"Wait," Kim said. "Sorry, sir. No, I wasn't meaning 'you.' Investigator McCallister just arrived. No, not Kou. I'll send him down as soon as he arrives. Yes, the new lead investigator. You haven't given her the grand tour yet? I'll remind her of your standing invite. I'm sure she's had her hands full getting settled. Takes a while to get one's sea legs. Yes, sir." She closed the comm and waved Janey over. "Henrys wants me to remind you that he's available for that nooks and crannies tour of the machine shop you requested."

"Thanks," Janey said.

Kim eyed her up and down. Here it came. "You may want to switch into something fancier. Or maybe add some sparkle."

"Do I have to?" Janey asked with a straight face.

"Yes. Paula says you don't dress with enough sparkle," Kim said. "She said to come in sophisticated yet understated chic."

"With sparkle."

"Of course." Kim held back her laugh.

"Fine. Only for Paula—though she's not my boss," Janey said. "Right after I add some sparkle."

"She's always testing our fashion know-how. Doesn't she know that she will always win at that game?"

"I'm afraid I'll have to fail that test today." Janey sighed. "Who knew this job required me to major in wardrobe?"

"You didn't get the memo?" Kim asked with a straight face.

Janey snorted. "Come on, you know I majored in jock and tech geek. And education. And military. But I'm good at taking notes." Janey winked at Kim and hustled to the anteroom to freshen up, using the auto-makeup kit to touch up her eyes and lips with sparkly eyeshadow and lipstick, leaving Kim's giggle in her wake. The fashion was lots of rainbow and glitter accents. Janey used the clothes-maker to add a glittery Hermes Nouveau scarf. Best she could do on short notice; she was on the clock. Still, to keep the peace with the head of hospitality, she could spare the few minutes. Plus, she had to admit playing dress-up was way more fun than being squared away in military blues.

She took a short vid waving Hi for Mom and sent it.

She stepped back into the front lobby and twirled under Kim's approving gaze.

"Good girl. Now, off with you. Don't keep the fashion goddess waiting."

"You mean fashion police," Janey said and flipped the scarf like a fashion model.

———

JANEY HEADED TO THE PUBLIC ELEVATORS, THEN

stopped beside a tall weeping fig tree that dominated a corner. The tree also conveniently created a visual buffer between the public side and the staff side of the hotel. Still on the staff side, nestled in the twining branches of the Ficus benjamina spread overhead and around her shoulders, she did a quick search via her wrist holo screen for Valdez.

She wanted to track him down, get a report, and confront him about how he'd run off without a word, how in the Venus hell had he disappeared so quickly when she'd run after him, and while she was grilling him, why in the multiverse did she have to find out from Mai that he was questioning staff? Even if it was an informal interview.

Who else had he interviewed without her? She needed his direct comm code links now.

She waved her hand over the light screen to search for his codes, again. No luck. Her wrist comm made a honking noise instead and flashed her a garish black screen with red font declaring a generic error message. What? Janey groaned and commed Kim again.

"Yes, Investigator," Kim answered, clipped and professional.

"Can you get me a location for someone?"

"Sure, who? Go ahead with the name," Kim said, all business.

Janey leaned against the wall and let the dark waxy green leaves of the weeping fig surround her, comfort her. "Investigator Orlando Valdez with Silverstein Insurance."

"Checking, hold please." Kim chuckled, her voice warm. "Oh! That Mr. Valdez!"

"Where is he, Kim?"

"He's a looker."

"Kim, his location."

"At SkyBar. Though I had to find him via face recognition. His biotag isn't in the network."

"I know. Your face recog is fast and precise. I'm impressed," Janey said. "You've made changes."

"Last night. I put in the next upgrade," Kim said, pride in her voice.

"Great job. Will you let me know when the new data crystal is ready? I need to be able to access staff files at will."

"Yes, it will be about another thirty minutes. Was there something else, Investigator?" Kim switched back to her professional tone. Was the chief in the office?

"Yes, do you have Valdez's private comm channel? It's not on file."

"Checking. Please hold."

Ethereal piano music played through the wall speakers, softly surrounding her like the ben ficus branches were. Then the music cut out and Kim spoke via Janey's ear hookup.

"No, sorry, I don't have that on record. I'll put in a deep search. Will that be all?"

"Yes, thanks." Janey closed the comm.

Paula Redstone at the lobby first. Valdez at the SkyBar second.

Janey smoothed her sleek pantsuit top, adjusted the sparkly rainbow Hermes scarf around her neck, and tugged on her diamond-stud earrings. Though the scarf was a quick knock-off from the clothes-maker, the diamond earrings were real—a going-away present from the aunties. They were so proud of her for taking this job and for looking after her mother "in the sky" while they took care of her "on the ground."

Mom would enjoy Valdez very much and not take

seriously for one second his pretty boy façade, though she would flirt mercilessly with him, teasing Janey in the process.

Taking a man home to meet her mom—she hadn't done that since her early twenties when she'd moved in with Danny Lau right after college a decade ago.

Janey left her tree enclave, passing into the public side of the hotel. The corridor walls shimmered with shades of light aquamarine. Delicate plants dotted the walls alcoves—miniature fig and olive trees. The air smelled of the sea—salty and warm—enough to make you want to take a deep breath and relax *everything* on the exhale. The corridors leading to the lobby evoked the Greek islands.

She turned into the round spacious lobby. A brilliant chandelier dominated the high-ceilinged domed space, spilling out a warm sunlight-like effect of mid-morning. Olive trees with the small dark green leaves dotted the edges of the lobby, and mosaics peeked through their branches, hints of yellow and green swirls revealed whenever the branches rustled in the breeze. There were no viewscreens of Earth or the stars, so the design made you think that around the next curve you'd see the Mediterranean Sea. Piped in sounds of the waves lapping on the shore completed the illusion.

Janey passed several hotel guests in their real fur coats following porters ferrying bags on hover carts toward guest elevators.

In the middle of the wide lobby, there was Paula Redstone—as confirmed by Janey's ocular scan. She was dressed in a crisp grey blazer, white blouse, and coral necklace, and she was conferring with a guest who looked upset, and then with her brother, Peter Redstone. Peter wore a grey suit with a coral tie. He strode away with the new guests toward the guest elevators as Janey approached the welcome counter. Paula returned to behind the barrier and studied a light screen hovering over a desk.

Janey leaned up against the tall counter. "Is everything okay?"

Paula glanced up. "Oh, yes, fine. We have our meeting. Right." She brushed a wisp of dark brown hair behind her ear and patted her tight bun. Her pearl stud earrings caught the warm chandelier light and looked burnished as if by a warm Mediterranean sun. Her screen chimed, and she frowned at it.

"Is there somewhere private we can talk?" Janey asked.

"Another group came unannounced, which is very unlike—" Paula peered up and stopped mid-sentence and sighed. "I apologize, Investigator. Can we do this another time? There are some last-minute guest requests I must attend to. Par for the course, I'm afraid. We have our hands full."

"No, sorry, it can't wait." Janey edged closer to the desk.

"I can spare you a few minutes." Paula waved her back to an office behind the registration desk.

As soon as they moved into the privacy of the small neat office with wallscreens of big fluffy white cats, Janey said, "I need to know where you were between the hours of 6 a.m. and 7 a.m."

"On the record?" Paula plopped down on her chair behind a sleek grey desk and pulled the pin out her bun. Her long brown hair tumbled down. Paula scrubbed her scalp, eyes closed.

"Please."

"Fine.

Janey hit the green button on her flipped-up holo screen to capture the interview in video and author. "Go ahead."

Paula slipped off one of her heels and rubbed the bottom of her foot. "At 6 a.m., I was at the front desk. Then I supervised the cleaning staff and the food delivery staff at the T-junction right here." With a quick wave of her other hand, she summoned up her schedule on her light screen and spun it around to face Janey.

A flashing red dot with a set of coordinates—a string of numbers—showed Paula's first location as she said in the lobby and then in the main corridor as she said—and as Mai had observed. Data flowed across the screen, names and suite numbers, food orders, and those special requests she'd mentioned.

"Anything else?" Paula frowned at her screen, and she slipped on her shoe. "I really need to take care of some onboarding."

"Did you see anyone coming from Mr. Bakaj's corridor before 7 a.m.?" Janey checked her timeline on her wrist holo. At least her case notes hadn't been affected by the staff directory glitch.

"Only foodservice personnel heading to and from that corridor and others."

"And why were you there?"

"I told you. I was supervising the cleaning staff and the food delivery staff." She puffed out a breath of frustration and slipped off her other shoe, rubbing the bottom of her foot. "I help foodservice staff find their way around on the first few days of their new shifts. The chef's assistant told me there would be a few new staff members. Not everyone has a thorough understanding of the layout of the guest areas."

"Seems like a bad use of your time."

Paula touched one pearl earring. "As Head of Hospitality, I make it a point to know everyone—back and front of the house. Doing my part to help everyone feel welcome and find their way around."

"Anything else? Anything at all out of the ordinary."

Paula stood, a glimmer of a smile in her lips. "I don't know if you could count this out of the ordinary, but you might want to let your Investigator Valdez know that I find him...intriguing. He can make any special requests he wants."

Janey frowned. "He is not my investigator. When did he come by?"

Paula waved her comment away. "You know what I mean. On your team. Now, if you don't mind. I really must—"

"What time?"

"Oh, about fifteen minutes ago."

"Thank you for your time, Paula." Janey held in her anger. She and Valdez were supposed to work together. They were duplicating work, wasting time. They needed to pool their resources. Divide and conquer. None of this Lone Ranger crap.

"Nice scarf," Paula said and hurried around the desk, toward the door, pointing for Janey to go ahead of her. "You know where to find me. Here. Always here." She rushed back to the front desk.

It was time to find Valdez and get their robots in a row. She had a case to solve. She turned away from the casino entrance, but something pulled her back. Valdez was hiding something. She needed to talk to him. She entered the casino, noisy and already full at ten in the morning, and wound her way around the gamblers, ignoring their admiring looks. She cleaned up nice when she had to, and she was having to a lot with this job.

She zigzagged through the card tables, on approach to SkyBar, and put fashion concerns out of her mind. Valdez leaned on the polished zinc counter, smiling at the retreating back of a tall woman with long black hair. The woman looked familiar.

Janey stalked up to him, her fists clenched. Why did she have to work with him? "Valdez, we have to talk." He was holding something back, and she needed to know what it was.

He turned to her and smiled. Filtered sunlight from the viewscreen above them highlighted his dimple. "Yes, we do."

Her stomach flip-flopped.

"Who was that?" Janey stood at the bar next to him, careful not to touch him.

"Chef Gina Gutierrez. The best in the biz. You must have met her by now."

She had but didn't recognize her from the back.

The bartender approached, and Janey ordered a fizzy water on the rocks.

"You're talking to people without me. Wasting my time. I'm doing double work. Why?" Janey asked.

"I thought I'd get a head start," Valdez said, leaning toward her.

She leaned back and sipped her water. "I didn't ask for this arrangement, but cooperate or you're off L'Étoile."

"That went harsh fast." He lifted an eyebrow.

"I work best one-on-one, but Milano wants you looped in. So—" She shrugged.

"You know I tried that, and it doesn't work so well," Valdez said.

"What? Working solo?"

"Yes." He stared at her intensely. "I need your help on this case."

"Then why did you run off."

"I told you, I had to check in with my boss."

"We have privacy booths like any workplace," Janey said.

"You do know how to work with a team."

"You're changing the topic."

"I know. Last night—you—" Valdez said.

"What do you know about that?"

"Only what I observed. You handled your team well and caught Lee. As a team. Well done." He sounded duly impressed.

"What are you playing at Valdez?"

"Not playing." That intense gaze.

"What do you know about Lee? Did you backdoor into our systems?"

He held her gaze—no increase in heart rate and no subterfuge. "We have a file on Lee. She's small-time but slippery." He relaxed against the bar. "Why don't you call me Orlando? I told you."

"I'd rather not. I told *you*. What are you hiding?"

Valdez stared into his drink, clear liquid on ice. She didn't smell any alcohol on him. She was guessing water.

"A lot," he finally said. "Bakaj is not at all who you think he is."

NINE

"WHAT DO YOU MEAN?" JANEY SAID LOUDLY. Heads turned.

"Not here," Valdez said, his voice low. "Is there somewhere we can talk privately, off-grid?"

"The conference room is shielded from all outside channels, except our own."

"Something more off-grid?"

"That's what's on offer."

"That'll have to do." He slipped off his barstool and stood close to her—too close. But instead of pulling away, she stayed put. She wanted to slip off her barstool and press against him. She could, but she didn't. Not even when he eyed her lips. They tingled, anticipating a kiss. Then Valdez spun and sauntered to the casino exit. Slow, deliberate, so self-assured.

He exerted an intense pull on her. He intrigued her. Who was he, really? All she knew was that he was quick and smart, outthinking her. Always a step ahead. He seemed at once honest and earnest and cagey as a grey fox. Something about him provoked her, set her on edge, and she didn't think it was only the sexual tension. He frustrated the cosmic filaments out of her. It had been a very long time since a guy intrigued her as much as Valdez did. When was the last time?

She had a hazy memory of a lovely week with a sweet corporate desk man at one of her Space Wing postings from three or so years ago. What was his name? Damiáo? Duncan? Daichi? From Rio? Cape Town? Chengdu? Yes, hazy and long ago.

She hurried to catch up to Valdez and tucked her feelings away deep in a trunk, far away from this case, and her job. Far, far away.

Five minutes later, Orlando, no Valdez—she had to keep it professional—stopped at the closed conference room door, waiting for her. She palmed the entrance pad, and the door whooshed open. She entered, and Valdez followed and strolled to the window, his back to her. Someone had set the wallscreen window to an Earth view of the entire Americas. Clouds covered the oceans and the landmasses from the northern top of Canada all the way to Cape Horn, Chile—the southernmost tip of South America.

A new pot of the dark coffee was brewing. The coffee maker percolated, its pungent, crave-worthy brew spicy and bitter filling the space.

"Sit, please. I need your comm channels and your biotag," she said. She could handle him and herself. For now, she needed to know what he knew. The sooner she solved the case, the sooner he could leave the station to distract someone else. Anyone else.

"I prefer to stand, if you don't mind." Valdez spoke into his wrist comm at too low of a tone, then turned back with a smile. "Comm channel sent." He slipped his hands in his pants pockets, relaxed, yet coiled, ready to strike or run—she couldn't tell.

"Thank you."

He nodded.

Her wrist comm vibrated against her wrist. A message from him.

"Thank you for your comm channel link and biotag."

"Of course. I am sorry for the delay. My lone wolf act wasn't helpful, I know that now. Please accept my sincerest apologies."

She glanced up at his courtly sounding words, wanting to judge them as lies, only to get caught in his intense direct gaze, long brown lashes, and dark brown eyes—a speck of gold in his irises. A flare of desire and wonderment. Almost as if he was peering into her soul with infinite curiosity and hunger.

Her chest warmed. Stars around. Why her? A voice whispered.

She cleared her throat—a nervous habit. "Well," she prompted, "who is Bakaj?

Valdez gazed at the wallscreen board, the timeline across it with Dima's picture at the top. "What do you have so far?"

Janey tapped the wallscreen to call up Dima's file. "Lots." Dozens of files flipped on the wallscreen—a mountain of data—starting with overly praise-worthy PR schlock of Dima's manufacturing and chemical companies. Pages and pages touted the life-saving qualities of products she didn't recognize. "Help me sort through all of this or cut to the heart of the matter."

"I need you to understand the why." He came to stand beside her, inches away. His body radiated warmth, strength, and a musk of something woodsy. Cedar maybe.

"The why of what?" Her palms tingled, wanting to touch.

"Why Bakaj's gem was taken," he said.

"Tell me."

"I'd rather show you," Valdez said. "Can you bypass all the PR fluff?"

The way he looked at her—with interest, as if she was the most intriguing person in the world—she froze for a second. "What?" she blurted.

"Where do you come from, Janey McCallister? What brought you to work at the 'Jewel in the Sky' 34,000 kilometers away from all that you know?"

Actually, she'd done a lot of work at other space stations. Mom had a wallscreen devoted to all her touristy vids.

"Focus, Valdez. What did you want to show me about Bakaj? Why was his gem taken?"

"Why did you leave the Space Wing Intelligence Corps?" he asked.

"What does it matter?" She had to sift through all this material for Bakaj, over four decades worth, and she'd do so with or without his help. She started with the most recent files and scanned them, speed reading as she'd been doing since she was thirteen and mastered her eye implant.

"I'm curious about you." He glanced at her, then turned to flick Bakaj's files to one side on the wallscreen.

She made a noncommittal sound. She didn't doubt him, she just didn't trust him. Time to do some snooping of her own. She tapped into her holo and commanded a search of a one Investigator Orlando Valdez of Silverstein Insurance, New York. A list of his cases pertaining to art and other artifacts scrolled on her wrist comm holo screen. She read his dossier on her ocular screen, behind her own custom-built firewall, in case he was inclined to eavesdrop. Though she doubted he knew she had an implant.

Her eye appeared normal unless you knew how to spot the odd glimmer on her retina in the back of her eye socket. She was used to keeping her enhancement hidden, so as not to be singled out for the wrong reasons. Only those who needed to know knew, and Valdez wasn't on that list.

Valdez had been with Silverstein Insurance for over five years, and in that time, he had made arrests all over Earth—and even on a few space stations around the planet. He hadn't been beyond Earth's orbit, but then again, neither had she.

To his credit, he'd handed his suspects over to the Sol Unified Planets' police force with a conviction rate over seventy percent. The other thirty percent of cases were either in progress or closed for no stated reason. All of the insured items he'd recovered were high quality, pricey, and sometimes one of a kind. Nothing odd stood out, and he didn't have any registered enhancements. She sighed. She was really hoping to see something shady in his record, but he was an exemplary investigator.

"Well?" he prompted.

"Well, what?"

She wasn't going to tell him how impressed she was with his work.

"Why did you leave Space Wing?"

"It was time." She also wasn't going to tell him how her commander had tried to frame her and her colleagues for mishandling evidence. That had been hell. "Did you find anything in Bakaj's files that could help this case?"

"Nothing yet. You?"

"Nope. Time to go deeper." She turned toward the wallscreen and punched in her security clearance at the first layer of Dima's corporate financial records. She navigated through layers of annual corporate financials filed with the Sol Trade Commission until she found Dima's private communications and financials. She studied the screen full of private messages from shareholders and myriad financial charts and graphs.

Valdez flicked through the files, making thinking noises. Then followed the sound of him grinding his teeth.

One graph caught her eye, and she tapped her fingers against her mug as she did some rough math.

"Dima Bakaj has a net worth of over... fifty-seven trillion." Janey paced the length of the room and back. "That's obnoxious. How many zeroes is that?"

"Twelve," Valdez said without turning around. "A trillion is twelve zeroes. A billion is nine, and a quadrillion is fifteen zeroes."

"That's what I'm saying," Janey said, pacing and waving her arms about to encompass the well-appointed meeting room. "So much wealth in the hands of one man. You could feed and clothe, educate and house entire corporate states for that amount. Several in fact."

People had to be mega-wealthy to book a stay at Bijoux de L'Étoile.

Valdez nodded as he flipped through more files on the board. Was he looking for something specific?

The income gap boiled her blood sometimes. She'd grown up on the other side of the spaceport, and Mom had three jobs to support them growing up.

"I had no idea you were a populist," Valdez said, his tone soft, neutral. Was that approval or disapproval in his voice? She couldn't tell.

"If wanting to make sure everyone is taken care of makes me a populist, then so be it." She glanced at him. "I didn't grow up with a rhodium spoon in my mouth. Apparently, you did."

Valdez turned away, stiff, and he pointed to the wallscreen board. "You don't know a thing about me."

True. Maybe he hadn't grown up with a rhodium spoon, maybe only a platinum one. Or maybe she was entirely wrong about him.

On the wallscreen, he moved some files around and tapped into one, grinding his teeth some more. His heart rate spiked, and the muscles in his neck went tight.

"You're angry," Janey said.

"Damn straight. Do you know how Dima made his trillions?" He glanced at her, a challenge in his gaze.

"The data has been opaque. Par for the course with corporate." Janey returned to the wallscreen board and examined the data, scrolling through it. "Holdings in manufacturing, mining, and chemistry plants mostly in Russia, Ukraine, Moldova, the -stans, and Armenia. Lots of company and product names here that don't mean anything to me."

"Keep digging." His voice was tight.

"What do you know that I don't?"

"Keep looking. It's there." He glared at the wallscreen. "Stop there. Open up Cheristyky Holdings."

"Never heard of them."

"You wouldn't have. You know how corporate entities hide what they really do."

"Some do." Some completely scrubbed all mention of themselves in the 'nets.

Janey clicked the Cheristyky line item, and it opened up. Financials popped up with terms she didn't recognize because they were written in Cyrillic—the writing system commonly used across Eurasia. She hit the translate app, and the terms flipped to English. She read, then her stomach dropped out, as if she was pulling five Gs, the truth finally emerging about Bakaj.

"Outlawed laser and sound weapons. A chemical plant that made FCN. What's FCN?"

She didn't know what FCN stood for, but the rest she recognized all too well. She jolted away from the wallscreen as if that could distance her from the fact that Dima was a weapons manufacturer and war profiteer. Or he had been, as all the records showed weapons sales over thirty years old. The chemical plant financial documents were all dated ten to twenty years ago. Who knew what else illegal he'd been involved in over the decades. That old sad man.

"Did you know this information would be here?" She turned to Valdez.

He paled, and his breathing shallowed. "I didn't. Lucky guess. Had a hunch. Heard unsubstantiated rumors. Lots and lots of them."

"Those types of weapons have been illegal since the Rio Convention of 2076." She squinted at him. "You've been investigating Dima before his theft."

He stared at her and blinked, his breathing calming. "Yes."

All his vitals pointed to him speaking the truth.

"So you were on the station to investigate Dima."

"Yes."

He was telling the truth.

She stepped toward him. "What are you investigating Dima for? I thought your company insured his valuables. Doesn't make sense."

"I can't say more until—"

"Until what?"

"I get approval." He held her gaze—truthful—then he glanced away. He was still hiding something.

"But why do I get the feeling you're using me, this case, to get what you want on Bakaj?"

He glanced back at her, his shock widening his gaze for a microsecond, then his expression went neutral. "Well, maybe a little. But—"

"I won't be party to some secret investigation." She waved to clear the screen and used a vocal command to lock it.

"Janey, it didn't start out that way. I needed to know —" He lifted a hand to brush her cheek, and she froze, caught in his magnet. Then he dropped his hand without touching her just as she breathed out, finding within a place of awareness blooming. He needed her. A thrill zinged through her.

"What did you need to know?" She moved closer so they were only inches apart. She eyed his mouth, then gazed directly into his brown eyes so full of yearning and something else—a hidden pain maybe. "Do you know who stole Dima's gem?"

His breathing hitched, and he eyed her lips. His readings were all over the place, but then again, so were hers. "Why else would I be here?"

Her breathing shallowed. "You didn't answer the question."

"Which one?" He leaned down, waiting for her to lean in.

She shouldn't. The job. The case.

But the man. Right in front of her. Alive, so alive.

She leaned in and kissed him. She wanted him, the kiss, the distraction, all of it—the pull of his gravity, his star, to have their heat meet and explode. She hadn't realized how achingly badly she wanted him until she pulled his body to hers, gave in to the kiss, and ran her fingers through his luscious brown curls. He groaned—a whisper in there somewhere of her name. And of yes.

Janey broke off the kiss and moved back. Goddess Inanna, help her. "No. Stop. We have to stop… this."

"I've been wanting that since that first night," he said.

She, too. But that didn't matter.

"We have a case to solve."

"I know." Valdez turned toward the door, a hard-to-read look on his face, and his vitals scatter-shooting all over the place on her ocular screen. She rushed to block him by the exit.

"Hey, you're not disappearing on me."

"You want to come with me to the lavatory?"

"Over there." Janey gestured toward the facilities on the other side of a row of tall potted ferns.

He nodded and disappeared behind the ferns. The door opened and shut. No other exits to the conference room, except for the main one she was guarding. He wasn't disappearing on her again. He was still holding the truth back. It was as if the kiss was the truth, but she couldn't translate it… yet.

On shaky legs, Janey reanimated the screen and brought her attention back to Dima's information. She systematically opened up each of his holdings, ignoring the flares of desire. She activated the app to automatically translate the Cyrillic to English, so she could read more quickly. By the time she was done, she felt Valdez's quiet presence next to her.

"I can't believe it. Dima Bakaj doesn't seem like a warmonger," Janey said.

Valdez snorted. "Appearances-deceiving." His voice was hard. "Crimes against humanity."

"That's for the Sol authorities to decide. Out of my jurisdiction," Janey said. "His financials and business communiques show that he's the richest and most secretive arms dealer the world has never known about. He has been illegally selling sound and satellite laser cannons to Russia's military oligarchy and other groups going back at least four decades. He seems to have funded the bulk of their military for almost as long."

Valdez had been nodding as she'd summarized, as if she was confirming what he already knew. Now he asked, "What do you gather from that?"

"I don't know. I'd leap to Bakaj being instrumental in installing the Russian dictatorship thirty-five years ago."

"My thoughts exactly. And?" He ran his fingers through his hair, blowing out a breath of frustration.

"The gem isn't just a gem." Her heart rate accelerated at her own words—a truth in them feeling right in her body, though she had no proof, yet.

Valdez's expression went to neutral, and his vitals cooled. "Why do you say that?"

"I'm speculating. What if? ..." She tapped her lip.

"Yes, what if? ..."

"If it's so important to him, and he carries it with him everywhere..." Janey opened a corner window on the wallscreen and called up media and gossip sites, searching for appearances of Dima. "Let me see." She scanned the data, her heart beating faster. There was something about the way Dima's personal information was shared, and the people involved, many of them his children and grandchildren, his wife too. Galas, public art gallery openings, holo movie premieres. They were all arts-related. Nothing business or military or science-related. And no mentions of his affiliations to Russia's military oligarchy.

"See." She pointed at different articles and pictures. Dima with his wife; Dima with other corporate heads; and Dima with his family. "There's never any visual or mention of this gem."

"So?"

"It's absent, entirely absent. Gossip shows don't even mention it."

"What does that mean?" Valdez took his coffee cup to the sink and rinsed it out, his back to her.

"The gem isn't just a keepsake. It's more. It holds something key to Dima and why it was stolen. Probably holds all the dirty business he's been involved in all these years. Maybe other secrets too." Janey blanked the wallscreen and locked it again with her handprint and heartbeat, in addition to the standard hand wave and voice code. She spun to face Valdez. "But you already knew that."

TEN

THE WATER TINKLED IN THE SINK, BUT VALDEZ froze, his back to her. He wasn't cleaning his coffee cup anymore. At least he didn't leave. That was hopeful.

"I had intel. Janey, we need to talk," he said and turned to her, his gaze earnest, his hands soapy.

"Fine, yes. Let's get lunch and go to a more secluded place. Stay here, please. I'll be back in a minute."

Janey exited the conference room. A private place, somewhere intimate, not work-related, but not her quarters. She knew just the place. They could get to know each other a little better, and maybe more than talk if that got him to open up. Her body warmed at the thought. She wasn't going to fight it.

She entered the security office two doors down. He wouldn't know what hit him. She'd get to the truth of his involvement.

"Ah, Janey, I was about to comm you." Kim beamed, then glanced over Janey's shoulder, a blush creeping up her cheeks. "Well, hello, you must be the insurance investigator I heard so much about this morning. I'm Kimani Iona, station security operations manager."

Stars. He didn't listen.

Valdez gripped Kim's outstretched hand in both of his and spoke in warm, rumbling tones, turning up the charm to eleven. "Indeed. So pleased to meet you, Ms. Iona."

Did he even know that he was doing it? Annoying jealousy flared in Janey's chest.

Kim giggled like a schoolgirl and eyed him coyly. She whispered to Janey. "Is he taken?"

"Kim!" Janey said. Her wrist comm vibrated. It was a video message from Mom. Janey ran the text transcription—Mom was taking her night dosages and getting ready for bed and was feeling okay, not great, but not horrible either.

"I know," Kim said and shrugged, enjoying herself.

"Never to be pinned down, not takeable, Ms. Iona." Valdez laughed and pecked Kim on the cheek. Very chaste of him. So unlike his kiss with Janey in the conference room only five minutes ago. "Not until the right one comes along." He said that last bit looking right at Janey. Yeah right. But the green monster of jealousy slinked out of her chest.

"You can call me Kim. Everyone does." Kim waved a hand in front of her large work screen and a standing desk, the giggles gone. She turned to Janey. "I have some extra lunches if you want them."

"I thought you might," Janey said. "Is that what you wanted to comm me for?"

"Yes, and the upgrades you requested. They're waiting for you in your private server."

"Thanks. You're the best, Kim." She leaned forward

over Kim's desk and dropped her voice. "For you. Special treat. Lower cupboard, bottom right corner, wrapped in brown paper." Kim loved Mai's handmade pastries but often missed out since she was so busy in the morning. Janey had set aside some for her in an out of the way spot.

Kim widened her eyes and tapped her nose. "Thanks, dear! You're the best too! Oh, and I'm looking into those glitches."

"What glitches?" Valdez asked.

"Administrative access," Janey said, jumping in.

She didn't want to share how she couldn't get into some employee files. Plus, it wasn't relevant to the case, as far as she could tell. While Valdez seemed sincere in working together on their joint case, there was something about him she didn't trust, as if he were running an angle she still couldn't see. She'd find out soon enough.

Kim brought out the lunches from beneath her desk. They were in a cloth satchel, stamped with a logo of an upright red phoenix surrounded by a crown of laurels. Chef Gutierrez's Red Phoenix restaurant logo.

"Thanks!" Janey took the bag lunches and exited the office.

In the corridor, Valdez tapped his nose, mirroring Kim's gesture. "What was that about?"

"Pastry talk," Janey said and headed to the service elevator.

A few minutes later, they exited the turbo into a grey passageway with no wallscreens, air plants, or piped-in custom music. Service panels lined one wall, and Janey led Valdez to a door at the far end.

"This looks like the back way into somewhere," Valdez said.

"It is." Janey opened the unmarked grey service door and waved Valdez in ahead of her.

Greenery opened up before them in a round room that could fit thirty people and still feel spacious. She sighed and breathed in the earthy aroma of soil and plants. Being in nature always relaxed her. Tall potted ferns gave the space a rainforest feel. Benches nestled in between plants and functioned as natural privacy screens. Discreet wall lights lined the walls, mimicking the faded light of dusk.

She glanced up and sighed again, tension releasing even more. Overhead was the highlight of the room. Broadcast from special cameras mounted on the outside of L'Étoile, bright specks of cold distant light blanketed the entire ceiling—a ceiling screen showing the Horsehead Nebula in the constellation Orion.

Valdez gave a sound of approval as he surveyed the room and the ceiling screen. "I love the Orion constellation. Alnitak, Alnilam, Mintaka."

"Who?" Janey stepped in and exhaled. Yes, a lovely oasis for lunch.

"The three stars in Orion's belt."

"Right. I love Betelgeuse and Bellatrix." The two stars in Orion's shoulders.

"Oh yes, *al-Jauzā'* and *Al Najid*."

The Arabic names.

"We haven't mentioned Rigel, the brightest star in the Orion Constellation," Janey said.

"Rigel gets all the glory," Valdez said. "This is a calm place. Is it open to the guests?" He slipped off his jacket and draped it on a bench nestled between two juniper bush hedges taller than they were.

"Yes, guests have access. Their door is across the way."

She took another deep breath, releasing tension in her neck and shoulders she hadn't realized she'd been holding, and peered at the stars, so she wouldn't stare at Valdez. He had her on edge in a way that was new. "Beautiful, isn't it?"

The domed ceiling, constructed from the most durable fabricated glass known to humans, was able to withstand micro space debris and larger impacts up to several kilotons. Not that anything like that could get close, what with the energy shield buffer zone and laser cannons at every external juncture. The guests didn't know anything about the anti-space debris methods, only that the station was protected from such debris by the energy shield and equipped with escape pods in the event of a catastrophic disaster.

"Yes, beautiful," Valdez said with awe in his voice. "No one else is here. Not many take advantage of this place?"

He sounded close. His heat seeped into her back.

"Not many," she agreed and leaned into his heat. Just for the moment.

They stood there, admiring the stars. Janey's stomach rumbled.

Valdez laughed. Janey sat on the nearest bench. Soon, she'd find out the truth. But lunch first. A sort of truce.

Twenty minutes later, after a hearty sandwich of beef and gravy and bitter greens, which she shared with Valdez, Janey sat back and took a quiet moment to savor fullness, and the stars, and Valdez—the way he draped his body across the bench and gazed heavy-lidded at the nebula. It was a study in elegant grace, like a big cat of the savannah after a rich meal.

She felt languid too and closed her eyes. The quiet

intimate space, the good food, and the intriguing company. She was still hungry though for something else. Her body flooded with tingles. No, not that.

The truth. She wanted the truth.

She heard rustling and opened her eyes.

Valdez had slid closer to her, his gaze boring into her, hot and intimate. "Is the door locked?"

"Why?"

He leaned closer and bent to nuzzle her neck. "Because."

He seemed to know exactly how she wanted to be touched. She closed her eyes and angled her neck to let him have better access to her tender, sensitive skin. "Orlando—" She put a hand on his muscled chest, her brain a little muddled. She whispered, "The truth. The truth about the gem. The case…"

But what about a little fun? Her heart whispered.

He spoke in her ear, his voice rumbling through her body. "This is about the case. Dima is a very bad man, who deserves to go to prison for the rest of his days. The secret holdings, the financials you uncovered, all point to his involvement in the illegal bio-chemical weapons trade." He slid a warm palm from her back to her waist.

"What illegal bio-chemical weapons trade?

"The FCN."

"What's that?"

He pulled away from her and scrubbed his face, looking at once tired and furious. "Felicitacin."

"Where did you get that?"

"It's circumstantial."

"What is Felicitacin?"

"A drug. Doctors gave it away like candy. It created a euphoria and then listlessness after a few weeks, quickly addicting, cheap, and plentiful. Well, it was until finally it was banned and went underground. Then people did things to get it…" He stared at the cushiony carpeting that mimicked moss in color and sponginess, looking lost.

FCN. Felicitacin. "I knew about it as Felice. That horrible drug ruined so many lives. Not much where I grew up," Janey said. "You were around it?"

Valdez said nothing.

"I'm sorry."

"Why do you say that?" he asked, his tone angry.

She held up her hands in surrender. "It sounds personal."

"It is." He sounded lost, so young.

"What happened?" she asked softly. Did he lose someone?

"It was a long time ago." He waved away her question, scooted closer to her on the bench, only inches away, and brushed some hair away from her cheek.

"You are telling me the truth."

"Of course, I am. Why wouldn't I?"

"I still feel that you're hiding something from me, about you, about this case. What does Bakaj's missing gem have to do with his alleged involvement in the illegal drug trade of FCN?" She shoved her lunch bag aside, leaned her chest against his, and whispered into his ear. "What is going on? Do you have proof?"

"Not yet. But…I need…"

"What?" She took in his warm gaze. "Tell me." She pressed a palm against his silky white shirt, his muscled chest so close.

"You're beautiful." His warm breath brushed her ear.

"You say that to everyone. The case…"

"…can wait one second. You think I am a flirt."

"You are a flirt." Had been from the moment she'd met him.

"So? You jealous?"

"No."

"Janey, open your eyes."

She hadn't realized she'd closed them. She opened them and took in his warm gaze, hungry and sincere. He brushed her cheek.

"Janey, you're beautiful."

"Thank you. No one has said that to me in a long time, but you said that already."

"I can't tell you again?"

"No, you can." She sat back. "It's just that…"

"You just want to jump my bones to get the truth out of me in a moment of vulnerability."

"That's not the only reason."

"Ah, the Ice Queen opens up."

She stood. "I am not—"

"You can be. Cold. Controlled. Smart."

She spun to him, her hands on her hips.

"Hot-headed, impulsive too. Passionate." All said with a teasing grin.

"Well, you're mercurial, unpredictable. Unreliable. Secretive. Infuriating. Why can't you just lay all your cards on the table?"

"Because this case means everything to me. I've been chasing Bakaj for—too long. And now I have him, with your help."

"You're nothing like the stuffy uptight insurance investigators I met in my travels with the Space Wing. Who are you really, Orlando? What is really going on?" She sat back on the bench—at the far end, two arms lengths away—and turned to face him.

He scrubbed his face again, stood, then sat down. "I

wanted to tell you last night, as soon as I saw you casing the casino and realized you were a cop here." He shook his head in exasperation. Maybe at himself. "After that first night, weeks ago, I couldn't stop thinking about you."

He must have caught her expression of disbelief because he said, "Janey, it's not a line, and no, I don't say it to everyone I meet."

He stretched his arm out toward her on the back of the bench. All she had to do was stretch her arm out and met him halfway. She felt the truth of his words, could read his quickened vitals or mild arousal, and aliveness.

"But…" Because there was obviously a *but*.

"I'm here on official police business."

"As in?" Which branch of the Sol government?

"As in Special Investigations Unit of Sol Unified Police."

"You're a cop." Of the most secretive spy kind.

"Yes, here to get evidence against Dima Bakaj for crimes against humanity."

"So, you've been lying to us all. What crimes?" Her stomach dropped. More lies.

"It was necessary for the job."

The job. She got that. But still. Still, there was something else—a slight holding of the micro-muscles around his mouth. "There's something else. You're still holding something back. What is it? What crimes?"

"No. Why do you say that?" He frowned.

"Because I can read it on your face. Here." She touched her own face around the lips.

He shook his head, huffed a breath. "It's just… as I said, I've been tracking Bakaj for a long time."

"How long?"

"A long time. I told you my secret, now you tell me yours." His tone was gentle, soft.

"I am who I say I am. I'm not hiding my identity like you are."

"I had to—for the case." He didn't meet her gaze, but his vitals didn't spike. At least that statement was true.

"What are you not telling me about the theft? You are hiding something. What crimes against humanity?"

Valdez stood, cool, tamped down.

The intimate moment was over. "Maybe you don't actually work for the Sol's investigative services."

He tightened his mouth, and his gaze sliced into her heart, cold and furious. "You don't know anything about me."

"No kidding. Whose fault is that? You hide who you really are to get into my investigation. Maybe you're here to steal trade secrets from a business competitor, for all I know." She crossed her arms over her chest, her body still buzzing from the promise of closeness. She locked down her emotions.

He choked out a laugh. "Check with Captain Kavya at the New York headquarters. You'll see I check out," Valdez said over his shoulder as he headed for the door. He stopped, turned toward her, a tortured look on his face, like he was about to spill something. He changed his mind and stormed out of the tiny observation room, making a strangled sound.

"Fine. I will!" she barked.

It was her job to question everything. He knew that, so what had she done to piss him off so much? Besides not trusting him. Maybe his anger wasn't about her. One thing was for sure—Valdez had his own agenda, and he was using her case to further it.

And in his anger, he'd left behind his jacket.

She dumped the trash in the wall recycler, then she grabbed his jacket and searched the pockets. Soft satin lined the breast pocket. The bright red pocket square was neatly folded there. Nothing else except for a small bump in the corner of the lining.

ELEVEN

TEN MINUTES LATER, NOW BACK IN HER quarters, Janey stared at Valdez's coat. Then she commed Kim. "Can you check for me—" Janey broke off.

A hidden object in the lining. Should she share this information with Kim? No, because then she'd tell Milano, and Janey didn't want the unforeseen consequences of that. Not until she knew what the object was and what the consequences could be.

"Check what?" Kim prompted.

She was about to say, never mind. It was at the tip of her tongue, but she had to know who the man was. Before he wasn't who he said he was. Why would this second identity check out? And if it didn't?

Then she'd personally escort him off L'Étoile and call her friend at Las Cruces Spaceport to cuff him at Arrivals.

Decision made, Janey straightened her duster. "I need an ident from the Sol Police Investigative Services. Ask if they have an agent aboard. Check only with a Captain

Kavya at the main office in New York. Secure channels. Off the official record."

"Kavya?" Kim coughed over the name. "Something in my throat. Hold on. Switching to privacy mode." Kim's voice went low. "Of course. Name of agent? And spell Kavya."

"Last name Valdez. First name Orlando. Middle name Indigo." Janey eyed the ceiling, ignoring the heat that flared in her chest and lower. The way he'd looked at her, as if he couldn't drink her in enough. Probably part of his playboy act, like one of his covers.

Kim whistled softly. "Chameleon, huh?"

"Seems like it. Keep this query quiet. Okay, Kim."

"Affirmative. Like a mouse. Be careful, Janey."

"I know."

"Seriously. That man is too sexy for his own good," Kim said. "He can get whatever he wants by batting his eyes at a woman. Really. What does he think this is, the twentieth century?"

Apparently, but Janey got what she'd wanted from him too—she hoped. "Don't comm me for about an hour. Send what you discover to my comm, secure—"

"Secure channels." Kim commed off. Janey hadn't spelled Kavya for her. Kim was smart. She'd figure it out.

Time to see what was in Valdez's jacket. She pushed aside the model of Saturn Station she was building in her off-hours. She lay open his coat across the table, smoothed it, and patted the inner lining. There, a bump about the size of a large marble in the bottom lining of the coat. She could carefully rip the fabric, but then she'd have to sew it up again, and sewing wasn't one of her strengths. The clothes maker concierge could do it in a jiffy, but that'd take her off course. Janey did have her mechanical engineering and model making skills. She'd glue shut the lining.

She turned the jacket inside out. From her toolbox, she grabbed a thin utility knife and made a careful two-inch incision where the silky lining met the finely woven linen. She brushed the lining, and something clunked against her wide-heeled ankle boots on the floor.

But she couldn't see anything. Nothing but the beige flooring. She thought-commanded her ocular implant to zoom in at five times normal. Still nothing. What the Venus hell?

She crouched, patted around her boot and the floor, and finally, she met smooth material, like touching cool water. She zoomed in tighter at ten times normal. Still nothing.

She scooped up the fine silky item, a rounded object in it. She still couldn't see what she was holding, but the answer was clear: cloaking metamaterial. It bent the light around it to hide its presence. This was a high-tech pouch—and very expensive to make.

That wouldn't stop her from seeing what couldn't be seen by normal people. That wasn't her. She had some mad high-tech tools of her own.

Janey set her implant to emit at the x-ray frequency for a milli-second—all that was safe. In black and white, she could finally see the two-inch-long pouch. It was rectangular with a thick thread to serve as a closure.

She pulled the thread and sucked a breath at a glaring white object no longer cloaked. Ouch! Pain shot through her temples. *What the Venus hells!* The object bobbled in her grip, but she managed to clench her hand around it in time. She stood and swayed, leaning on the table for support.

Stars alive. She hadn't adjusted the magnification and had let in way too much light. Rookie mistake.

Panting, she shoved away the pain and blinked to reset the implant to her normal vision. Time to see what refracted so much light and nestled in her hand.

Eyes closed to give them a rest and reset, she shook out the pouch onto her palm. Plain as Sol herself, it was a gem. Cool and smooth, an oval diamond filled her palm. Although not particularly beautiful, it was mesmerizing, its many facets polished and sparkling in the daylight setting of her room lights.

Dima's gem.

She sat heavy and snorted. Valdez. That clever devious man. It had been in his coat, hidden in a highly sophisticated cloaked pouch in the lining.

Part of her wanted to admire his tradecraft. The other part of her—space dust, black holes, and quasars. Playing her. Her chest heated with anger. She tightened her grip around the diamond.

He'd had it all this time.

If he was who he said he was—an agent with Sol's Investigative Services, the world government's spy and law enforcement service, and he really was investigating Bakaj for crimes against humanity, then maybe he had a good reason for his sophisticated game.

He certainly had ample opportunity since he was on L'Étoile. Right place and time.

Did he have the means? Assuming he did, did he steal the gem himself? Or had someone else stolen the gem and delivered it to him?

How did someone steal it? Valdez would have had to travel undetected in the halls. Cameras were all over, and biotrackers were always on. The only way to move undetected would be to tamper with

L'Étoile's security system. Or maybe Valdez had access to other tricks of his spy trade that she didn't know about.

Using her table as a monitor, she called up his where-abouts last night. She'd seen him in the casino at twenty-two hundred hours and then at Bakaj's suite at zero-seven-thirty-two. Where was he in the interim?

Hotel records showed he was in his suite during that whole window of time.

Then how did he or anyone else get the gem?

Whoever they were, they were good. Very good.

She stared at the gem.

She opened the comm to call security and have them haul Valdez in for questioning. Served him right to treat him as a common criminal.

She stared at the gem again, flipping through the different light frequencies with her implant. There it was, an ongoing transmission on very low-frequency wavelength—radio waves. Data was transmitting via the gem. What data she couldn't tell.

What the—

She closed the comm, her anger cooling, and her curiosity sparked.

Anyone with the right frequency could receive the information flowing out of the gem. Who could be receiving it? Was this the information Valdez wanted for his case against Bakaj?

Only one way to find out.

She needed to decipher the data and then find the receiver. She set her database to search for the receiver, opened a dresser drawer, and stared at her tools.

Maybe she should return the gem to Dima. That was protocol after all. Then this theft case would be closed. Or maybe Valdez had a worthy case, and she could help him bring down the world's biggest arms dealer who looked like someone's genteel grandfather.

Either way, she had to know what information the gem possessed. It was the crux of this whole affair.

Her wrist comm vibrated against her skin—a message from Kim. She switched to a secure channel to listen to Kim's voice message. Kim shared that Valdez's identity was correct. Janey let out a deep sigh. So, this identity stuck. Maybe there was a moral center to this man, after all.

Kim said she'd used some of her secure sources to double-confirm, and she cautioned Janey *again* to be careful. She ended the message by saying that Janey owed her enough credits for another case of cream-filled donuts.

Janey wanted to trust Valdez, and she now had no reason not to. Her deep-dive records search revealed Dima had been an arms dealer, who had sold to the Russian Empire, to their enemies, and to other military regimes around the planet, fostering the ongoing civil war in the Russian Empire.

She needed to know what was in the gem.

She needed a few supplies first, so she slipped the gem back into the pouch, stashed it into an inside pocket of her flowing jacket, and left her quarters, making sure to put the double lock fail-safes in place. If Valdez could get into a guest's suite undetected by the best-in-class security system, then he could make an attempt to break into hers. But she was smarter than the average bear about tech. He'd be in for a surprise if he tried to get into her room without her permission.

She hustled to the office and the lab to get a few supplies. In fifteen minutes, she was back in her room, and no one had tried to break in. She used her supplies and tools on hand to engineer her makeshift data-suck and turned it on.

Data spilled on the table screen, flashing by too quickly for her conscious mind to make sense of. She couldn't slow down the feed; her set up was too clumsy. Yet she was able to glimpse spreadsheets, chemical formulas, data sets, and reports. Ten minutes later, the gem stopped broadcasting and stayed on a final holo image for a full sixty seconds before looping to the start of its manic flashing broadcast. That was a lot of data—a lifetime's worth. What was so precious about it? She was no closer to its secrets than before she unlocked it. It'd take her hours to wade through all this data. She stopped the data from looping.

"Rhea," Janey said to her personal AI wired into the room, "cross-reference all case files on Dima Bakaj with the data pull from the gem," Rhea could do the work outside of the security department. Janey couldn't afford discovery—not until she knew what she had stumbled upon. "Estimate time of sort."

"I won't know until I calculate," Rhea said in natural female voice.

"Then calculate."

"Hold on, Janey."

"Holding."

While she waited for Rhea, she examined the final holo image projected from Bakaj's gem. In a studio portrait, twelve children, from infant to about fifteen years old, grinned toothy grins and sang in overlapping child voices. She ran their words through a translator. They were singing, "We love you, Grandpa Dima."

How very adorable.

In one corner of the family image, words were hand-scrawled in Cyrillic. She scanned her holo screen over them and hit translate. The scrawl said, "For you, my dear great-grandchildren."

How sweet. Dima loved his great-grandchildren. He couldn't be all evil, could he? Even warlords had families they loved and who loved them.

This was an image normally given to an elder from family. Why was his message to the children?

That didn't matter. What mattered was that she'd recovered the gem, could return it to Dima, and could arrest Valdez for obstructing the investigation. Case closed.

She ignored the twinge in her heart that whispered he perhaps had just cause and that overrode her case. Her station, her case. She couldn't afford to fail.

Valdez would just have to wrangle with someone else on this one.

"Rhea, time?"

"Still calculating, Janey."

"Let me know the minute, Rhea."

"Of course, Janey."

She stashed the gem back into the cloaked pouch, slipped it back into her inside jacket pocket, and dismantled her supplies, storing them in her underwear drawer to return later. She needed a proper lab—and a proper office.

She scanned the map for Valdez's location. Finally, the bio-locator was working and showed he was in his quarters, five doors down from hers. Oh, so now he was treated like staff. How had he snagged staff quarters when he said he was in a guest suite? One of the many things she'd ask him after she confronted him about the theft and arrested him.

Janey left her room, locked tight as usual, Valdez's coat in hand.

"Two hours" flashed on her inner screen. It was a message from Rhea on how long the cross-referencing analysis would take. Too long, but it would do no good to ask her personal AI to work faster. Rhea couldn't, not unless Janey asked her to skip details, and Janey didn't know what details were important until Rhea presented them to her. She sent the thought command for Rhea to drip content every ten minutes.

In less than a minute, she stood in front of his door. She palmed the keypad for request to entry. The door beeped, but there was no answer. She palmed it again.

"Valdez, you in there?"

"Coming!" he shouted.

The door opened and there he was, practically naked. She swept her gaze over him— dark curly hair, tousled wet, his bare chest still damp, a towel wrapped low around his waist, and his slow smile of pleasure when her gaze popped back to meet his. Intent, hungry, yearning, a hint of despair quickly erased, he drank her in, without moving from her face.

Oh for star's sake, he was too—everything.

"I guess I interrupted your—" She clasped her hands behind her back.

"I guess you did." He returned the favor and looked her up and down, a wolfish expression in his gaze, skimming over his jacket she carried.

"I have to talk to you. May I come in?"

Valdez stepped back. She entered and the door shut. His quarters were as small as hers, but not as neat. Slob would be putting it mildly. She'd thought he'd be ultra-organized, but instead fancy suits and dress shirts were strewn over the table and chairs, the bed, the kitchenette counter, and the bathroom door. "Reorganizing?"

"I like knowing where things are." He winked at her,

then spotted the smoky grey jacket she was holding, snagged it out of her grip, and muttered under his breath. "Mierda. That's where it was." He rooted around in the pockets. "Where is it?" He narrowed his gaze at her, hot and demanding.

"What are you playing at?" She wanted to cross her arms but held her ground, hands at her side. She'd left her cuffs and firearm in her room. She wouldn't regret that choice, would she?

"What are you talking about?" He stalked toward her. She stepped back until she was pressed against the shut door.

"You know what. The gem."

He was good. He went for her lips, without touching her, his body an inch from hers. Warm, hot, fire—all sense fled as she met his kiss. She burned for him but held herself back. To run her hands through his tousled silky hair—one last time.

No, that wouldn't do.

She slipped out of his embrace, a little dizzy, and turned away, wrapping her flowing jacket around her. The pouch was still in her jacket, safe from his not-yet-roving hands.

"Janey," he said, his voice soft, vulnerable. She had to turn and see this soft version of him.

He gazed at her, still dazed from their kiss. Good, he was affected as much as she was. He blinked, saying nothing, waiting for what she wasn't sure. Watching her as if he could gobble her up, not as prey, but as a lover. As if she wasn't a small-town cop and him a Sol Unified Planets heavy. As if they were two people who made a new kind of whole that could face anything and everything together in a new reality.

Not here, not now, and probably not ever.

That reality could never be. A blackness of solitude opened up before her, painful and heart-breaking. Too bad. This was her life, for a reason.

Janey straightened her shoulders, her spine, and found her fortitude. "I'm here to arrest you."

"You can't." He didn't move but stilled, slowed his heart rate and breathing, and went cool. His camouflage. "On what grounds?"

A faint hum took over the room. It was the station's quantum generator, always on, but usually masked by ambient noise of the casino or the piped-in hallway music.

"Obstruction of justice. I found the gem in your jacket pocket, hidden in an invisibility pouch. I'm going to report you to Chief Milano as the thief. I wanted to tell you first, then escort you off the station."

He frowned, looking pained. Blood flowed back into his face. He made a growling noise of frustration. "No, you can't tell him. I'm investigating Bakaj for crimes against humanity. You can't, Janey!" He reached for her cheek. "Please."

Janey stepped out of his reach, skirting him to stand in the middle of the small room, and hugged herself. Chemistry did not equal relationship. She gathered her aching heart, stuffed it away, and faced him.

"This robbery investigation has been a way for you to get past Dima's privacy firewalls. Hasn't it?" She waited for him to confirm.

Instead, he turned away and tossed clothes around and said, "I have a warrant."

"What? Why didn't you come clean with me, with the chief, in the first instance? Why all this secrecy? Under-cover—sneaking around?" She bunched her hands into fists, wanting to swing at something, someone.

He sat on the bed between piles of clothes and stared off into nothing. "This was the only way. I needed to get close to Bakaj. I still do. He's been a slippery one. All previous evidence has been only circumstantial and thrown out of court, repeatedly. I need to crack the code and open the gem and get evidence—"

"I cracked it."

"What? You did. Let me see. What does it say?" He stood and his towel slipped, revealing more of his washboard stomach and the muscles of one hip. He stalked toward her, intent.

"Put some clothes on."

"Why? I'm going to take them off again, now that you're here." He smirked.

"Would you stop it?"

"Janey, I'm hurt. You don't find me attractive." So he was going the charm route, but she'd seen past that. His charm was only another camouflage.

"Not working." She spun, her back to him. "Put some damn clothes on."

"Oh, I think she likes me."

"*She* is right here." She hugged her arms around herself again and listened for signs that he was complying. Some rustling, a closet opening and closing, the water running, the tantalizing sound of a zipper being fastened, and the shur-shur whisper of socked feet slipping into shoes. That and his faint perfume of cedar wafting around her.

"You can turn around now," Valdez said quietly, all heat and teasing out of his voice.

Janey turned around. He had on a tailored black jacket, a red pocket square neatly in place. His black slacks and shiny black shoes completed the urban look— the outfit he wore last night at the casino show. "You clean up real nice"—she lifted her chin—"but I still need to escort you off the station. Then I'm returning the gem to Dima."

"No, Janey. I told you, I have a warrant. The case is bigger than a theft." He picked at an invisible speck from his coat.

"Crimes against humanity. I understand. Fine. Let's confront Bakaj." She checked the bio-tracker. Bakaj was in the casino, near or in the restaurant. "Let's go. There's a private room we can speak to him in off the casino floor."

"No, wait." He sat at his messy table, strewn with plates and cups and utensils.

"Why?" At the door, she stopped.

"It's bigger than this—theft." He brushed an errant strand of wavy brown hair off his forehead and looked at her in earnest.

Don't. Just don't look at me with those eyes—she wanted to say as her heart cracked a little. His mission was big—it had to be. Yet, she couldn't be sucked in.

She put her hands on her hips. "You said that already." But she didn't leave the room. How could she? She needed to march him off this station. What was she doing? "You need to come with me to the hangar. Next departure is in a few hours."

"No. I haven't come this far…" He blew out a breath and wrapped his hands around a mug. His vitals were normal. He wasn't hiding anything in this moment, but he stared into the near-empty mug as if it held all the secrets.

She waited. They had a few hours to spare before the jet took off for Spaceport Las Cruces.

Finally, he spoke. "Janey, I need you to understand— it's important that you understand—" Then he stood and bussed his dishes to the recycler, one trip with everything stacked. He returned to the table and wiped it down. "I can't believe it... it's so hard to talk around you sometimes..."

"What are you trying to say? That you stole Bakaj's gem?"

He held her gaze, his expression neutral but not cool.

"You did, didn't you? How did you do it anyway? There was no trace of you on the vids."

He waved his hand, brushing off her question. "Tradecraft."

"Valdez." She stomped her foot. He brought out the tantrums in her. "Enough with skirting the issue."

"What's on the gem?" he asked.

"Not sure."

"What do you mean, not sure?"

"Lots of documents. I haven't had time to sift through it. It did have a picture of his great-grandchildren. What's so important about the gem?" She sat at his now-cleared table, hands clasped on the faux mahogany. She was flying blind without the details from Rhea.

"I need it as evidence so I can to arrest Bakaj for crimes against humanity. You saw his file. I need to arrest him now. I've been on this case too long to waste another day in bureaucratic wrangling. Please." He reached out to touch her but stopped short.

"Those files were only circumstantial."

"That's why I need the gem. What's on it? Please transfer me the files." He asked her again, heated, nostrils flared, as if he was holding back desperation, anger, despair.

"Wait a minute. If you stole it, why couldn't you

crack it? You're obviously very good at circumventing hard-to-crack security."

He ground out. "Faulty intel. I knew it was a small exceptional item, but I didn't know what it was exactly."

"You didn't have the proper tools." She barked a laugh but didn't smile.

"Where is it?" He sat back, cool, the color still high on his cheeks.

"I have it. Safe. What do you expect to find on it?"

"Direct evidence of his crimes against humanity."

"There's lots of files and an image of his great-grand-children, just as he said." With that inscription to them. "I have no idea if the gem contains your evidence or is as he says it is—mementos."

"What I need is there."

"How do you know?"

He gave her a look as if that was a stupid question.

"Right. Tradecraft." Janey sat back and sighed, feeling as if she'd been in a wrestling match with no clear winner. "So where does that leave us?"

He gazed at her as if she was the loveliest flower in the garden—precious and one-of-a-kind. "Work with me, Janey. Help me crack open the biggest case of your life. Not for me. For the Sol."

"Work for the Sol again? Tempting. But not properly closing my theft case? Not so much." Mom was counting on her to do her job right, to keep her job.

"File your report, but I need that gem for my case," Valdez said. "And I need to see what's on it, to confirm. The evidence has to be there." He said that last bit under his breath.

"Of him being a warlord?"

"Yes." He blew out a breath and got up, paced, and then kicked a lone shoe into the closet.

"If what you say is true, about Bakaj being a warlord behind the Russian Empire, I want to ask him," Janey said. "He has the right to face his accuser."

A shadow passed over Valdez's face. "I should be so lucky."

TWELVE

"What does that mean?" Janey asked. "You should be so lucky?" More layers. Who was this man?

Valdez waved her off and said nothing more. He tidied up, calm and cool, his movements efficient and fast. So he did know how to fold clothes and put things in drawers. And keep himself masked. Maybe his messy room was part of his act.

Fine. She had a case to solve, not a man to—what? So what if she wanted to peel back his layers, see his true heart, his true self. Maybe at core, he was as complex as he was to her now— ever-changing, evolving. Not so much as a man as a force of nature, ever-shifting like the solar wind. Maybe that was his true self, never to be pinned down.

Didn't matter. She had a job to complete, not daydream about what her life could be like.

She wanted to return the gem to Bakaj. She wanted to know what was on his gem, even though her case was essentially over. When Bakaj had given her permission to deep-dive into his life for the purposes of finding the gem, he had to know he was opening himself up, exposing himself as the criminal Valdez said he was. Still, she itched to crack the secrets of this case —to be a part of a large case again and to get to the heart of what drove Valdez to be so covert. A Sol agent wouldn't go to such lengths unless there was a good reason.

She clicked her wrist comm to call Kim. Valdez opened his mouth and shut it when Janey glared at him. She too was good at shutting out her heart, but maybe that wasn't such a good thing anymore.

When Kim picked up, Janey asked for a private room where a guest would feel comfortable meeting her, and not the security conference room. That would be too official.

"I have just the space: The Betelgeuse Suite. What guest would you like to have meet you there?" Kim asked.

"Dima Bakaj. Please contact him and have him meet us there." The Betelgeuse Suite was on the mezzanine, above the casino, a private lavishly-appointed suite in honor of the massive red supergiant star in the constellation Orion.

"Checking." Kim put her on hold. The comm went silent.

"Janey, I need to see what's on that gem. Now," Valdez said, suddenly standing too close to her. The room was tidied.

"We're doing this my way, Valdez." She moved toward the door. "And stop calling me Janey."

"I commed him," Kim said, "but he didn't confirm receipt. This is strange..."

"What?" Janey asked. He could be busy. Bakaj did say he had meetings.

"I have two bio readings for Mr. Bakaj. One at SkyBar and one in the Red Phoenix's kitchen."

"Both? Weird." Janey double-checked her readings. They confirmed Kim's.

"Impossible," Valdez said. "Even I can't spoof the bio readings to be in two places at once."

"I'll check the coding," Kim said grimly. "Possibly a glitch in the station's AI. Quantum weirdness. It happens... sometimes." She sounded frustrated.

"We'll check both places," Janey said. "Thanks." She closed the comm and turned to Valdez. "We'll check both places, together."

"We should split up to save time," he said at the same time.

"No way," Janey said. "My case, my way. Locality first."

"Actually, it's my case. The warrant, remember? Sol Unified Police jurisdiction trumps the locality in cases of crimes against humanity." Valdez crossed his arms over his chest. "Which this is."

"Crimes which we have no proof of."

"Yet." His glare could melt asteroid ore, but not her.

"The financials we reviewed show transactions but not how the weapons were used. You could get him on weapons trade."

"The statute of limitations has long since passed on the weapon trade. That's why I need what's on that gem. I have it on good authority that what I need is on it."

"I thought you said Bakaj was the warlord behind the Russian Empire."

"You came to that conclusion."

"What is his crime against humanity?"

Valdez peered at her but said nothing.

"Fine. Once I close my case, my way, you can pursue

yours." She left his quarters and headed toward the security section. Valdez caught up after a few strides. Did they just have their first fight?

"I was on my case until—" Valdez said.

"You got careless."

"That wasn't what I was going to say, but yes, I didn't plan for every contingency." His tone was pensive, not at all flirty. And he was accompanying her. That had to count for something.

Once he arrested Bakaj, provided the evidence he needed was on the gem, he'd jet off L'Étoile back to New York.

First fight. Last fight. Relationship over before it began. What had she been dreaming about? You couldn't tame nature. Besides, she was flying solo, and that was how it had to be. She didn't even feel good about doing things her way. She was only doing her job—one she needed to keep.

She knew what she signed up for when she said yes to the very generous job offer to be lead investigator of Bijoux de L'Étoile. Mom would be well cared for as she followed the expensive treatment protocols. The treatment had to work. They had to beat this disease.

Hopefully, Mom wouldn't wake up with the night sweats again tonight. The new meds had crappy side effects. The very expensive experimental medication had better work.

The man who ultimately paid her—the reclusive Frederick Schoeneman—was one of the richest men on the planet, if not the richest. He'd made his massive fortune with his conquests in asteroid mining and had who knew how many holdings all over Earth, on the moon, in the asteroid belt, and beyond. The hotel had started as a waystation for asteroid miners. There was still a bare-bones eat-and-sleep on the hangar level.

But even with all his wealth and holdings and the influence that came with it, Schoeneman wasn't above Sol Unified Planets law—the governing body that regulated Earth's planet and off-planet-wide trade and the judicial system.

She could do right by her job and properly close the case. Then the Sol lawman could swoop in and leave.

Janey stopped at Milano's office and knocked but got no answer. She commed him and interrupted his lunch, somewhere with old piano jazz in the background, possibly his quarters.

"Go ahead, McCallister," Milano said and chewed.

She told him she'd found the gem and would file the proper forms for recovered stolen property soon and close the case.

"That's good news," Milano boomed. "That's two in less than twenty-four hours. Great job, Lieutenant."

"Thank you, Chief. We're on the way to return it to him now," Janey said, and she turned around and headed to the staff turbo elevator.

"We who? You're still working with Valdez? Good work, you two. I want to see you both in my office by 5 p.m. local time to present your report. And Frederick can receive it with his morning espresso."

"Yes, sir." Janey commed off, and they stepped into the staff turbo elevator. It smelled faintly of lemon cleanser. The bot cleaners had just been through. The grey door whooshed closed and the turbo headed up, a faint vibration through her feet the only signal of their movement.

"Why did you tell him that we were returning the

gem?" Valdez turned to her, frowning. "I don't want to return it. I need it for evidence."

"It's the right thing to do. Then your boss can take it up with my boss." She crossed her arms. She stared at the grey turbo walls. "Case closed."

"Where are we going? The casino was one level down." Valdez moved in front of her, leaned in, and paused for a second, waiting, refusing to be ignored.

She held her ground, notched up her chin, and didn't lean in even though his lips looked delectable. "To check the Betelgeuse suite on the mezzanine. This turbo will get us there without going through the casino." His brown eyes had flecks of green in them. He stared at her lips and licked his.

"I wouldn't dare think of changing your mind." His voice was velvety smooth and held a purr. His scent of woodsy aftershave surrounded her, drawing her in. It seemed at odds with his cosmopolitan demeanor, but it seemed to suit him and hinted at something wild and mysterious. And that heat radiating off him—so male, so sure, centered, grounded, and ready for anything. Who was this man?

She'd never see him again. Didn't matter.

"You're lying." She closed the gap and kissed him, hard. He returned the kiss, then pulled back and searched her face.

Closeness was closeness, if even for an exploding moment.

"Trust me," he whispered. Was he referring to the case now or to them? He caressed her cheek, as if she were the most precious thing he'd ever gazed upon, and sighed, as if he'd found whatever he was searching for.

But she wasn't precious. She was hard edges and need. "I don't." She ran her fingers through his silky, curly brown hair. Stars! She'd wanted to do that since she'd first laid eyes on him. She pressed her body against his, her hands over his muscled back, his firm butt, need spiraling through her. He held her head gently and deepened their kiss. She was lost into sensation. Her heart beating against his, together against the world.

No. No, that couldn't be.

"No," she said aloud. She edged back farther from his heat, faced forward, and patted her hair.

What was she doing? Messing about like a lovesick teenager. She'd never lost control like this even when she was a teenager. He brought out the wild in her, the deep yearnings, the parts of her that wanted all of it, to embrace life, and race a jet to outer planets and beyond and back again, high on reaching further, farther, faster— to explore all the unknowns of their precious Sol system. She swatted away that old dream from childhood, inspired by the adventure vids she devoured when she was innocent and when the Sol and its wonders was first opening up to her.

This elevator was too small for them both. The Sol system was too small for them both. She combed her fingers through her hair, finding knots.

"Now what, Janey? Leave it. You're beautiful."

"What?" She brushed a stray tear. Stardust. She blew out a breath and shook her head. She couldn't do this— whatever this was between them.

When would the damn door open?

And then it did. The turbo doors slid open onto an empty mezzanine walkway, the buzz of the casino low in the background. She jumped out.

"I said 'you're beautiful.'" He spoke softly, all smooth charm and artifice gone from his voice. He was at her side, peering at her, open and ready for anything it seemed. "Is there any chance for us?"

"I don't—" The casino games popped and whistled. The huge viewscreen was set to a space jet race in the asteroid belt, and people cheered, laughed, and bet on the race.

"Janey," he said her name like a prayer. "You challenge me like no other. And you excite me. It's wonderful. So alive. My life is crazy. But with you I feel... complete. I can't explain it."

Then he was quiet and waited, still and focused on her, his magnetic laser attention—all on her. For one breath. Then another. She held the third breath and closed her eyes to search within. She focused on releasing the tension in her body and sent out her fears and worries.

May the stars guide her true.

She could do this—whatever this dance was. Whatever this life threw at her, she would catch and throw back and survive. As she had many times before. She turned to face him and gazed into his dark eyes. "You're done playing me?"

"I've put all my cards on the table, McCallister. How about you?" He tugged her back into his arms.

She let him, her heartbreaking. This could never be real, whatever fire zinged and combusted between them.

Yet what if it could?

Then it was time to lay all her cards on the table.

"I need to show you something." Janey blinked, making her ocular implant visible to him for the first time.

A look of shock flashed on Valdez's face, and anger sharpened his features. He quickly masked his face with an expression of neutrality—his coolness.

"You have an eye BCI," he said.

"Yes, an ocular implant."

"Since when?"

"Thirteen."

"You were just a kid. Why? How? What happened?" His gaze softened a little.

"An accident. One I caused. Trying to fix our home robot."

"Oh, Janey." He folded her in his arms again, his voice warm in her hair. "That must have sucked."

She lowered her guard just long enough to hug him back—to be sheltered from the harsh world. No one had ever had this reaction to learning she had her ocular implant. A few had treated like she was a god; some feared her; still others hated her or were jealous or wanted to use her.

He leaned back, gave her a bright smile, and pretended to lift a cap off his head and swept his arm out, all bluster. "Milady, the casino awaits." His vitals read cool and calm—his hiding mode.

What was this calculus? That he could bare his heart, then slip into a role?

Two could play at that game. "One moment." She backtracked to one of the several doors on the mezzanine. She unlocked it. A suite opened up, the sitting room furnishings all red velvet and gold and silver accents. The suite smelled of whiskey and faint lemon cleanser. The room was empty. No Bakaj. It was a gamble to double check the suite before continuing their quest for him.

She checked her internal screen for his location. He was still showing up as being in the kitchen. At least only one location was showing now.

"Very nice," Valdez said at her shoulder.

"Milord." She brushed past him to the top of the stairs that led to the casino floor. Tiny white lights twinkled up the edge of each stair. She headed down the steps, and the little lights flashed in pattern ahead of her.

She stopped at SkyBar, crowded with ladies and gents drinking, all flirty and falling over each other. It was only fifteen hundred. Above the bar, a lowered ceiling display showed a distant galaxy in blue and white. The bartender served several drinks, then came over to them and smiled.

"Hey, Janey!" Faizah commanded such a welcoming presence, as if you were stepping into her domain, and she was always happy to see you. She was a tall, trim Ethiopian woman, goddess-like in her spiral galaxy tattoos and multi-colored bead necklaces. They'd chatted when Janey had come by the bar late at night after her shift.

"Hey! Have you seen this man here?" Janey showed her Bakaj's image on her holo screen.

Valdez cozied up to the zinc bar beside her. Faizah studied the image and didn't glance at Valdez.

Faizah washed a glass with quick efficiency and nodded. "He passed by with Chef Gina. They headed that way." She waved deeper into the casino, toward the restaurant and high roller tables.

"How long ago?" Valdez asked slowly, his voice dripping with charm.

The bartender lifted an eyebrow at him. "Well, you certainly know how to turn it on, but save it for your lady friend." She winked at Janey.

"How long?" Janey asked, suppressing a smile.

The bartender looked her up and down, making a show of it for Valdez's sake. "For you, anything."

"Thank you." Her cheeks heated. She could take the compliment. "Well."

"Well what, gorgeous?" Faizah smirked.

"Faizah! Come on." Jane fanned her face and gave the bartender a fake pout.

"About fifteen minutes ago."

"Do you know where they were headed?" Janey asked, all business.

"They were talking about food, so perhaps Chef's kitchen." Faizah leaned closer to Janey. "I know there's not supposed to be any fraternizing during work hours, but if you wanted to, you know... Then you know where to find me. I have the 3 p.m. to midnight shift almost every night." She winked.

Janey leaned in and whispered. "I'm flattered, but no thanks." Janey winked back.

Faizah patted her hand. "I'm keeping you from your— work. And don't tell Chef Gina that I, uh, propositioned you. She hates fraternizing, except if she does it."

"Of course, Faizah. We gotta do what we gotta do."

Faizah blew her a kiss, and Janey pretended to catch it and stick it into her bra.

Faizah laughed and waved her off.

"Should I be jealous?" Valdez draped an arm across Janey's shoulders as they left the bar.

"I don't know." She shrugged his arm off and led him through baccarat and roulette tables toward the kitchen in search of Bakaj. They could go back to the staff side and take the staff turbo to the kitchen, but they were here now, so they may as well enter through the public side.

Traveling the length of the curved casino, she barely glanced out the wide floor-to-ceiling window that made up the entire wall. She had her eye on the swinging door that came into view, where servers rushed in and out with full or empty trays.

At the final curve, the restaurant came into view perched on an elevated level. Tables were nestled here and there behind potted ferns to give guests privacy, while still enjoying being in public.

There was something about hiding in plain sight. She could see the appeal, and the excitement, to snuggle with the one you desired while you fed him delicacies, touching him delicately or not so delicately, near so many people who didn't know what you were doing. There she was going wild in her fantasies. She swiped them aside and strode into the restaurant. Ms. Bartlett, the maître d', didn't stop her.

Janey navigated around the low tables and tall potted ferns, peeking past the plants, searching. When she'd done a full circuit of the sparsely populated restaurant, she breezed past the frowning maître d' and said with a pouty face. "Ah, he's not here."

Valdez met her at the bottom of the stairs, a frown of his own on his face. "Well, that was a bratty thing to do."

"Part of the act," she said under her breath and flipped her hair. "I was looking for you know who." She poked him in the chest like a jealous lover.

Some women laughed at her display and nodded, sipped their drinks, and went back to playing cards.

She had no idea she was such an exhibitionist. Stars above, she enjoyed it.

There was that one time, when she streaked across campus with her girlfriends, but she was eighteen then. They'd been new Granton citizens, and she'd felt so free. Now she was an overly responsible thirty-two-year-old supporting her mother, searching for an old man to lock up for crimes against humanity, and over-acting for those present. Or maybe loosening up a little and having some fun.

Valdez grabbed her around her waist and growled possessively. In character, Janey laughed, spun out of his grip, and sped up her stride. She got to the swinging door to the kitchen first.

A big man dressed in ninja black stopped her with a hand up and a stern look in his eye. The tight jaw was a good indicator, too, of the blaring "No" his body language radiated. She knew the type.

THIRTEEN

JANEY HADN'T MET THE GUARD BUT HAD SEEN him from afar in the commissary. He was ex-military, like she was. Plus he had an extra foot in height, an added one hundred pounds in girth, and bulging tattooed biceps.

Maybe he'd see her for who she appeared to be and not who she really was. Worth a try. Maybe she was caught up in the charade, having some fun on the job for once.

"Oh, sweetie, can't we just go in and get us some extra—what were those—canapés with caviar and Scottish cheese?" Janey batted her eyes at Valdez. He picked up on her cue and grinned and smacked his lips, wiggling his eyebrows suggestively. A bit over the top. She didn't need to play an act, but Valdez brought it out of her.

Janey suppressed a giggle, as if she'd had too much champagne. That was what it really felt like—a bubbling up of something from her belly. Who knew improv on the job could be this fun and a little disorienting, but in a good way?

"I don't see why not. If you'd let us in, my good man..." Valdez moved in front of Janey and motioned with one hand behind his back for her to slip around them.

Janey tried it, but the big man was too smart. He side-stepped to block her path, peering down at her a bit bored as if he could do this all day.

"I didn't want to do this, but—" She crooked a finger in the big guy's face. Time for the direct approach.

He leaned in, expressionless, his pulse normal.

"I'm Station Security Investigator McCallister, and we need to get into the kitchen." She spoke in a whisper and flashed her holo badge. "We're undercover."

"Is that so?" A flicker of concern crossed his face. Then he went impartial and cool again. "Thought I recognized you. That's right. I saw you shadow sparring the other day in the gym. Nice job." He almost smiled, then shut that down. "Doesn't matter. Chef's orders."

"Since when?"

"Since always. Didn't your chief tell you? We're separate security departments."

"Chief Milano may have mentioned that." She didn't remember. Janey crossed her arms and accessed the encyclopedia-sized files via her implant and searched for the rules and regulations concerned. Who heard of a kitchen having their own security crew? When you ran a six-star restaurant on the world's classiest space station hotel-casino, maybe you needed to. Why would Chef Gutierrez need to?

Ah, there it was—a one-page mention amongst all the gigabytes of contents on the casino contingencies and emergency security protocols.

"He's security too?" The guard gestured to Valdez with his chin.

"Yep, him too. Sol Unified Police. Joint task force," Janey said.

The guard frowned at Valdez, scanned him from head to toe, and glanced back at Janey, suspicion in his gaze.

"You don't believe us." Not exactly joint, but at least they were working together.

Big guy leaned back, grinned, and crossed his arms against his massive chest. "I do believe you, but the answer is still no."

"Come on." Janey put her hand on his muscled forearm, bigger than her mother's Gratitude Day ham.

He uncrossed his arms, brushing off her touch. "No. Chef Gutierrez is clear on this rule, as she is on all others. No non-kitchen staff beyond this point."

"Shall I call Chief Milano? I'm sure you know who he reports directly to."

"Call him. Won't make a difference if you do. I still can't."

Milano would not want to be bothered by so trivial a matter, nor would he call Schoeneman about it. Dumb move, McCallister. But it was worth a try, to test the boundaries and see what kind of security Chef Gutierrez had. Excellent, so far.

Janey motioned for him to come closer again. He leaned down. "Then please get someone to search for a guest. We think he's in there, and we need to talk to him."

"No guests have gone past me. I've been here for hours." He stiffened, as if insulted.

"What's your name?" Janey crossed her arms, nudging her breasts up a bit to reveal more cleavage.

Big Man's eyes didn't roam from her face. Darn. You used what you had.

"Why? So you can report me to Chef?" His pulse kicked up a notch, and his cheeks reddened.

He wasn't afraid of Milano, only of the master chef extraordinaire, Gina Gutierrez. She sounded like a real tough cookie.

"No. Why does everyone think I'll report them to the chef?" Janey blew out a breath. "I want to know your name so we can have a more humane conversation. I told you my name. It's common courtesy where I come from for the other person to share their name too. Isn't it like that where you grew up?"

The big man's face softened, and his vitals calmed a little. He held out a meaty palm. Janey shook his hand. He could crush probably every bone in her hand but seemed to know just the right pressure to make it a firm, friendly handshake.

"Mutu, Tomika Te. Nice to meet you." He leaned in for the last bit, so no one passing by could hear. "Investigator McCallister." Mutu turned to Valdez. "And you are?"

"Valdez, Orlando, Special Agent with Sol Unified Planets, undercover." Valdez wrapped an arm around her waist and pulled her close.

"You two didn't waste much time." Mutu chuckled.

Janey ignored that remark and the buzz that fluttered through her chest and lower, and she checked her holo for Bakaj's location. Now Bakaj's biotracker showed up in the kitchen and also in the spa. Really? What the quasar was going on with his bio-reading? Was this a system glitch or only something affecting Bakaj?

She hit her comm. "Kim? Can you confirm Bakaj's location? I'm getting two readings—again."

"On it. Stand by." Kim muted her comm so she could

search without the cacophony of the casino blaring in her ears.

"If we've lost him..." Valdez scrubbed his face and turned toward the massive wallscreen where a new space jet race was ending and announcers yabbered about the results. Gamblers laughed and chatted at the card tables, and a waitress bustled through the swinging doors from the kitchens five feet away, tray held high. Janey caught a tantalizing whiff of a fried, doughy something that reminded her of beignets.

Waiting for Kim's reply, Janey joined Valdez, leaving Tomika to guard his swinging door, oh so close, yet off-limits. "How could we lose him? There isn't another space jet or StarEl arrival until this evening."

"Not true."

"What do you mean?"

"I sent for a jet as soon as we dug into Dima's files."

"When you went to the bathroom," Janey said.

He shrugged, not looking at all apologetic. His team commanded a lot of resources if he could call a space jet to pick up one person.

"Not cool, Valdez. You should have told me."

"I have a job to do." He gave her a cool unreadable look, his vitals calm.

"So do I," Janey said. How did a simple theft case become so complicated? What was the proof hidden on the gem that Valdez wanted so badly?

Janey checked the internal scan she'd set running to translate the gem's files. Only a small portion had been translated. She wouldn't know what to look for once it had. She'd have to let Valdez have access. Then he'd leave, and she'd stay.

Kim came back on the comm. "Mr. Dima Bakaj and Chef Gina Gutierrez are indeed in the kitchen. The spa signal blipped. I'm looking into that glitch. Shouldn't happen." Her voice was tight.

"Thanks, Kim," Janey said. "Any ideas on how to get around Mutu?"

"Oh, Tomika? That big teddy bear is on duty?"

"Yah."

"No way to talk your way through, if that's what you mean. But you know there's a back entrance through the storeroom at SkyBar, don't you?"

"Right, of course." Janey accessed the schematics. There was a huge storeroom connecting the bar and the kitchen. Right. Damn fun and games.

"You'll have to get past Faizah. Have you met her? Can you handle that?" There was a laugh in Kim's voice.

"I have met Faizah and can handle her, no problem," Janey said.

"Another thing, McCallister." Her voice was serious. "Tell Valdez that his jet is here, but Milano ordered for the dockmaster to keep the agents in the hangar. He won't let them into the hotel. Something about jurisdiction. And Milano wants to see you two pronto. Iona out." Kim commed off using her last name before Janey could ask any questions. Milano was probably standing right in front of her, peering over his ridiculous old-fashioned and inoperative eyewear.

Janey relayed the messages to Valdez along with the other way into the kitchen.

"Milano and the jet can wait. We need to get Bakaj now." Valdez headed toward the bar, and Janey hurried to catch up with him.

A few feet from SkyBar in the middle of the poker table area, Valdez slowed then stilled her stride by pulling her to him in an embrace. The kiss was for show. And then it deepened, and the kiss was for them, wet and heavy. Connected in the moment, even if it was only temporary. Even if was only an illusion.

"What was that for?" she asked, breathless, hot all over.

"We're a team, right?" He whispered into her ear, echoing her thoughts. "How do you want to play this?"

"Straight. Tell Faizah we need to get behind the bar, that we're on the job."

"I want to play it up."

"Why?"

"For fun. Together. With you."

"You just like to draw attention to yourself." The fun was over.

"To us."

"No need. Not efficient."

"But it's fun. Come on, Janey." He caressed her cheek, so sincere.

She paused a bit, finding no strong reason for no. "Why not?" Either way they'd find Bakaj and the case would be over, and he'd leave.

He grinned wide and gave her a quick kiss.

She managed to grin back, but only for a second. "Is Faizah watching?" Janey's back was to the bar.

"Faizah is washing a glass and taking an order and laughing at something a guest just said," he said, squeezing her tight and nuzzling her ear. "How does she do all that?" he added with admiration in his voice.

"Practice." Janey pushed against Valdez's muscled chest, spun, and strode toward the bar gate.

"Hey," Valdez said and followed.

She was improvising, acting on gut instinct. She lifted the bar gate, keeping her face away from Faizah. Maybe she wouldn't be recognized and only be considered a rogue, overly eager, thirsty customer who wanted to get her own bottle.

Janey pushed the swinging door to the storage room, Valdez right behind her. Faizah didn't follow. Maybe she saw who it was and wouldn't raise the alarm. Maybe she would and she'd call Janey. SkyBar was part of Janey's jurisdiction.

"I thought we were a team," Valdez said tightly. "That was your play? Barging right in?"

Janey said nothing and perused the storage room. She hadn't been here before. The large room had four or five aisles of floor-to-ceiling shelves, stocked with liquors of all kinds and colors, the edges of the high-ceilinged room off in the darkness. The space smelled of onion and wine and spices. Janey adjusted her ocular implant to brighten the darkness. There was the door to the kitchen at the end of the center aisle.

She picked up the pace and jogged, Valdez keeping pace behind her, trusting her in the dark. In her quick sweep of the cavernous room, she didn't spot any security measures. There could always be alarms she didn't anticipate, security sensors hidden even from her implant. Clearly, kitchen security and main hotel security needed to coordinate better.

She reached the end of the aisle and pushed the swinging door into a very busy kitchen, full of shouting commands, the pungent smell of garlic, searing meat, and cilantro.

FOURTEEN

REAL FLAMES FLASHED ON THE STOVES UNDER enormous vents, and sous chefs wrapped in white long aprons yelled orders to servers in black aprons and to each other. In the middle of it all, a statuesque Latina woman, in a ruby red evening gown, barked commands. The legendary and Sol-renowned chef—Gina Gutierrez.

From eight feet away, she looked straight at Janey and boomed, "What are you doing in my kitchen?" The woman must have had a sixth sense or super-sharp hearing enhancements to hear Janey enter.

Janey approached Gutierrez through the crowd of kitchen workers that got ever thicker, pressing close, glaring at her, barring their teeth like a pack of wild dogs. When Janey was four feet away from Gutierrez, she stopped. Kitchen staff hemmed her in, knives and other sharp implements in their hands. Street fighting style.

"Station Security Investigator." Janey slipped her physical badge from her clutch—no way the holo badge would have the same impact—lifted it high, and spoke in a loud voice, "Chef, tell your people to stand down.

There's no cause for this behavior. We're on the same side."

Gutierrez glared at her. "This is *my* kitchen."

"I know, Chef. I'm not disputing that. I'm looking for a guest. He's a person of interest." That seemed to have no effect—in fact, the opposite of what Janey expected as a hotheaded cook lunged at her with his paring knife.

What the—

Janey grabbed his wrist and twisted it, forcing him to release the knife. The weapon clattered to the floor. She twisted his arm behind his back for good measure. "Really? Anyone else want to play? This isn't the barrio."

What was wrong with him? With all of them?

"Chef Gutierrez," she yelled, but the chef only glared at her.

She heard a punch behind her. Valdez shook his hand and grimaced down at the sous chef coldcocked at his feet. "He thought I was a pansy and came at me with a pan."

Janey rolled her eyes at his bad pun, then she turned to the chef and raised her voice again over the kitchen din, keeping her tone conversational—in an attempt to de-escalate this aggressive behavior. "Gina, is this what you want? A brawl in your world-class kitchen? We're not here to hurt you."

"What *do* you want?" the chef said.

"I told you. I'm looking for a guest. Where can we talk privately?" Janey said, keeping her tone light.

But it wasn't over, apparently.

A middle-aged woman built like a linebacker nearest Janey swiped at her with a knife, one of those big ones used for chopping carrots and potatoes and other thick things, maybe even meat bones. Janey jumped out of the way just in time. With a strong overhand, she whacked the sous chef on the elbow with the flat of her palm, and the woman cried out. The cleaver banged on the floor. Janey held in her wince of pain. Hitting a sharp elbow with the flat the palm hurt.

"Everyone, stop," Gutierrez commanded, loud as any one of Janey's drill sergeants. "Give them safe passage to my office. Johnson and Ramirez, to the infirmary, now. Say nothing." The chef had spoken, and the sea of kitchen staff turned back to their work like obedient soldiers, leaving the aisles clear. "Follow me, Investigator." Gutierrez frowned, her steely gaze pointed at Janey.

Janey did as the chef commanded.

Off of the kitchen, the chef entered the small office and took a seat on a stool behind a wide bistro table. Two barstools were in front of the table.

"Close the door." Gutierrez waved. "Sit."

"I prefer to stand. This won't take long," Janey said.

"Good." Gutierrez eyed her. "What do you want?"

"I'm looking—we're looking—for Dima Bakaj, a guest on this station. Have you seen him?"

"He and I had lunch together today. I gave him a private tour of the kitchen, and then he left." She tapped a clear keyboard on her desk and the screen shimmered in front of her. She eyed the screen, as if checking her calendar. "Only twenty minutes ago. What is this regarding?"

"We'll ask the questions," Valdez said, his voice hard, all business.

"Who are you?"

Janey jumped in. "This is Investigator Valdez, and we're following up on a theft. We would like to know what you and Bakaj discussed?"

"That's confidential. Business."

"At what time did you meet with him?"

Gutierrez huffed a breath and tapped on her keyboard. "Twelve noon station time."

"And you say he left your side twenty minutes ago, so..." Janey said.

Gutierrez huffed out another breath and checked her screen. "Yes, three-ten station time," she said in a snippy voice.

"Do you know where he was headed?"

Gutierrez splayed her hands on her desk, as if stretching them. "How should I know?"

"You two just spent over three hours together, and you showed him your sacred domain. I'm sure you have some insight into the man."

Gutierrez clamped her lips tight, a quick gesture, but often a sign of holding back something.

Janey leaned back on her heels. She could wait out the moody chef for as long as it took. "You look like someone who knows her business associates quite well." Janey dropped her arms at her side.

Valdez mirrored her relaxed and open stance, thankfully getting her message to let her take lead. It was her damn case, after all.

Gutierrez turned to a mirror on the sidewall and fiddled with her black hair done up in a tasteful bun, red jeweled pins holding it up. She applied another line of ruby red lipstick on painted lips.

She spoke nonchalantly without looking at Janey. "He invited me to the spa, but I am far too busy to take the afternoon off." She turned to face them, looking like a high-end model for beauty products, and not the head chef of a premiere restaurant.

"We have a report of him being here only five minutes ago," Janey said. "Are you sure he's left the kitchen?"

"Of course. I escorted him past the bar myself, past dozens of witnesses." She narrowed her eyes at Janey. "What do you mean a report? Are you spying on guests?"

"We need to search the area."

"No. No way. You'll only be underfoot. We're in full dinner prep. And we don't like *others* in our kitchen." She wrinkled her nose at Janey and ignored Valdez.

Janey was used to people not liking law enforcement. Whether or not Gina Gutierrez had a good reason for her behavior remained to be investigated, later. "Chef, we'll stay out of the main kitchen. We need to check the storage areas, freezers, stockrooms, that sort of thing."

Gutierrez stood and smoothed down her gorgeous dress. "Five minutes. That's all. And escorted by one of my people." She tapped on the table in a one-two beat, and one of her staff appeared in the doorway.

"Torres, escort these two to storage areas one and two and then out of the kitchen via the stock room. Or staff hallway. I don't care, but make sure you have your eye on them the entire time. Avoid the main kitchen."

"Yes, ma'am."

Janey followed the young woman, sidestepping the kitchen to storage areas one and two, which were mini-vertical gardens along two walls and contained shelves full of labeled bins against the other two walls. Staff coming in and out of the storage areas for supplies ignored them, but Janey felt their furtive gazes on her. No trace of Bakaj.

Janey checked the young woman's personnel file. Juanita Torres, a twenty-two-year-old recent culinary school graduate with average scores. That was all. No place of origin noted.

When they stepped into the final cavernous stock

room behind the bar, Janey asked, "Torres, do you enjoy working for Chef Gutierrez?"

Torres nodded and pushed open the stockroom door to the back of the bar. She lifted the wooden hinged counter and waited for them to pass through to the public side, but she didn't meet Janey's eye. The young woman had probably been told by the chef to not engage in small talk.

When Janey didn't advance, Torres frowned and waved toward the casino.

What was Gutierrez hiding in her kitchen?

"Thank you, Torres." Janey stepped through the opening.

The young woman didn't reply, lowered the counter, and returned to the storeroom.

Janey passed the bar and glanced at Faizah, grimacing. "Sorry," she mouthed.

Faizah shrugged but didn't stop her work to come over. SkyBar bustled with guests lingering and casino servers waiting for their orders.

"Well, that was a bust," Valdez said and leaned on the bar, all playful pretense gone.

"Not exactly. I think we should head to the spa," Janey said, stopping beside him.

"Gina did say Bakaj had invited her there," Valdez said. "We could take a nap. That'd be nice." His mouth curved in a teasing grin.

"No naps. Let's go," Janey said and headed back through the loud casino and into the bustling lobby, glancing about at the guests crisscrossing the open space.

For a second, a wave of dizziness descended on Janey, and her vision went fuzzy and red-tinged. She swayed and felt herself tipping over. Valdez caught her before she hit the floor.

"You okay?" Valdez draped an arm around her waist, an undercurrent of panic in his voice. "What's happening?"

"Minute. Need a minute." Janey closed her eyes, counted to ten, and then opened them again. Everything looked normal. She blinked through the optical wavelengths to make sure everything was working properly, ignoring the panic in her gut. Her screen read green—all functions nominal.

She pulled away from Valdez. "I'm fine."

"What's wrong?"

"Nothing. A glitch. It happens sometimes, but it's fixed now," Janey said. "Let's get to the spa." She put a hand on her stomach to quell the queasiness.

The last time the dizzies had hit her this hard was when she was thirteen and adjusting to her implant. What could be the cause this time?

"How do we get to the spa? I don't see any signs." Valdez peered around the lobby.

"It wasn't in your case prep?" She gave him a half-smile.

"No need." He looked at her funny.

"It's…" Janey called up the station map. It was upside down on her screen. "Weird," she said under her breath.

Okay, so something *was* wrong with her implant or the screen or the brain-computer interface. And she couldn't recall the station map from memory. She had toured in the day or two after she first arrived on station. This wasn't good.

The flutter of panic burst through her, spreading across her chest, and spots of light flickered in her periphery. Her fingertips tingled —all symptoms of a crash.

"Janey? You okay?" Valdez had her arm in a firm grip.

"Fine." She breathed in, out. Her vision returned to normal. She could do this.

FIFTEEN

Out of her periphery, Janey saw a shimmery black shape hurrying across the lobby. She turned to focus on it—him—a pasty-faced man in the silver and black uniform of housekeeping, carrying a handful of plush towels. Out of place. Housekeeping was supposed to take the staff lifts. She didn't recognize him. But she'd probably only met a quarter of the staff, and there was regular turnover. It was impossible to meet everyone.

Still, she had to check him out. Janey stopped him with a wave. Richard was the name on his silver-plated name tag. He approached, and his personnel file scrolled on her ocular screen. Richard Bander, forty-nine, from New Jersey Protectorate, employed for the last ten weeks at L'Étoile, and he had a decades-long string of housekeeping jobs at other posh hotels under "previous work."

Tipsy persona in place, Janey asked, "Where's the spa, young man? The signs seem to be missing. Probably stolen by the young colts who party all night long." She squinted at his nameplate. "Richard."

The man kept his expression neutral, polite. "That

way, behind the fig tree, ma'am. Down the spiral staircase. Unless you want to walk to the other end of the station and use the aft elevator bank by the suites. Up to you."

"Of course, it's up to me," Janey said haughtily.

The man turned to go, but she caught his frown as it flashed for a millisecond. She'd have missed it if she wasn't trained to notice and interpret micro-expressions. So, he didn't like rich snobs. She understood where he was coming from.

"Please excuse madame," Valdez said. "She's had one too many… or ten." Disapproval dripped from his voice, the perfect image of the reproachful mate.

"Yes, sir." Richard's frown flashed again as he glanced up at Valdez.

So he didn't like Valdez either.

"I'm sorry," Janey said and dug deeper into her persona. Maybe this Richard would reveal more. "I know I really need to sober up. But when? Life is too short, or too long." She giggled and blinked to see if there was more information in the man's file. "There's just too much fun to be had. Must spend hubby's money!"

There was one past infraction in his record from another hotel, for using the wrong elevators, crossing the public space when he hadn't needed to. Same behavior as here. She'd have to have a word with Paula to keep an eye on him. She blinked again for more information, but a pain shot across her temple. Hell. She gasped and sagged against Valdez.

He caught her smoothly around the waist and pivoted, turning her away from the man and directing her toward the fig tree. "Enough, dear. You need that cure and now." At a whisper, he said, "What's wrong? Do you need a doctor?"

"Yes, no. I'm fine. Yes, the cure." In that last millisecond before turning away, she caught the fact that Richard's expression of disdain had stayed plastered over his face. Not everyone liked the super-rich, even though one felt obligated to work for them. She could understand the dislike and anger but not disdain. Unless he had disdain for drunk women.

"Come along, *querida*," Valdez said, guiding her around the fig tree in a mosaic planter, and pushing open the door to the stairwell. "You sure you don't need a doctor?"

"I'm fine," she said.

They clipped down the two dozen steps of the iron spiral staircase, Valdez's arm around her waist.

"Sure?"

"Sure." The banister was smooth and cool to the touch. The stab of pain was gone, a dull thud in its place, but all her inner diagnostics were green.

"The hotel doctor can check you out. I'll call."

"No, stop, mother henning me. I'm fine."

They reached the bottom of the stairs and took a set of double doors that led them into a cocoon of a lobby, humid and full of eight-foot-tall palms, ferns, and other tropical plants.

Valdez gave her a worried look, but thank the stars, he didn't ask her one more time if she was sure she was okay.

From a back room a woman arrived, dressed in a sparkling green pantsuit, sleek and low-cut. She was dripping wet. In an instant, the dress wicked dry. Janey recognized her from her great karaoke singing in the mess hall last week. What was her name? The woman had no name tag on, but facial recognition popped her personnel file up: Maryanne Umbanto,

L'Étoile's spa manager and professional masseuse. Right.

"May I help you?" Maryanne said smoothly.

"Hi, Maryanne. We're looking the guest, Mr. Bakaj..." Janey rubbed her temple. She blinked, and her vision blurred. She glanced at Valdez, and he put an arm around her. She leaned on him. Why not? He was warm, steady. And for the moment, she was not.

"And we'd like massages," he said.

"We would?" Janey straightened and blinked again. She had to talk to someone. This wasn't good, not remembering.

Valdez laughed. "Yes, dear."

"You okay, Janey?" Maryanne asked.

"She will be, I hope." Valdez squeezed her, eyed her concerned.

"Right this way," Maryanne said. "Scan your bracelets for the registry, and we'll get you set up."

With every step into the welcoming spa, Janey relaxed, and her headache receded. Her dizziness too. She breathed in the balmy sweet warm air. The spa walls were decorated with flowering hibiscus and wisteria. Sunlight filtered in through the ceiling, refracting into this part of the station through a series of mirrors.

Maryanne waved them toward the changing rooms and invited them to get comfortable in the adjoining massage room.

Where was Valdez? What was he thinking? As much as she'd love a massage, she had to find Bakaj, if he was even in the spa.

As much as she wanted to strip under the warmth of piped-in, diffuse sunlight, she slipped thick, soft bathrobe over her clothes, and cracked open the door to the massage room. The aroma of lavender and home-made oatmeal cookies permeated the room. It smelled lovely. Tall ferns softened the corners of the white-walled room, and so did the vid images of waves crashing on beaches, the sound a low background ambiance.

Valdez chuckled. He was already positioned on a nearby massage table, under a blanket. "Want to join me?"

"What are you doing? I don't understand you. We have to find Bakaj," Janey said.

"I know. But you didn't say no," He smiled and popped up, fully clothed. "Gotta catch some winks when I can."

"Two seconds' worth," Janey scoffed.

"More like ninety. You coming?"

"You go ahead. I'll catch up. Need to check in with my office."

"Fine."

Janey stepped through a different door into a new hallway, with treatment rooms no doubt behind the closed doors on either side. She moved to the next door, and the door slid open with a lovely little chime. A person was under a blanket.

A woman said, "Is that you, Marcie?"

"Uh no, sorry, ma'am," Janey said and stepped away from the door. It shut automatically.

She padded from door to door. Each one opened with a chime. She'd only discovered one other spa guest, a woman, who must have been napping because she didn't respond. One of the rooms had a staff member cleaning it who asked if she could help Janey. Another was a steam room with only two young men relaxing against the tiles. Still no Bakaj.

The last door to check was at the end of the hallway. She opened it and found herself in a white and blue-tiled atrium, filled with ferns. The atrium opened onto a large Olympic-sized pool that filled the vast room and scintillated in the soft light. She entered the domed space and sucked in an awed breath. The far edge of the room and where the pool met the wall was floor-to-ceiling glass. You could do your laps and feel like you were swimming in space amongst the stars.

There was Bakaj, swimming laps, goggles on, the only one in the pool.

She sat at the edge of the pool and slipped her legs in and waited to catch his attention when he swam back toward her.

He moved his arms through the water with strength and grace. That had her thinking about the amphibian-like chemical trace Soren had analyzed for her. There had been rumors of people using salamander-like genes to encourage limb and even organ regeneration. But, as Doc informed her, those enhancements were illegal and dangerous.

"Janey?" Bakaj's voice brought her back from her roaming thoughts.

He was treading water in front of her, his goggles on the top of his head.

"Hello, Mr. Bakaj. How are you?"

"Getting my daily constitutional. Are you here with news of my gem?"

"In fact, I am. We found it."

"Oh, I am so relieved. When can I have it back?" He planted two hands on the side of the pool and lifted himself out in one swift move. Was this man really ninety-years-old as his record stated?

Bakaj grabbed his towel and wrapped it around his body and under his armpits. His skin was bronzed from the sun or from an artificial bronzer. He was toned and muscular, at the peak of health, but he had the skin elasticity of an older man. His physical condition wasn't her concern, Janey reminded herself.

"We need to talk privately about all that." Janey stood. "Please come with me."

Dima frowned. "You looked into my records." He stated it.

"You knew I would," she said softly. "I also looked inside the gem."

Dima swore. "Could you decipher it?"

"Not yet."

"I need my gem back," he insisted and headed for the exit. "And I need to dress."

Janey followed, then called out to him, "Mr. Bakaj, I'd like you to stop there."

He did. "Where are we going?"

She joined him in the atrium. "I have a private suite reserved for us above the casino."

"I'd rather we talked in my room, if you don't mind."

Janey weighed the fallout of Bakaj's potential complaints to Schoeneman about being grilled with the benefit of being in a comfortable environment while they did so.

"Okay," Janey said. "But Valdez—"

"Valdez, what?" Valdez said as the door to the hallway opened.

"Please take Mr. Bakaj to the men's changing area and meet me at the lobby. Five minutes. We'll do the interview in his room."

Bakaj headed for the changing room exit, and Valdez lifted an eyebrow in question.

"Keep an eye on him," Janey said.

"I'm not a flight risk," Bakaj said without turning around, and he headed into the changing area.

Valdez watched him go, frowning, his heart rate kicking up.

"You really hate him," Janey said.

"No, I don't." But his heart rate and blood pressure increased by five percent.

"Liar."

"Stop reading me, Janey." He followed Bakaj into the changing room, leaving her with a wake of mixed signals.

It didn't matter. She probably wouldn't see him again after this case closed. It didn't matter what he thought of her.

Liar. It did matter.

SIXTEEN

IN THE QUIET OF THE GREEN HUMID LOBBY, while Janey waited for Valdez and Bakaj, she commed Kim.

"We found him," she said. "There's some kind of glitch in the system. It shouldn't have been that hard to locate him."

"Where was he?" Kim asked softly.

"Swimming in the pool."

"Oh dear. I've heard that some bio-trackers won't work submerged in water," Kim said.

"Right. I bet they're purposely built that way," Janey said.

"Why?"

"To hide from bio-tracking systems like ours." Janey scrubbed her face. Why would Bakaj go to such lengths? "Is Milano still there?"

"No, but he was only a minute ago, and he's pissed."

"Understandably so, but I thought Milano wasn't so hands-on. What is it about this case? Or is he concerned with something else."

"It's the case, I think, and he won't say what," Kim said.

"Well, we're wrapping it up. We're interviewing Dima in his room soon. I'll keep you posted."

"You and—"

"Yes, McCallister out."

Her and Valdez. What were they? Did it matter? They were two investigators, using—no, helping—each other to close their cases. She had to decide. She had decided. She was going to let Valdez take Bakaj into custody. She had to do what was right for the greater good.

Valdez entered the lobby, Dima right behind him, both of them dressed. Valdez looked restrained, Bakaj pensive. Janey took the stairs first, Dima behind her, and Valdez bringing up the rear.

They'd traveled halfway across the busy lobby full of guests and staff when they crossed paths with Richard from housekeeping again. This time he was carrying a covered meal tray.

"Did you enjoy the spa, ma'am?"

Janey stopped and flipped her hair over her shoulder. "Refreshed, yes. Sorry about earlier."

"She feels much better now," Valdez said and put his arm around her waist. "You are, aren't you?" he whispered into her ear.

"Fine," she whispered back.

"Good." Richard glanced at Bakaj then hurried toward the staff elevator.

"Courteous staff," Dima said, beside them.

Janey shook her head slightly at Valdez.

"What?" Valdez mouthed.

She firmed her lips. Something struck her as odd about Richard, but she couldn't put her finger on it yet.

Five minutes later, they were in Bakaj's suite. Bakaj

pressed the room comm and ordered some tea and sandwiches from the chef's room service. "It's better than *that*." Bakaj pointed to the wall Meal Maker. "I know many people love the in-room appliance, but I'm old-fashioned. I prefer humans making my food from scratch."

A full pitcher of ice water was already on the table with some glasses. Without a word, he poured each of them a drink and took a sip.

Janey waited until he'd set the glass down with a clink on the glass-topped table. "Before we return the gem to you, we have some more questions," she said.

"Of course." Bakaj folded his hands in his lap. "May I see it?"

Janey pulled Valdez's cloaked pouch out of the inside pocket of her wrap and set it on the table. Bakaj looked at her quizzically. He'd seen her movement, but he couldn't see the pouch. Neither could she, without adjusting her ocular implant. She upended the pouch, and the gem dropped into her palm. She set it atop of the pouch, and Valdez shifted in his seat.

"Where did you find it?" Bakaj reached for the gem.

Janey pulled it closer to her.

Bakaj sat back and sighed. "I knew this day would come, but not so soon. I hoped to do a few things first."

"What do you mean?" Janey asked.

"Like what?" Valdez said, speaking over her, his voice hard.

Bakaj stared at him. "You. You're not really an insurance investigator."

"Why do you say that?" Valdez crossed his arms. He was not cool and calm but flushed, his heart beating fast.

Bakaj shrugged and sipped his water. "Swimming always makes me thirsty," he said to no one in particular.

"Mr. Bakaj—" Janey tapped her wrist comm to prime the recording.

"Call me Dima, dear. Remember?"

"I do. Dima, I'm recording this interview. Do you understand?"

"Of course, I do." He smiled a bit sadly. "But this conversation must be off the record. For you two only. Turn off the recording."

"Why?" Janey asked.

"We can't do that," Valdez said.

"Let's hear what he has to say," Janey said.

"It's not that. We need it on the record," Valdez said. "For my case."

"What case?" Bakaj asked. "What I have to say to you two is"—Bakaj stared up at the ceiling—"sensitive," he finally said. "And not a matter of public record."

"This interview won't go into my final report," Janey said.

"But it is a matter of public record," Valdez said and shot out of his chair.

"What do you mean, Valdez?"

He glared at her.

The door chimed. "Who is it?" Valdez barked.

"Room service."

"That was fast." Bakaj smiled.

"Maybe too fast. I'd better check." Janey rose to take care of the door with her security override.

It was Richard with the tray.

"Oh! Why, thank you, you sweet man. This suite will send you a tip," Janey said and handed the tray of lavender black tea and egg and salami finger sandwiches to Valdez.

"Thank you," Richard said as he glanced over her

shoulder. Janey stood in the entrance so Richard couldn't enter.

"Thank you, my good man. That will be all." Janey closed the door without waiting for him to reply. Something about him rubbed her the wrong way. She didn't want to drop her persona for him like she had for other staff.

She set a security lock on the door and returned to the table. Valdez had poured tea for each of them.

"How civil of you," Bakaj said to Valdez as Janey sat at the table. "What do I call you? You mentioned your case. Doesn't sound like we're discussing insurance anymore. Are we?"

"Investigator Orlando Valdez, same as before."

"And?" Bakaj prompted.

Janey turned to Valdez. "Can I talk to you? Over here?" She tapped off the recording and turned to Bakaj. "Would you excuse us, please?"

Bakaj served himself a few finger sandwiches. "Of course. I'm not going anywhere."

Janey pushed her chair back, stood, and walked to the far side of the living room, near the entrance to Bakaj's bedroom. Valdez followed her, his expression neutral, his respiration slightly elevated, and his heart rate accelerated above normal.

"What?" He slipped his hands into his pants pocket. "I thought we were working together."

"We are. I know you have a bigger agenda here, but let me conduct the interview. What he says can help me sort through his files, make connections." Rhea had been sending her bits and pieces but nothing definitive yet.

"I get it. But let's not delay. I have a jet standing by, and I'd like to close this case without alerting anybody."

"Who?"

"Anybody who's watching Bakaj," Valdez said, and he bit his lip like he wanted to say more.

"Okay, secret agent man, understood." She gave him a little smile.

His eyes widened a little, a sign of surprise or shock. He smiled back. "Team?"

"Team. Stay cool and we'll all get what we want."

Janey returned to the table, sat, and sipped her tea. "Thank you for your patience, Dima. This interview won't go into my final report, but we do need to record it for my notes."

Valdez sat, and Janey clicked back on record. She stated her name and rank and the date and time. "Interviewing, Dima Bakaj, off the record. For my ears only." She glanced at Valdez. "Anything to add?"

He shook his head, frowning.

"Dima, is that satisfactory to you?"

"Which part? Your timestamp or the fact that Mr. Valdez is hiding something?" He shrugged. "He's welcome to his secrets. I have plenty of my own."

"I know," Janey said. "This is a delicate interview because you were the victim of a theft, and Investigator Valdez was the one who stole it."

Bakaj widened his eyes. "That explains… Wait, young man. Who are you really? No more obfuscation. Why did you steal my gem?"

"You first." Valdez straightened.

"Valdez, please," Janey said.

"I didn't steal the gem," Bakaj said.

"But you encrypted it with more than photos of your grandchildren," Valdez said, a bite to his voice.

"Great-grandchildren." Bakaj frowned. "Have you figured it out already? The tech *is* beyond most everyone." He eyed Valdez, then Janey, finally coming back to Valdez. "You? I didn't peg you for the type."

"The type for what?" Janey asked.

"Complex data decryption," Bakaj said.

"I cracked it," Janey said.

"Well done. Do you know what you have?"

"I do." Valdez shot out of his chair again.

Janey went with what she'd gathered from the deep dive into Bakaj's files. She was still waiting on Rhea's final analysis.

"From the shadows, you single-handedly supported the military regime of Russia," Janey said, "despite the UN's best efforts to stop the illegal arms trade. Your weapons were, and probably still are, the cause of so much suffering."

"That was thirty years ago," Bakaj said. "Statute of limitations and all that." He said that last part sadly.

"You shut those factories down and began to manufacture something else." Janey blinked to see the data as Rhea dripped it to her implant. So much. She zeroed in on the chronology. All that data was what was probably causing her dizzy spells and headache earlier.

"That was also a long time ago." Bakaj sighed, suddenly showing his age. "That doesn't matter now." He turned to Valdez. "Investigator Valdez, how did you manage to steal my gem anyway? You left no clues I presume, or the very smart Investigator McCallister would have certainly discovered...wait, she did discover... how?"

"A careless mistake on my part," Valdez said.

"Certainly, or perhaps you wanted her to discover the truth about you. The truth will out, and all that."

Valdez glared at him.

"Dima, I see you went to the Max Planck Polytechnique and graduated with highest honors with dual degrees in Computational Analysis and Neuro-Technical brain chemistry," Janey said.

"Yes, so? Lots of people did. And my education is my personal files that I assume you accessed."

"It is. I also see that you patented like a fiend for the next fifteen years and perfected brain-blood carrier for airborne chemicals, specializing in neurotransmitters to evoke endorphins and serotonin."

"That is not in the file."

"But it is on the gem." Valdez sat back in his chair and nibbled a sandwich, the picture of cool, but his heart rate kicked up a notch.

"You did crack it," Bakaj said.

"She did," Valdez said.

"According to the files I've unlocked on your gem," Jane continued, "I see that twenty years ago your company shipped en masse the weaponized compound FCN to the Russian Empire and the Russian separatists under the guise of humanitarian aid. Then via proxies, you shipped FCN to every major metro area around the world."

Valdez fidgeted in his chair and set his teacup down with a clatter. Tea sloshed over the rim.

"FCN is not a weaponized compound. It was designed to ease the suffering my weapons caused."

"How could you say that?" Valdez spat out.

"FCN was designed to make people happy. I wanted the war to end. Too many people had died—have died—already. I want people to be happy. Only to be happy."

"Bullshit. What do you mean?" Valdez shouted. "Your awful drugs make people not care, about anything. Or anyone."

"Valdez!"

"No, Janey. No." Valdez leaned across the table a shook a finger in Bakaj's face. "You're lucky I don't kill you right now."

Bakaj nodded as if Valdez's words were reasonably expressed. "I know how you feel, young man."

"How could you know?" The despair was thick in Valdez's voice.

"One of my granddaughters... she—" Bakaj sipped tea. "I can't speak of it, not yet."

"So you lost someone. Big whoop! I lost my whole family. My whole family. Goddammit!" Valdez shoved back from the table so hard the tea service rattled. "The cost of your happy drugs..." Valdez spun and stalked toward Bakaj. He stopped inches from him, his hands clenched into fists, as if he wanted to take a swing at the older man.

Janey rushed to hold him back. "What are you doing?"

Valdez twisted out of her grip and stalked to the other side of the room, breathing hard.

"The young man has the right to his emotions. Leave him be," Bakaj said.

"You—you have no right," Valdez spun to face Bakaj and stalked over to him. Janey rushed to put herself between the two men.

"Valdez, I thought you have a warrant. Sol rule of law, all that," Janey said.

"A warrant. I'm impressed," Bakaj said, smoothing down his red brocade vest, identical or the same one he was wearing that morning when Janey had interviewed him about his gem theft.

"Nothing you can do can make up for the destruction your drug caused." Valdez walked away and assaulted one of the plush royal blue pillows on the couch.

"My happiness drug was supposed to make things better—"

"Not for me." Valdez glared at Bakaj, his hands still clenched at his side. But at least he was across the room and could punch another pillow if he needed to.

"What happened?" Janey asked.

Valdez softened his gaze when he turned to her. "Nothing good." He slipped his hands into his pockets and paced the thick carpet, his head down and sadness bowing his shoulders.

"I am so sorry for your loss, young man, but I'm afraid your warrant is flimsy. No judge would have issued it without just cause, and I doubt you have it. Not with the lengths you've gone to," Bakaj said.

"My warrant is legit—from the highest authority in the Sol."

"Uh…" Bakaj said, his voice full of disbelief.

"It is legit isn't it, Valdez?" Janey asked.

"Of course. You doubt me too?"

"No, I don't," Janey said.

"How could you have gotten the warrant if you're only able to unlock the gem now for the evidence you need?" Bakaj said coolly.

"Six weeks of undercover work with your bratty spoiled grandson-in-law. He's provided a notarized record of your illegal sales of FCN and told me you carried direct evidence on you."

"I should have cut him off… but I hadn't the heart…" Bakaj said.

"Under Sol Judicial Authority," Valdez said, his voice loud and commanding, "I am placing you under arrest, Dima Bakaj, for crimes against humanity." He clutched a pair of handcuffs.

"I suppose you have proof now that you decrypted my

diamond," Bakaj sipped his tea, his heart rate a bit elevated, but his hand steady.

Valdez glanced at Janey, pleading in his gaze.

"We do," Janey said.

"There is no statute of limitations on the destruction you caused with FCN," Valdez said.

"It was legal when I made it," Bakaj said.

"But not for long. You could only con the Sol for so long, but by then the damage—millions of lives ruined, cut short."

"I'm sorry—"

"You don't get to be sorry. You get to pay for what you've done." Valdez snapped open the cuffs.

"Please, at least let me wrap up my affairs with dignity," Bakaj said. "Put those away, young man. I can't go anywhere."

"You slipped our search earlier today," Valdez said.

"I know how to turn off biotrackers—my own design. Come sit down. Have some tea and I will tell you my sad tale, then you can arrest me. Once you do me the courtesy of telling me who you really work for."

"Sol Unified Planets Investigative Services as a special investigator."

Bakaj nodded sadly. "Well done, young man. You have gone to great lengths—"

"You don't deny what you've done?"

"No," Bakaj said.

"That doesn't excuse you as the responsible party," Valdez said, bitterness in his voice.

"I know that." Bakaj dabbed his lips with a fine linen napkin, then twisted it, distorting the fabric's warp and weft. "But if it helps, I didn't learn of all the lives destroyed by my drug until later... much later. My own company, my partners, my direct reports, they hid it all from me. That's why I compiled everything into the gem and told no one."

"What?!" Valdez slapped the table, and cups clattered in their saucers. "You didn't know you created a drug that made people stop working, stop feeding their children, and neglect everything, even their own health. I don't believe it."

"I didn't know… not at first."

"How could you? So irresponsible." Valdez choked on his words. "All those deaths. On *your* hands."

"When I found out, I made a cure. I created an antidote."

"What antidote?" Valdez asked. "Really? When?" His eyes went wide with anguish.

"Yes, really. It's on the gem," Bakaj said. "I just created it. Took me five years."

"Is the antidote on the gem?" Valdez asked Janey.

Janey input a search for the antidote to FCN. "I don't see it, but Rhea hasn't finished. There were several terabytes of data."

"It's there," Bakaj said. "I came here to make things right for my beautiful great-grandchildren. You saw them, didn't you, Janey?"

"How are you making things right?" Janey asked.

"You two would make beautiful babies." Bakaj ignored her question and gestured to Valdez and then pointed to Janey, as if drawing a line between the two. "With your Latin looks," he said to Valdez. He glared at the older man. And to her, Bakaj said, "And your eclectic mix. Your ancestry is English, Scottish, a touch of Mongolian by way of Eastern European Jewish, I surmise, and Romani, definitely."

Janey didn't know what to say. Her cheeks heated, and she breathed to calm herself. But he'd guessed right.

Mom's family was mostly Scottish. She never knew her father. She was an IVF-er, like lots of her friends—Mom's genes mixed with anonymous father genes. She grew up in a tight community with her mom, her aunties and uncle-moms, and a pack of kids.

"All I want is for the young ones to be happy." Bakaj threw his mangled napkin on the table and smoothed the tablecloth flat.

"How are you making things right?" Valdez ground out through a clenched jaw.

"If only you had children, you'd understand," Bakaj said, his eyes watery with unshed tears.

"I get it," Janey said. "The next generations are important to you. You want to leave a legacy. But why now? Why not sooner? You have great-grandchildren now. I counted twelve in that photo."

"What does it matter? You have already done so much damage," Valdez said.

"It matters," Bakaj said. "Righting wrongs always matters."

"Twenty-five years too late," Valdez choked out.

"I can see you're hurting," Bakaj said.

"What do you care?" Valdez ground out.

"I care, despite my past actions." He stared into his tea. "I made my bed, now I must lie in it." He daintily wiped his mouth with his crumped napkin. "But I would like to ask a favor and indulge in your kindness."

"Please ask, and I'll see if I can help you," Janey said. "But no guarantees."

"No way," Valdez said. "You need to come with me now."

"I understand." Bakaj wiped his sandwich crumbs with the napkin onto the tea saucer. "I need twenty-four hours. To finish my business."

Janey checked the time. It was seventeen hundred, and Milano would be expecting to see her and Valdez in his office by now. Right on cue, Milano commed her.

"Report," he said without preamble.

"I'm in the middle of an interview, Chief Milano, with Dima Bakaj. I'll get you my report as soon as I can. McCallister out." Janey tapped her comm bracelet to end the link.

"Mighty cheeky of you," Bakaj said. "You'll go far."

"I don't need to go far. I only need to do the job I have," Janey said. "I can give you thirteen hours—until eight am."

"No, Janey. No." Valdez stood, handcuffs rattling at the ready.

"What will you tell your chief and your investigator?" Bakaj asked.

"That you're not going anywhere," Janey said. "We recovered your gem. Case closed. And that you're wrapping up your affairs."

"Can I have my gem back?"

"No, it's evidence in an ongoing investigation." Janey stood and swooped up the pouch and gem and handed it to Valdez. "You have the gem. Let him have a few hours. Stay here and watch him, if you like."

"I desire my privacy," Bakaj said. "Personal matters to see to."

Valdez growled and scrubbed his face, then he stuffed the cuffs back in his pants pocket. "I'll be here at midnight local time to escort you personally to the jet."

"Thank you—" Bakaj started.

"Don't thank me!" Valdez snapped.

SEVENTEEN

JANEY HEADED FOR MILANO'S OFFICE, NO GEM in hand. Best to get this over with. There was nothing to do but face her boss.

For a split second, she had the irrational desire to flee. What was going on with her? She liked her job, needed her job. Besides, there was only so far you could go on a space station, unless you wanted to go for a space walk. She shivered at the thought.

She'd been top of her class in everything, but only a few knew how deathly afraid she'd been of the space walk training and final test. It had only been by sheer will and plenty of de-phobia work she'd done that she'd been able to sublimate her fears enough to pass the final. But her fears of the black were still there.

She blew out a breath and blinked to focus on the minute details of the wall ahead, at the ever-advancing curve always out in front of her, like a horizon, always there always out of reach. It was a calming technique she'd learned back at the academy when her fear of the blackness of space first reared its ugly head.

Far ahead, at sixty feet, the speckles that she knew were caused by the refraction of the light shifted and danced as she approached. She picked a new spot in the distance, reminded herself to breathe, and kept going.

One foot in front of the other, as Mom always said when things got tough. Speaking of, hopefully her mom wouldn't call her wanting to chat. She had a report to write. It was the middle of the night in Las Cruces, and sometimes Mom would wake up for no reason. No one knew if that was a side effect of the new meds or something else.

She stepped into the staff elevator. There was nothing she could do about Mom for the moment. Milano was waiting for the case report. She'd uncovered the culprit of the theft, who had his own explaining to do. Where was Valdez anyway? As soon as they'd left Bakaj's quarters, he'd split in the other direction saying he had to debrief his boss.

She commed him and leaned against the grey elevator wall, dizziness pressing on her. Symptoms of something off with something she didn't have time to check right now. That's right. All that data Rhea was still sorting, compiling, analyzing. Valdez didn't reply.

Kim commed her. "Where are you?" she asked, her voice tight.

"Service elevator double-oh-five. Why?" Janey straightened, shoving back against the fogginess in her brain.

"Can you talk?" Kim said in a whisper.

Suddenly alert, Janey said, "Alone for another sixty seconds. Go."

"Milano is steaming mad, steaming. He's in his office."

"I'm on my way there now."

"Investigator Valdez is there too."

"Good. I need to talk to him."

"I hear lots of shouting in there. From across the hall. Milano is pissed about something."

"Thanks, Kim. I can handle it." Janey breathed, releasing tension in her shoulders. She got this. "Thanks for the heads-up."

"Anytime," Kim said.

Felt by one, felt by all, her childhood martial arts sensei always said. What was going on? Her dizziness, Milano's tirade, and now an argument. Were the sunshields acting up?

The elevator opened on the security floor, and Janey rushed to Milano's office. She passed security staff on their way to evening posts, and they nodded in greeting as they passed.

Thankfully, Milano's door opened as soon as she arrived. Soren was there, reviewing his holo screen. Janey was not sure why he was there.

Valdez stood, feet planted wide, his arms crossed over his chest. He was in tightly fitted workout clothes, showing off all his muscles, a damp towel around his neck. He was frowning, and his vitals showed elevated heart rate, respiration, and blood pressure, as if he'd come from his workout or was pissed—or both.

How had he had time to work out? He'd only been gone five or so minutes. Had Janey lost eight minutes? It only took seven minutes to get from Bakaj's suite to the security wing.

Milano was tapping on his keyboard, loud, banging, unnecessary typing. He didn't like to dictate or hand-wave. He glared at her over his defunct, old-fashioned glasses. "Take a seat."

Why did he wear those glasses anyway?

"I'll stand," Janey said.

"I'll stand too," Soren said, moving to rise.

Janey put a hand on his shoulder to stop him. "You're fine."

"It is not fine," Milano said with a bite to his voice. "I told you two to be here, what, fifteen minutes ago."

"My fault, sir," Janey said, as Valdez said the same thing.

"Well, which is it?" Milano volleyed a glare at each of them.

"I was conducting—" Janey started, but she stopped when Valdez put his hand on her arm.

"No, sir. It's my fault. This entire case is my fault."

"Yours? Explain, Investigator Valdez."

"My superior should have filled you in," Valdez said.

"Nobody has told me anything," Milano said. "All I know is that there is an official Sol jet parked in our hangar. They won't talk to me because I won't let them out of the hangar. They want to speak to you, but they won't say why. There you go. I have Schoeneman expecting a report in thirty minutes, and I want to tell him what he wants to hear, and that's only good things."

"Well," Valdez said, "I actually—You're not going to like this, sir." He broke off and shot a glance of apology at Janey. What had he done or not told her now? Would she ever be able to trust he was telling her the truth?

"Spill. I need to know what's going on," Milano said.

Valdez nodded and turned to face the chief. "I understand. I don't actually work for Silverstein Insurance. That was a cover. I'm an investigator for the Sol Unified Planets Police Investigative Services, here to gather the evidence I needed on Dima Bakaj, so I could arrest him for crimes against humanity. I used your office, and I used Investigator McCallister's investigation."

Milano sat back, frowning.

"And now, with McCallister's help, I have all I need to bring Mr. Bakaj to justice. I called the Sol jet here, and now I can arrest Mr. Bakaj and bring him in."

"At zero-six-hundred," Janey said.

"No. At midnight."

"Right," Janey said.

"Work it out you two." Milano breathed out. "Investigator McCallister, your report in fifteen minutes."

"Yes, sir."

"I gave you a wide berth. You need to report on time or else. I've noted your delay in my records. If you were anyone else, I'd fire you," he said under his breath, not looking at her but at his holo screen. "Schoeneman's pet project."

"I'm no one's pet project, sir. I'll get you the report now," Janey said. Since Schoeneman had hired her, only he could fire her. Yet, another negative report in her dossier from Milano wouldn't help her standing.

"After Mr. Bakaj leaves the station"—Milano turned to Valdez—"I want a report from you too, about the gem theft and subsequent investigation for our records. And I'm calling your S.O."

"I'll have to clear that with my boss."

"Fine." Milano turned to Soren. "Why are you here?"

"You called me here, sir."

"Oh, yes, I did. I wanted you to tell us what you found. But now that the gem has been recovered, we can call that case closed, and we don't need any more leads, now do we?" Milano checked his holo. "I need to finish this report for Schoeneman." He turned away and pounded on his table keyboard. They were dismissed.

Janey lifted her eyebrows at Valdez and motioned for

the door. She left the office without a word, Valdez behind her, and Soren scrambling to keep up.

In the hallway, Soren bounced on his toes. "What was all that about?" He eyed his holo screen. "You gonna fill me in?"

"It's not my case anymore," she said.

"Can't say much. It's mostly classified," Valdez said.

Soren looked crestfallen.

"But I can tell you about the time I chased a fugitive from the Tianhe space station almost to Lagrange Point One."

"Oh! Dangerous! Trying to make a run for Lagrange Four to escape into the Trojans asteroid cluster, I bet. Did you catch him?" Soren asked.

"I'll tell you over a beer," Valdez said.

Soren brightened. "Sure, mess hall, say 7 p.m.? Janey, you joining?

"I don't think so. I gotta get this report in and do some personal work," Janey said.

"Okay, well, the lab calls," Soren said, and he waved with a cheery grin and headed for the staff turbos.

Valdez turned to her, concern in his gaze. "Take a break, McCallister. I bet you haven't stopped working since you got to L'Étoile."

"I take breaks."

"My place? We can work on our reports together."

"No, thanks."

"I'll be perfectly polite."

"I don't think so."

"It's good-bye then."

"That's right." Janey bit back a sigh. There really wasn't a future for them. How could there be? Her last long-distance relationship had fizzled, and they'd had years together before that. Valdez and she had known each other only a day—if you counted all the hours playing poker that first night and then all day today since zero seven-fifteen.

Valdez lifted his hand as if to brush his knuckles against her cheek, and she pulled back. Sadness flickered across his eyes. "I'm sorry things turned out the way they did."

"I closed my case. You're closing yours. What is there to be sorry about?"

"Janey, there's no need to leave things like this."

"You're right." She held out her hand for him to shake.

He shook it and nodded. "See you around the Sol, Investigator McCallister."

"Likewise," Janey said, and she turned and hustled to her quarters without waiting to see if he was heading to his, only around the bend from hers.

Once in her quarters, Janey locked her door with extra security measures. She still didn't know how Valdez had broken into Bakaj's room. So frustrating. She didn't know everything that was on the gem either. Rhea, her personal AI, was still crunching through the files. Didn't matter now anyway.

Her head ached—a residual of the dizziness. She had to siphon that data out of her head and over to Valdez. But first, the damn report. Janey changed into her favorite Space Wing sweatpants and sweatshirt, zapped a cup of decaf tea from the food crafter, and powered through the report. She added an addendum for Milano to attach Valdez's official report and commanded it to send to Milano at seventeen twenty-five.

She stripped off her clothes, threw the lot on a chair, and headed to the shower. Time for a break or she'd fry some circuits, and there wasn't a doctor on board who could fix her. Well, maybe Doc could, but she probably hadn't worked on live people in a long time. She didn't want to risk it. She'd do what she could on her own, until she went back home for her first leave scheduled in eight weeks to visit Mom and check in with her regular doctor.

She slipped off her comm bracelet and turned on the shower. In a few minutes, it steamed up the bathroom. Janey stepped under the heavy pounding stream and let out a deep breath.

"Rhea, stop compile," she said. "Back up into personal server and delete all files from my link-up."

"All right, Janey. Are you okay? Your cortisol levels are high. Shall I play some Baroque for you?"

"Sure, and dim the lights by one quarter. Block all calls except for Mom's."

"You got it, Janey."

Twenty minutes later, Janey was refreshed and at her table, dressed in clean and comfy study clothes, frowning at her ocular implant screen. Her peripheral view on both sides was black, indicating that those areas of her screen weren't working. From the table, she waved to lift a two-foot-wide holo screen in front of her so she'd have a larger work area. On the widescreen, she examined the brain-computer interface controls.

She sighed. Everything looked normal as far as she could tell. She fiddled with some of the controls, but there was no change. The doctor always hooked up sensors to her for their tests, but she didn't have that equipment. She hadn't anticipated needing it.

She yawned.

"Rhea, outside of my linkup, do a search for salamander-like life extension drugs or treatments correlated with Myasthenia Gravis." Mom's illness was scary hard to treat, but maybe this new search would find some obscure paper a grad student had filed that her previous searches hadn't found.

"Sure thing, Janey. You got a call while you were in the shower."

"Play message."

A short nap was in order. Then she'd go down to the mess for dinner and stop by the shop for sensor supplies to see if she could repair her ocular implant herself. Ill-advised, but she'd done it before.

"Video or audio?"

"Audio only." She stretched out on her bed, her head resting in the crook of her arm, and she stared at the ceiling.

Mai Chen's voice came on, a little impatient, and a little teasing. "Where are you, Janey? We had a tell-all date at SkyBar. If you're with your hottie, don't call me back. Have a great time. But if you're not, why not?" Mai laughed a giddy laugh, probably already into her second round of Kaoliang Wine. "Really, no biggie. Just wave at me when you can."

Right. She'd forgotten about their date made that morning—which seemed like two or three days ago. She'd make it up to Mai later with a round on her, because there sure as Venus hell wasn't going to be a juicy story to tell.

"Rhea, lights off. Turn on raindrops."

The room went pitch-black. The patter of raindrops landing on the earth soothed—a soundtrack she captured from her mom's backyard during a muggy summer rainstorm.

How different her life was now than what she imagined it would be when she was thirteen and hopeful for a life of service and fulfillment in Granton San Francisco.

Then all she'd wanted was to be a teacher, settle down with a man who liked the same kind of food she did, have a dog and a pleasant life filled with friends, students, visits to mom on holidays, and maybe start a family one day. That dream life was far away, as if it had been imagined by a different person.

The next thing she knew she was hearing a high-pitched whine. She opened her eyes to psychedelic flashes of red and orange and an excruciating headache at her temples.

"Rhea, stop sound!" she shouted.

"Who's Rhea?" It was Valdez, somewhere near her door by the sound of his voice.

"My personal AI." She groaned and sat up in bed, holding her head, her heart racing, and she was sweaty. "Valdez, what are you doing here? Get out." She checked the time on her implant screen. It was eighteen forty-five. She'd slept for almost an hour.

"You didn't respond to my comms. I let myself in."

"You can't."

"I did." He moved closer and reached for her.

She batted his hand away. "But I set up my security..." She rubbed her temples. "What is that sound?" Some sound waves created light effects and vice versa.

"You can hear that? Most people can't."

Valdez waved over his holo, and the sound stopped.

"What is that tech?" she grumbled.

Valdez brushed loose strand of hair from her forehead. "Let me help you up."

"No." Janey got up and rushed for the bathroom. There, she fumbled with her medkit, fished out a med spray, inhaled a shot, breathed, and then counted to five. Her heart rate slowed to near normal, and the drubbing at her temples dulled to a quiet roar.

"What's that?" Valdez said, his voice cold. He snatched the meds from her. "Are these legal?"

"Of course, they are. What's your problem?" Janey held out a hand to steady herself on the door jamb as a wave of dizziness crashed over her. She swayed. Instead of the door, it was Valdez's chest she touched. She slipped. Her legs weren't working. Rubbery.

Valdez swept her up in his arms, and in four strides, he deposited her on her bed. "What is wrong with you?" His voice was tight, edged with concern.

"Nothing's wrong. A side effect. Triggered by that sound. That's how you did it. The door." Janey closed her eyes against the glare.

"That's not good. I'll page medical." His voice was suddenly too loud. The thunder in her head would pass, soon, she hoped.

"Shhh. No. No doctors. I'll be fine. Give me a minute." Janey licked her lips. "Water. Just water. Give me five minutes. I'll be fine."

"You're not fine." He put a wrist on her forehead. "You're burning up. Even I can tell that, and I'm not shot full of enhancements or drugs."

"Shhh. You're shouting."

A warm hand stroked her forehead and her cheek and stayed there. She turned her head to rest it in his palm— so warm and tender—and drifted on the crashing waves of dizziness and the feeling that her heart would thump out of her chest.

She had to get under control, calm the haywire symptoms, and then diagnose.

She focused on the pain. It was centered behind her eyes, in the center of her head. It was an orange that shrank to a plum and then to a pea. And then the pea-sized pain pellet shrunk smaller until she was drifting on a slow-moving current.

She let out a breath and tested her vision. Blurry and dim. She blinked a few more times and focused on Valdez's face hovering above her.

"Hey, you. Are you back?" Valdez said softly.

"Yes. Now go away." She tried to sit up, but something was pressing on her side.

"McCallister, you're a piece of work, aren't you?" He frowned at her.

Not half the piece of work he was. "I want to sit up."

His frown deepened.

"You're leaning on me, Valdez."

"Oh." He took his weight off her side.

She sat and scooted to the edge of the bed in a smooth move, her equilibrium back. She sipped from the glass of water on her bedside table. Better. The room was crystal clear, her screen blackness no longer, and the dizziness was gone. She headed to the table and sat. Maybe if she adjusted the BCI-implant link at her temple the headaches would stop long enough for her to run a diagnostic.

"Did you forget we had a date? What did you inhale back there?"

"I told you. Meds. And I didn't agree to a date." Janey leaned back in her chair and crossed her arms.

"If I hadn't been there to catch you—"

"I would have crawled to the bed, or passed out."

"You act like you have no feelings."

"I do. I'm fine." She picked up her laser tool. "Valdez, I have work to do. Don't you?"

"I filed my prelim report. Do I look like I'm on duty?" He was wearing casual attire: black jeans, a black sweater, and a leather jacket.

"I don't know. Are you? You broke into my room." She wanted to pace, but her legs didn't quite feel steady enough for that. She needed another ten minutes and then she could move. "How did you do that?" She tapped on her holo to study what he did. Her tracers should have tracked his every move on the lock, but the data looked like a random jumble of numbers.

Valdez scrubbed his face and blew out a breath. "Trade secret."

"Really? That again."

Janey turned back to her work. Why hadn't her implant been working properly? Something Valdez was doing, perhaps. Some undetectable new tech. Venus hells. Her chest tightened, and her breathing came shallow.

"Janey, we have something…" Valdez said. "We work well as a team."

"But we're not. You couldn't even tell me the truth about the simplest thing, like why you were really after Bakaj."

"It's not simple. I didn't even tell my boss."

She rubbed her temples again. "I don't know whether to admire that you could keep such a vendetta away from your boss or hightail it in the other direction. What is even real about you?

"Are you all right?"

"I don't know, Valdez. Why do you even care? We hardly know each other." Janey wanted to snarl, claw, fight, but instead, she turned away from him. "You're leaving. Why start anything?"

"I think we already started something." Valdez sat at the table across from her and stretched out his arm toward her, palm up, inviting her in. "Friends?"

"You're leaving."

"I know. But my work may bring me back. We can stay in touch when I'm not here." He wiggled his fingers at here, inviting her in. "We had fun. We had more than fun, I thought."

Janey sighed. "You're a thief and a sneak."

"Yes, I am." He had no shame in his gaze, only a bleak look, as if he'd beheld the blackness of space and it had peered back, swallowing him whole. Maybe she was catching a glimpse of the real Orlando Valdez.

"It *was* fun." She eyed his hand. The strength in his fingers, the competence and vitality there. It drew her. He drew her. Maybe it was his willingness to do what it took for the greater good. No one was perfect after all. "But I may never see you again. Your work may not bring you here again."

"You will see me again. Plus side, there's always vid calls. Besides, life is short, McCallister." He wiggled a "come here" gesture with his fingers. "Don't wait to live it."

You had to enjoy the life you had. It could be gone tomorrow, Mom always said. And she should know.

Janey placed her palm in his. "I don't know where this is going." His warmth seeped into her.

"Do you always need to be in control?" He squeezed her hand and brushed his thumb on the back of her hand.

"As much as possible." She intertwined her fingers with his.

He leaned over the tools on the table and kissed her, gentle and light. She melted into the sweetness of his lips. She wanted heat. She wanted one last kiss.

She deepened it, and Valdez met her fire.

She pulled away and sat. "Why do you even care about me, Valdez?"

"You're strong, brilliant, persistent, beautiful. What's not to love?" He fiddled with a stray stylus.

"Love?"

"Yes, love, like, lust, all of it."

"I can't. Not now." Maybe not ever. And certainly not all of it. Not any of it.

He was not going to throw her life into chaos. She had no room for love. How could she? She stood and paced, straightening her room as she went, putting away her clothes, stacking her tools in a neat pyramid.

He sat, quiet. Her ocular implant revealed his vitals at slightly elevated from normal. "Janey, come here, sit with me."

She shook her head and re-stacked her tools into a straight line. "I can't. I have to keep this job. It's the only thing that's supporting my mom."

"What does that have to do with us?" he said softly.

Janey made the bed with tight military corners, pulling, smoothing, tightening. Battening down the hatches. "This is fine for now."

"Fine? What about you? What do you want?"

"This." She waved her arm around her quarters to encompass her life on L'Étoile. "Why do you do what you do?"

"To put men like Bakaj behind bars."

"I saw how upset you got back there. This case is personal for you."

"Every case is."

"No, you need to be dispassionate, cold, gather evidence."

"I do all that too. But if your heart isn't in your work, there's nothing else. I see how you are. When it comes to your work, you're a one-track mind." Valdez swiveled in the chair to watch her pad into the bathroom.

She wiped down the counter, stashed her toiletries back into the cabinet and drawers, and hung up her towel. She brushed her hair. Fatigue and stress showed in her eyes, but not in her face yet.

Stress caught up to all of them. She'd seen how it had affected her mother, and it was probably a factor in her mom's debilitating illness, though the doctors weren't certain.

The room was straightened. There was nothing else to hide behind. She sat back at the table, crossed her arms, and addressed Valdez. "Do you have a woman in every port?"

"I wish."

"Don't play dumb with me, Valdez? You're the type."

"I only flirt." He met her gaze. "I have dated—years ago. But right now, there's only you."

"And when you're not here? If I'm going to take our relationship further, I want..." She straightened a diagnostic board that didn't need straightening.

"What do you want, McCallister?" He waited, open and curious.

"I know what I don't want," Janey said. "I don't want the secrets and lies and false promises."

"Okay. That's great. And you want?"

To have her mother cured.

Valdez stood and came around the table. "Come on."

"What? You're ordering me around now? I am your superior officer—" She protested, but it was weak.

"Not anymore. The case is closed, remember?" He held out a hand. "Stand up."

She stood, but she didn't take his hand.

"Great. Now, put on some walking-about clothes, unless you want to be seen in those schleppy things."

"Why? I love my schleppy things. Mom gave me these. Where are we going?"

"And the sweet schleppy things will be here when you return. For now, pizza, beers, friends, you know, Soren, Kim. To celebrate a case closed. No man or woman is an island. Come on! Let's have some fun. I'll only come on to you in fun, flirty, public ways. Okay?"

"Okay. Fine. I'm on call tonight anyway." She grabbed her jeans, favorite shirt and jacket, and she headed for the bathroom to change.

When she came out five minutes later, Valdez was lying on her bed on top of the covers, eyes closed, breathing long and slow. He was asleep.

A moment later, he must have sensed her presence, because he yawned, stretched, and sat up.

"You clean up real nice." He scanned her up and down hungrily.

"You're only being nice to me because you want to sleep with me." She wanted to run her fingers through his already tousled brown curly hair. She strapped her on-call kit around her waist instead.

"And you don't?" He raised an eyebrow.

Janey's cheeks heated.

"You know you wanna," he said with a teasing lilt as he headed for the door.

"You're insufferable, Valdez. I don't need to feed your ego like a million other women have."

"Way more than a million." He smirked at her.

"Oh stop."

"Are you going to unlock the door?" He waved at the door.

"You can only unlock it from the outside?" Janey asked.

He stuffed his hands in his jeans pants pockets and

quirked an eyebrow in an unspoken challenge. "I can't reveal my methods."

"I will discover them. Your unlocking mechanism is perhaps interfering with my implant."

"Sorry. I didn't know. Really. I—I can make adjustments." He looked stricken with pain. "But I still can't tell."

"Why do I put up with you?" She unlocked the door with her light screen controls.

"Because I'm sexy." He flashed a grin and there was his dimple. She wanted to wipe that smirk off with a mind-numbing kiss, but she held herself back. The case was over, but the allure was not.

"No comment." She waved him ahead of her into the corridor.

Valdez let out a hearty laugh and exited her quarters. "The woman doth protest too much."

"Let's get some grub." She set her triple lock controls on the door. "But that's all we're doing together."

EIGHTEEN

THE CALL CAME AFTER THE SECOND ROUND OF snacks and beverages and the teasing and laughter about Soren needing a girlfriend and Janey needing a full night's sleep.

The mess, a large hall filled with long tables, was raucous with day staff eating dinner and drinking. A space jet race in the asteroid belt was turned up high on the vid screens, but Janey still heard the distinctive beep of the night security desk over the din of fans whooping in joy and hollering at their team to swerve around the latest ice rock.

She turned to shield the hubbub and answered. She was the on-call investigator on duty.

"Night duty manager Quincy here, ma'am." He spoke in the clipped, clear tone of a New Englander.

"Yes, Quincy." Janey stabbed at her coleslaw with her fork. She'd been picking the salad that came with her burger, even though the fresh station food was great. Post case blues.

"An anonymous call came in about Suite 52. Only said that they heard cries of distress."

Bakaj's suite. Her heart sped up. Janey dropped her fork beside her plate, the clatter muted by all the yelling over the game, and surged to her feet.

"What was the nature of the call? Was medical called?" Janey asked. She checked the time. Twenty-three thirty, or 11:30 p.m.

"Yes, they're on scene, sir. The guest is dead. Call was untraceable, but I'm working on it."

"Dima Bakaj?"

"Yes, sir."

Foul play? Suicide? Chief Milano would not like this, and neither would Schoeneman. Neither would Valdez, currently getting another round of chips and salsa with Soren. His case against Bakaj over.

"COD?" she asked. Cause of death.

"Medical said undetermined."

"Understood. I'll head over there now. Please secure the scene and send me the anonymous call."

"Yes, Investigator. Medical will secure it until you get there, keeping it quiet. They notified Doctor Running Feather too."

"Good," Janey said. "Milano would not want this getting out."

"Schoeneman either. Per station regs, in the event of a murder or suspicious death—"

"We'll have to close down traffic in or out of the station, correct. I'll keep you informed," Janey said quietly. The morning jet was due to arrive at zero six hundred.

Luckily, no one could easily overhear in the noisy mess hall. Staff gossip could easily spread to guests, and

Schoeneman wouldn't be happy about that. "Have Security Agent Meilani Shawhan meet us there."

"Would you like me to inform the rest of the on-call team?"

"Only her for now."

"Yes, sir," Quincy said, clipped.

Janey closed the comm and stared at the table, no longer seeing the remains of her burger and slaw.

Soren and Valdez came back with the chips and salsa.

"What is it?" Valdez asked.

She spoke into his ear. "Bakaj is dead."

"Oh shit." Valdez bobbled the chips and salsa as he plunked back in his chair. Salsa sloshed over the sides of the crockery.

Janey motioned Soren closer and spoke in a low voice. "Soren, we have a 10-10." A death of a guest or staff member onboard L'Étoile.

Soren paled, nodding to show he was listening.

"Medical isn't sure of cause of death," Janey continued. "They've secured the scene and alerted Doc to expect the body." No need to alert the guests or most staff while they sorted this and possibly searched for a killer.

"Is somebody going to wake Chief Milano?" Soren glanced at the snacks with longing.

"Only if Doc concludes it's a homicide." Janey stifled a yawn. "Let's go check the scene." She turned to Valdez. "I'm sorry."

"Me too." Valdez blew out a breath and seemed distant. "I really wanted to bring him to justice." He eyed her, steely-eyed and determined. "I can lend a hand on yours."

"You don't have to."

"I know, but I'd like to. I want to know what happened."

Janey nodded. "Then let's go."

Four minutes later, they arrived at Suite 52. Janey waved at the front door pad with her wrist comm, and the door whooshed open. A petite woman in a tailored black suit ushered her in—Chief Medical Officer Tseng.

"Investigator." Tseng nodded.

"Hello, Doctor Tseng. Cause of death?" Janey took in the scene. The elegant living-dining room looked the same as when they'd been there earlier, except there were three matching valises of various sizes parked at the end of the real leather couch. Bakaj's body must be in the bedroom.

"That's for Doc to determine. I'm only here to declare it a death and make the initial assessment as a L'Étoile representative," Tseng eyed Valdez.

Janey introduced them and then asked, "Has anyone touched anything? And do you have TOD?"

"Time of death, to be determined," Horsely said, one of the two medical assistants on scene. "Rigor hasn't set in, and there are no signs of lividity, but we guess about forty minutes to an hour, based on body temp."

"We've confirmed the victim is dead," Tseng said. "Too far gone for resuscitation efforts. I examined the body. Fully dilated, fixed pupils, and no signs of brain stem activity. EEG shows no signs of brain activity either. Plus, there are tiny puncture marks on his neck. He's fully clothed, sitting on the floor, beside his bed. I consider it a suspicious death. That's why we called you."

"Understood," Janey said. Still, a suspicious death wasn't a homicide. She couldn't call for the lockdown of the station yet, but the clock was ticking. The sooner she knew one way or another, the sooner she could make the decision.

Soren said to Janey. "Where do you want me?"

"Sweep the rooms for particulates and collect any anomalies," Janey said. "We'll compare them to the first readings I took. When Shawhan gets here, have her help you."

She turned to Valdez, and before she could say anything, he called up his holo screen from his wrist comm, saying, "I'll do a spectrum analysis and a DNA RNA sweep."

"Thanks." Janey slipped on gloves from her kit and turned to Tseng. "Show me the body."

NINETEEN

JANEY PAUSED AT THE THRESHOLD OF BAKAJ'S bedroom, hit record on her wrist comm and implant, and scanned the scene. The bedcovers had been thrown back, as if Bakaj had been about to get into bed. But he'd never made it there. Instead, he was sitting on the floor, his back against the bed, and his head crooked at an awkward angle.

She crossed the room and crouched to study his body up close and examine that side of the bed. Fully clothed in his shirt, vest and slacks, but with no shoes, Bakaj faced the wall, his eyes staring at nothing. One leg was stretched out and the other was bent at an angle, as if he was lounging on the rug. She inspected his face and noticed two distinct puncture marks at the base of his neck. Her ocular implant revealed a luminescence on the right side of his neck, running the length of his jugular vein. Other than that, his face showed no visible marks of trauma.

Something was crumpled in one hand. She zoomed in. It was a tiny piece of lined paper, but she couldn't see any text. Why would Bakaj grip it in his final moments? Soren would collect it soon, if he could safely do so, or Doc would extract it once she had the body for the autopsy. For now, she needed to finish her three hundred sixty-degree visual of the body on the horizontal plane.

That thought sounded so cold, even to her.

She gulped past the lump in her throat. It wasn't that she hadn't seen a dead body before. She had, a few times, but it was never easy or pleasant.

She'd never known the victims in any other of her cases, except for the first, even though it wasn't technically her case. Her best friend, Christine, had disappeared one day from her happy life in Granton San Francisco. Weeks later after desperate searching, Janey had been the one to find the body. There'd been signs of a struggle, visible marks of restraint on her wrists and ankles, as if she'd been held captive for a while, and the unmistakable odd bend in her neck. Someone had snapped it; Christine had been murdered. She'd never figured out who did it, and the police in Granton San Francisco hadn't either.

She pushed away thoughts of the past to focus on the here and now and laser in on what she did best: evidence gathering and connecting the dots to unravel the mystery.

She crouched again in front of Bakaj to get another good look at his face and the front of his body.

The pallor of death struck her. Bakaj's skin was sallow, gray even, and he hadn't been dead more than an hour. How quickly death robbed a human of color.

His clothes were not torn or stained, and there were no visible signs of struggle. One button of his red vest was partially out of its buttonhole. She scanned it and saw no fingerprints, not even Bakaj's. That was odd.

She blinked rapidly, running her implant through the different light frequencies, an ultraviolet osteo-scan for the bones, slightly higher ultraviolet for skin lesions. Nothing appeared.

The man looked like he was napping, except for the absence of color, breath, and a certain something that separated the living from the dead. Was it spirit, soul, the anima/animus? Janey didn't know what it was, only that it was in all living creatures while alive and suddenly gone in death.

Her vision blurred with tears at the encroaching memories of her friend's death. She blinked rapidly to clear them, stood, and pivoted to examine the rest of the room.

The bedside light was on. Nothing was on the table. A deeper scan of the surface of the bedside table revealed minute traces of cleaning spray and a faint ring of a wet glass not more than an hour old. Could be evidence. She looked in drawers, under the bed, and under the bedding, but no glass was there. Nothing else was under the bed. Not even dust bunnies. The cleaning bots were thorough.

She'd have Shawhan check the kitchenette and track down how recently the room had been cleaned and when room service had last been here.

Next, she scanned the carpet surrounding Bakaj's body. On the carpet peeking out from under his leg, there was a tiny piece of torn paper. Perhaps a part of the paper Bakaj had clutched in his hand. She collected it into an evidence bag.

She came around to the other side of the bed but saw nothing out of the ordinary. A bedside table, a lamp that was turned off, and no unusual tread marks on the carpet. The path from the door to Bakaj had been walked multiple times. It was impossible to tell how many prints beyond hers, Tseng's, and Bakaj's. Even those weren't distinguishable with her implant.

She backed out of the room, called Soren over, and handed him her evidence bag. He signed off on it for chain of custody. "If you can, bag the paper in his hand, and, of course, anything else you find. There's a missing drinking glass. Find it."

"Right away, boss." Soren hustled into the bedroom.

Shawhan approached. "I got everyone's statement, sir."

"Thanks, Shawhan. I need you to vid the bedroom, the body, and the entire suite, and get the hallway footage. Check with other guests if they heard anything, discreetly. Pull in Lane and Kou to help."

"Yes, ma'am. You think it's a crime scene?" Shawhan slipped on gloves and pulled her slim recording glasses out of her pocket.

"Hope not," Janey said. "But it probably is."

Valdez was at the holo wall painting of a van Gogh sunflower that undulated as if in a summer breeze. The holo painting covered the wall safe. "McCallister, check this out."

Janey approached, and Valdez pointed to a tiny chip in the ornate real wood frame.

"That wasn't there this morning," Valdez said.

"You think someone tampered with the safe?"

"I do."

"Let's find out." Janey changed her gloves, so she wouldn't cross-contaminate. Valdez did the same. She opened the painting at the frame, scanning the whole time for anomalies via other wavelengths above and below normal vision. Besides the chip in the frame, there were no other marks of damage, except for normal wear and tear.

Behind the picture, the safe door was shut but the readout screen was smudged and covered in a thin layer of a waxy white substance. She scanned it. A carbon-heavy chemical formula showed on her screen, though she didn't recognize it.

"Soren, come take a sample," Janey called.

"Be right there," Soren said from the bedroom.

Valdez held up his holo to the safe door and keyed in a command. "That residue contains DNA. Whose I can't tell."

Soren approached and took a sample with his reader. "Shawhan's still working on her recording. I'm done in there."

"What is it?" Janey asked.

"The salamander-like DNA in a wax—paraffin to be more precise. There are also traces of Bakaj's DNA in it," Soren said.

"What are the uses of paraffin?" Janey asked.

"Common applications include lubrication, electrical insulation, and candles. My grandparents used candles."

Janey moved out of the way so Soren could collect a sample in a test tube. Once he was done, she nudged open the safe door. It hadn't been fully re-latched. The safe was empty. All the bearer bonds worth millions of credits were gone and so was the black book—the items they'd seen when Bakaj had shown them the safe that morning.

"A robbery gone horribly sideways?" Janey said quietly.

"Possibly," Valdez said.

"I don't see fingerprints, not even Bakaj's. Do you?" Janey asked.

"No. Whoever was in here was using gloves."

"Maybe Bakaj packed the safe contents." Janey waved toward the three matching bags by the couch. "And that's why it was unlocked."

"McCallister, you ready for us to take the body to Doc?" Tseng asked. Doc rarely left her lab.

"Yes, thanks." Janey turned to Tseng. "I assume you have a discreet way of taking the body out of here. We don't want to spook the guests."

"Of course," Tseng said and nodded to her team who headed for the bedroom, carrying a folded-up hover stretcher that would float the body out of the suite under a cloaked covering. Anyone looking directly at the stretcher would only see the wall on the other side and not a shrouded body.

"I need to accompany the body," Soren said. "Unless you need me for something else."

"We're done with our prelim scan," Janey said, "And I didn't spot any other odd materials. We're good for now."

Soren nodded and left with Tseng and the medical assistants.

Janey turned to the luggage and scanned the exterior for prints and saw only Bakaj's. She hoisted one bag onto the brown real-leather couch and opened it. There was the thick three-inch stack of bonds on top of neatly folded clothes. She let out a breath. "Okay, so not a theft of the bonds. We'll need to count them to be sure and match that against what Bakaj declared when he arrived on board."

"Where's the black book?" Valdez asked.

"Still looking." She scanned and vid-documented, then went through Bakaj's clothes, suits, and shirts of the softest silk and finest wool. "I don't see it here."

"I'll look in the other two." Valdez videoed, then went to work on the second suitcase, lifting out toiletries. "Nothing."

Janey searched through the third suitcase full of fine shoes and boots. "Not here." She sat on the couch. Straight ahead was the ornate chest of drawers.

Valdez saw it too. "I got it." He stood, scanned with his holo, then tugged open all the drawers and small cabinets. "Nothing here. He could have given away the little black book, thrown it away, or even couriered it to himself." He sighed. "Bakaj was ready to leave the station, as promised. I have to give him that."

"We need to retrace his steps from the time after we left this room and determine the importance of the missing black book." Janey stood and surveyed their mess. "We have evidence of an unusual, possibly suspicious death. We need to rule out foul play."

"I'll let the jet know to stand by," Valdez said.

"Why?"

"I'm staying to assist you on this case."

TWENTY

"LET'S REVIEW THE ANONYMOUS CALL, AGAIN," Janey said to Valdez. They were back in the conference room, steamy mugs of pungent coffee in hand.

For the *nth* time, she waved over the audio file on the murder board to play it and studied the visual representation of the sound waves undulate as a voice, not identifiable as male or female, speak in a monotone.

"I hear yelling next door," it said.

"Which suite are you calling from? Your ident is unclear." That was Quincy's clipped voice, practically melodic against the anonymous caller's flat speech.

"I said I hear yelling from 52."

"Please identity yourself," Quincy said. "Where are you?" But the comm channel had ended from the caller's side.

"Anything?" Janey turned to Valdez who was running the audio analysis with his two holo screens at the table. She could have asked one of her on-call team to work the analysis, but Valdez had offered.

"Not since the last time you asked me two minutes ago," he said without looking up from his work.

Janey growled and paced the length of the quiet conference room. It was zero hour—midnight station time—and the night security staff were at their posts throughout the casino and other parts of L'Étoile, all quiet there. At least Mom was sleeping soundly in her bed since it was 4 a.m.—twenty hours earlier the previous calendar day—in Las Cruces Spaceport, New Mexico. Hopefully, she'd sleep through to the morning.

Janey stared at the timeline she and Valdez had created. It was too quiet here with no clear leads yet. It was going to be a long night.

Chief Medical Officer Tseng determined Bakaj's death as suspicious, and now it was up to Doc, the forensic pathologist and coroner, to decide the cause and manner of death. Schoeneman wouldn't like the lockdown at all. He'd want this case wrapped up as soon as possible, so they could open the hotel and docking station to the morning arrivals, due by space jet at 6 a.m. Also, a new batch of staff and the next shift of asteroid miners was due to arrive by 10 a.m. on the StarEl.

She reviewed again what she and Valdez had noted on the wide wallscreen.

TOD was in the hour or two before 11:30 p.m., based on body temp.

The disturbance call from Anonymous had come into Quincy at 11:21 p.m. The medical team had arrived at 11:24 p.m. and 11:25 p.m.. She'd been called at 11:30 p.m. and arrived at Bakaj's suite five minutes later at 11:35 p.m..

"I have to account for your movements this evening," Janey said to Valdez.

"I'm a person of interest?" Valdez leaned back in his

chair, his holo screens hovering over the table behind him.

"No, sorry. We were in the mess from nineteen hundred, I mean 7 p.m. But we need to account for the whereabouts of everyone on the station." She was grabbing at straws here with no evidence yet, but she needed to start somewhere. Janey paced the long room, swinging her arms. "Anything on the audio?"

"No, Janey." He shoved out of the chair, stood, and stretched. "And I don't think we're going to. The voice is entirely mechanical. I can't get a human voice print for identification. We're up against a pro."

"Takes one to know one."

Valdez lifted an eyebrow at her and closed up his screens.

"You did steal from Bakaj, undetected," Janey said. "If I knew how you broke in, that might help me—"

"Possibly. Then there's his black book which is still missing."

"A robbery gone wrong?" Janey said and paced. He wasn't going to tell her how he broke in. "The book could be squirreled away somewhere else on the station."

"Possibly." Valdez munched on a pastry at the counter.

She stared at his pastry, and her stomach growled. "What is that, and where did it come from?"

He shrugged and handed her his half-eaten pastry. "Some kind of donut. It's good. Why? You want some."

"Yes. No. I need to know cause and manner of death. Unless he died..." She took the pastry and bite into it, chewed. "...of natural causes in a way that appears suspicious."

"This your medical examiner would know."

"Yes, she will. In the meantime, Shawhan is gathering details on Bakaj's movements after we left his room at 5 p.m." A data box flashed on the wallscreen murder board. She popped the rest of pastry into her mouth and moved to the board and waved open the data box. Lane was reporting that no one else heard a scream or any unusual noise. Maybe the call was faked and the murderer wanted to announce the murder, like a boast or a taunt.

In the timeline, there was a gap from when she and Valdez left Bakaj's suite and the time they returned at 11:35 p.m. A six-hour hole they needed to fill.

Valdez joined her at the board. "In the six intervening hours, someone killed Bakaj, took the black book from his safe, left the bonds where they were, and then disappeared from the suite, leaving it as-is except for a smudge of the salamander-DNA on the safe."

"Right. So this person was after information and not money. Like you were. Perhaps another undercover operative?"

"That's a possible motive. But I was the only one assigned to Bakaj."

"You sure?"

"Yes. It was a highly sensitive case. Need to know, etc."

"Can you check with your boss? Just in case."

"I can." Valdez moved to the end of the table near the vid screen window displaying a distant field of stars Janey didn't recognize. It was 12:30 a.m. on station, so it'd be 6:30 a.m. in New York. He waved over his wrist comm, turned his back to her, and spoke low so she couldn't hear the call. He was still on L'Étoile. He was helping her. What was in it for him?

She turned at the case board and frowned at it, fisted a hand on her hip, and then commed Shawhan.

"Compiling all the vid for you, boss. Almost done, but I need a little more time."

"Can you give me a summary? I need to start interviewing those who saw Dima Bakaj last."

"Now? I can come to you."

"Yes, now," Janey said. "No, over the comms is fine."

"The guest, Dima Bakaj, leaves his suite at 7 p.m. and has a drink at SkyBar, alone," Shawhan said. It sounded like she was reading from her notes. "Door lock shows he returns to his suite at 7:30 p.m. No one enters until 8:15 p.m., when Chef Gutierrez enters with a covered tray. Then they leave the suite together at 9:15 p.m. and go to a room on the mezzanine above the casino. Mr. Bakaj returns to his suite at 10:21 p.m. That's all I have so far."

"Good job, Meilani. Get me the vid as soon as you can. Need more help?"

"No, I got it, boss," Shawhan said.

"Thanks." Janey commed off and turned to Valdez. "And now we wait for Doc's results."

"My boss said that I was the only one assigned to Bakaj," Valdez said and headed back to the counter, "but he's going to check with some of the other clandestine services. Some of the military branches do off-book operations, and then there's private corporate. He'll let me know what he finds."

"Thanks." She paced in front of the too-empty board. She didn't have all the facts. "Let's go to the lab. You can meet Doc, and we can breathe down their necks, waiting for results."

Valdez set down another pastry he was munching on and brushed the pastry crumbs into the sink. "Yes, let's go bug Soren and the Doc. I know how you get if you aren't taking action."

"You know me well in such a short time," Janey said as she set her coffee in the sink and headed for the door.

A few minutes later, Janey entered the lab and led Valdez down one of the aisles to the back of the lab crowded with equipment. No one was there. Soren stepped through two sliding doors. He wore full scrubs and a mask molded to his face.

"Suit up. It's a clean room." He gestured with his head to an anteroom and a door labeled "Scrub" and went back into the morgue.

Janey led Valdez into the scrub room. They changed and entered into the morgue. Her breath misted the air in the cold room.

"Doc, what do you have?" She wanted to ask why the morgue was a clean room, but now was not the time. They had more pressing matters.

From behind her protective mask, Doc peered at her. "I do. And hello to you too. Who is your friend? Only station personnel allowed."

"I'm Special Investigator Orlando Valdez, with the Sol," Valdez said.

"He's been cleared by our office." Janey peered at the body, splayed and cut as if part of a lab experiment.

Bakaj wasn't Bakaj anymore, she reminded herself. Now he was a hotbed of evidence. "I need to know if it was a homicide."

"I can't manner it just yet, but cause—take a look at the neck, left anterior side, past the midline," Doc said. "What do you see?" Doc couldn't yet rule on the manner of death, but she was pointing to the cause of death, what started the lethal sequence of events that led to Bakaj's death.

Janey approached the table and scanned the body's neck, the left side, which she hadn't been able to see when in his room while his head was tilted that way.

Janey peered up at Doc. "A puncture. Made with some kind of high gauge needle, half a millimeter in diameter, and larger than what I saw on the right side of his neck. We didn't find any needles at the scene."

"Soren ran toxicology on Bakaj," Doc said, "and came back with a high concentration of Felicitan mixed with—"

"High-grade pot," Valdez said. "Ghost."

Janey couldn't see his mask, but she could see his eyes, and they were hard like marble.

"Yes, I was going to say, 'premium *Cannabis x intersita Sojak*,'" Doc said, her tone sharp. "How did you know? Have you seen this before?"

"I have," Valdez said. "A common mix. Gives people a long mellow high that lasts for a few days, sometimes a week. It's a way to cut down on quantity of both and prolong the stupor, or high. Called a ghost high because they feel so light they could fly and because they ghost on the rest of their lives. Just disappear right in front of you." He sounded so sad and resigned.

"So, is that cause of death, Doc?" Janey asked. "A drug overdose?"

Doc glanced at Soren, who picked up his cue and spoke grimly from behind his full protective face mask.

"From the tox screen, I found lethal levels of Felicitan mixed with high-grade pot in his blood. This Ghost drug."

"The overdose caused myocardial infarction, a heart attack, and then cardiac arrest. His heart stopped," Doc said.

"Administered by whom?" Janey stated. "I highly

doubt Bakaj would inject himself, though I saw no visible signs of struggle. He cared about his health. He was ninety years old but easily looked fifty.

"Due to the angle of entry, and the faint pressure outline, it was likely administered by someone else," Doc said.

"Explain," Janey said.

"The angle of thrust determined by the puncture wound at his jugular vein and the needle track into his body—it comes from below," Doc said and made an upward thrust with a gloved. hand.

"Any indications of a struggle?" Janey firmed her jaw.

"Yes, there are contusions, blunt force trauma, and bruising here and here," Doc pointed to the front of Bakaj's forearms and shoulders that showed faint bluish bruising.

"So intent to kill," Janey said. "Murder."

"That for you to determine, but the evidence is showing that," Doc said. "I am ruling it a homicide."

"I have to call Milano and Quincy and get the station in lockdown."

"Soren found one other thing you might be interested in," Doc said.

"I scanned his clothing and found a partial fingerprint on the underside of a button," Soren said. "I think someone dressed him in clothes, at least his vest."

"Why do you say that?" Janey asked.

"Well, there's that partial on the button and a speck of DNA on the collar that isn't his," Soren said.

"Are the prints or DNA in the system and crossed checked with the paraffin on the safe?" Valdez asked.

"I'm running the data now through the ident databases," Soren said. "Nothing yet."

"Anything else?" Janey asked.

"The man was in excellent health, besides the poisoning," Doc said. "Death occurred in under a minute. But that's not what I wanted to point out. Here. Look." She pointed to his open chest cavity. "This may not be relevant. His organs had been replaced in the last ten or fifteen years."

"From donors?"

"Yes, grown in live hosts—people—but created from his own tissues. They're his own, but new. No wear and tear of a ninety-year-old."

"That's illegal," Soren said.

"It is," Janey stated. "And isn't that a long and painful process for the organ host?"

"I hear the people are sedated most of the time. They can't feel the organs growing at an accelerated rate inside them," Soren said. "But there is another process done in a lab with donor organs and the patient's stem cells. The scientist directs the donor organ to morph into the patient organ, effectively creating a brand new organ. An accelerated process. Very expensive, highly regulated, but legal."

"Donor organs?" Janey asked. She shivered. Her friend Christine's organs had been taken. She'd heard of organ harvesting, but she thought that had only happened in the past, decades before her time.

"Donated from accident victims," Soren replied.

"But isn't that rare?" Janey asked, dread in her chest. Had she stumbled on an illegal organ trade? Christine's death had been nearly six years ago.

"What are you thinking?" Valdez asked.

"I don't know. It could be nothing." Despite the cold, sweat trickled down her back. She wanted to get out of the morgue, run on the treadmill, and process these new facts that could relate to Christine's murder. But she couldn't. She had a case to solve. Her first murder on the station. Her first murder as lead investigator. The clock was ticking. She had to call in the homicide and catch a killer.

"Let's hear it, McCallister," Valdez said.

"After I get out of this clean suit. Can't think." Janey breathed out. Panic was setting in. The med clean suit reminded her of the skin-tight space suits.

Valdez said and turned to Doc and Soren. "We're done here, yes?"

Sweat trickled down her back.

"Yes, that's it for now, Investigators," Doc said. "We'll call you if there's anything else, including a specific time of death."

"I'll send the DNA results as soon as they're done processing," Soren added.

Janey closed her eyes and panted. "Any idea when that might be? I need to call Milano. I'd like to tell him we have a suspect." She'd didn't want to say that everyone on the station was technically a person of interest.

"Hard to say. I'm on it, Janey. Rest assured," Soren said.

"Thanks, Soren. I know." Janey said her good-byes and rushed for the scrub room.

She heard Valdez's footsteps behind her. He said nothing as they stripped off the scrubs, throwing them in the recycle bin. She shivered. Her systems were all wonky. She felt Valdez's gaze on her and glanced over her shoulder.

"What?"

"Nothing." He kept his gaze averted.

"Your heart rate was elevated...is elevated. Never mind. Mine too." She sat on the bench and clicked up the heat on her jacket. That was better. She rubbed her eyes and hit the comm.

"What is it?" Milano said, his voice slurred with sleep.

"Sorry to wake you, Chief. McCallister here. There's been a death on the station. Doc confirms that it's a homicide. We need to put the station in formal lockdown. I need your approval."

"Yes, you have it. Che cavolo! Dammit. Schoeneman is going to hate this." He blew out a breath. "Who was the victim?"

"Dima Bakaj, sir."

"Dio santo! Call the on-duty and get the lockdown taken care of."

"Will do, Chief. Sorry to wake you."

"Hell of way to start a day, McCallister," Milano said. "Do you have a suspect for me?"

"Not yet. We're running down the DNA we found at the scene, gathering footage. I'll report when we know more."

"The Sol investigator with you?"

"Yes."

"You'll need to search his people's jet, just in case,"

"Haven't they been regulated to the hanger bay?"

"Do it anyway. Cause of death?"

"Doc says a heart attack brought on by a massive overdose of the drug Ghost."

"Just find out who did this," Milano said. "Work fast. Schoeneman will be on his way here as soon as he hears."

Oh great. That was what she feared. Having the big boss breathing down their necks and scrutinizing her every move.

"Of course, sir. McCallister out."

TWENTY-ONE

Janey rushed out of the scrub room, past the lab shelves crowded with gadgets, and exited the lab. Valdez followed, without speaking—thank the stars. She kept up her long-legged pace.

What she needed was to run down the long, curving corridors—to think—to go over everything she knew about Christine's case. She should've requested the case files years ago, as soon as she got her investigator's badge in Space Wing. With this new insight into stolen organs, maybe she could finally bring justice for her friend.

But not right now.

Right now, she needed to catch a killer.

Without breaking her stride, she commed Quincy. When he answered, she said, "Please implement lockdown."

"Yes, sir."

"And assign the rest of the on-call security team to the hanger, just in case."

"Expecting trouble from miners waiting for StarEl Earthside?" Quincy asked.

"No, not expecting, but—"

"Better safe than sorry."

"Exactly." She commed off and ramped up to a jog.

"We're in a hurry? Or you running from something?" Valdez kept pace with her.

"Yes," Janey said. "Need to think."

He gave her an understanding look.

Before she knew it, they were back in the conference room. It was 1 a.m.

"Coffee?" he asked, standing in front of the auto-brewer.

"No, thanks. I only need to solve this homicide before zero six tomorrow, I mean 6 a.m. I mean today. In five hours. Sure, no problem." She scrubbed her face and stared at the murder board, not seeing it.

Christine, what did you get mixed up in? Was this case connected to her?

"Why, Janey, what's up? You sound positively frazzled, defeated even." Valdez struck a light tone, leaned on the kitchenette counter, and crossed his arms. "We've barely begun."

She paced in front of the murder board, unlocked it, and stared at the timeline. No clear suspects, and she needed results. They all did. Frustration roiled in her chest. She shoved Christine's case out of her mind and took a few deep breaths.

Handle what's right in front of you.

She could do that.

"We? Why are you still involved in this?" she asked. "This isn't your case any longer. Yours was over when your suspect was murdered."

"I told you—to assist. Plus it's too late to leave. You

know two heads are better than one. Besides"—Valdez stepped closer to her—"we're good together." He raised a hand, as if he was going to touch her cheek, but then dropped it at her somber glance. "How can I help?"

"I need to figure out what I don't know and what I need to know. We need a suspect pool." Janey turned to pace the length of the room. The eggshell-colored recyclo flooring of the conference room was oddly attractive. The tiny dots in the faint patterned soothed her.

"Okay. Talk it out," Valdez said. "I'll take notes." With a hand hovering above the wallscreen, he drew a horizontal line under hers from 5 p.m., when they both last saw Bakaj, to 11:21 p.m., when the call came in and near the approximate time of death.

"Out loud?"

"That's what I mean by talk."

Janey made a face at him.

He quirked a smile. "Come on. Time waits for no investigator."

"I know." She blew out a breath. So much was at stake. What if they didn't find the killer? What if he or she killed again? What was the motive? The questions kickstarted her brain.

"We know Bakaj had dinner with the chef. We need to talk to her. He may also have spoken to the bartender."

"Gina and Faizah, noted," Valdez said and wrote their names. He knew their first names.

"I'm waiting on Shawhan for the compilation of footage of Bakaj's movements. Then there's the hallway traffic to examine."

Valdez wrote "Footage" and "Hallway."

"We can do that here, yes?"

"Yes." She tapped her chin. "There's the DNA sala-mander-like trace we found on the safe."

He wrote "DNA."

"The partial fingerprint on the button."

He wrote "Partial print."

"The DNA trace on the collar."

He wrote "DNA collar."

"The scrap of paper that was in Bakaj's hand," she said and then commed Soren and asked him the status of the DNA trace on the button, the partial print, and the scrap.

Valdez wrote "Scrap."

"I'm finishing the analysis as we speak and sending it to you … now," Soren said and the murder board pinged. "No dice on the partial. There was no core or delta, and the quality was too low. Just an edge." The core was the center of a loop or whorl, and the delta referred to the triangular ridge pattern of the fingerprint that went in different directions above and below a triangle.

"Either the person had a glove with a tear or—" Janey started.

"No prints. I've seen it," Valdez said.

"Did you get the scrap?" Soren said.

"Got it," Jane said and opened the image. It was an enlarged scan of the scrap of paper, along with details on the paper content—ordinary; writing ink used—also ordinary; and transcription of the text, written in tight, square capital letters.

"DNA is still processing," Soren said and commed off.

"It's a list of eleven names." She read aloud, "Jonatan Petrovich; Pierre Rainier; Seranjo Vossinick. Mikhail Andropov. Who are these people?" All traditionally male names.

"Either Bakaj's allies or enemies, debtors, or trade partners, I'd guess," Valdez said. "I recognize the sixth name down, Spelto Ceriseo. He's been a person of interest in the Bakaj case for a long time. I haven't been able to track him down."

"Seems like a made-up name. Could that be an alias?" Janey asked.

"Could be. We've worked that angle but haven't been able to find his true identity. These industrialists are extremely cagey and secretive to protect their massive wealth and shield their companies from taxes," Valdez said. "I'll run down the other names in the Sol CID and search for connections between them and Bakaj." He waved in the names to his holo screen to search the Sol Unified Planets Criminal Investigative Database and returned his attention to her. "What's next?"

Shawhan breezed into the conference room. "I just posted the footage to the board and wanted to let you know in person," she said breathlessly, as if she'd run full tilt from the bullpen two offices down.

"Great!" Janey said. "Walk us through it."

Shawhan cleared her throat and glanced at Janey nervously. Janey nodded to give her the go-ahead. Shawhan pointed to still shots of Bakaj arranged in a line across the board and spoke, at first softly, then louder as she seemed to gain confidence. "He left his suite here, went to the SkyBar, and ordered a drink from Faizah, here. Faizah said he didn't speak to anyone, not that she could tell. I knew you'd ask me that." She glanced at Janey for confirmation.

"That's right."

She gave a small smile and continued. "He took his drink, a Lunar Rise Martini—that's a martini with aged lunar scotch—over to the lounge by the casino screen."

She pointed. "He spoke to no one, and no one approached him. I clipped vid of that, just in case you wanted to see for yourself." She waved over a still image, and they watched twenty seconds of Bakaj sipping his drink and staring at the viewscreen.

"What's he watching?" Janey asked.

"He called up the asteroid race on the guest screen. It's the semifinals," Shawhan said and blushed. The same game that had been on in the mess earlier that evening, and Shawhan had been loudly cheering on her racer.

"Run it again at half speed," Janey said.

"Did you see something?" Shawhan asked. "What did I miss?"

"Yes, his lips are moving," Janey said.

"Barely, wow, you saw that. I didn't notice." Shawhan set up the vid to play at half speed, and they watched again.

Guests strolled behind Bakaj. Servers rushed past with trays held high.

"He *is* saying something," Shawhan said with awe in her voice.

"I can read lips," Valdez said.

"What's he saying?" Janey asked.

"Not English," Valdez said. "He's saying 'pora pretty chisto.'"

"What does that mean?" Shawhan asked.

"I don't know. It's Ukrainian or Russian," Valdez said.

Janey waved the transliteration into the database. "Here's the translation," she said. " 'It's time to come clean.' " She thought about that for a moment. "What if he told someone you were bringing him in? That'd be odd. He seemed so secretive. He said no one knew he had the encrypted gem."

"And that got him killed…" Valdez said. "Perhaps."

"I'm sorry," Shawhan said. "I didn't realize he was talking on his comm."

"No need to apologize," Janey said.

"I'll get into his comms traffic," Shawhan said and scurried out of the conference room.

"I can get into his comms faster than she can," Valdez said.

"No, let her do her job. She needs the win," Janey said.

"Confidence builder. Understood," Valdez said and studied the other stills of Bakaj. He waved over a vid to play it.

They watched Chef Gina Gutierrez arrive at Bakaj's door, covered tray in hand. She wore a long, flowing black dress. Bakaj greeted the chef with a kiss on each cheek, and the vid cut to them leaving the suite together. It then jumped to another cut of them entering a lounge above the casino, the viewscreen set to the Earth from space. Again the vid cut to the chef departing the lounge and Bakaj a few minutes later. The next bit of the reel showed him weaving through the busy casino crowd, not speaking to himself or anyone else, and not stopping. When he entered his suite six minutes later, he looked healthy and calm.

The next bit of the reel showed only his door, then the medical team arriving.

"What's that?" Janey said. "Back up to the start of that clip, before the medical team arrives."

"What do you see?" Valdez frowned at the screen.

"The view of his door goes grainy and grey for a millisecond. Can you slow that down?" Ceiling cameras were mounted above each suite entrances and at three-feet intervals down the hall.

"It could be a smudge on the camera, a malfunction, or tampering," Valdez said.

"Could be, but I know what I saw."

"Your super eye."

"Yup."

Valdez adjusted the controls and ran the vid again at one-quarter speed. A grey blur passed in front of Bakaj's door. The moving image was faint, wispy like smoke, but more coherent and moving together, in the size and shape of a person's head and shoulders. A person hiding in plain sight.

She turned to Valdez. "Tell me about full-body cloaking."

In front of the murder board, Valdez snapped his gaze to hers. His movements stilled. All his vitals dropped, even his respiration slowed.

"Really? You're pulling a cold front on me?" Janey narrowed her eyes at him. "You know a lot about full-body cloaking, and you used such a device to get into Bakaj's suite to steal the gem. Didn't you?"

After a few seconds, Valdez blew out the breath he'd been holding. "Yes, I know about them." His vitals settled closer to normal.

She shook her head. "You're going to have to teach me that cold front trick."

He frowned at her. "I can tell you this. The cloak the killer likely used is not top of the line. Otherwise, we would see no trace of him at all."

"We don't know that it's a man," Janey said. "Bakaj was poisoned. Poison is more often than not a woman's method of choice for murder."

"Yes, but the force needed to overpower a strong man like Bakaj—puncture the jugular vein—"

"Would take a strong man or woman." Janey glanced

at the grey blur still image. "From the camera angle on the ceiling, it's hard to tell exactly how tall the person is. Maybe between five feet five to six feet. Great, we're looking for a person on the station, man or woman, staff or guest, in that height range. That's at least half of the population of L'Étoile. Five hundred people—give or take."

"True, but I may be able to narrow the suspect pool if I can sharpen the image," Valdez said.

"We need more footage for that," Janey said and checked the timeline. "From the time Bakaj came back to his suite until medical arrived, 10:21 p.m. to 11:24 p.m., roughly an hour." Janey contacted Shawhan to have her send the raw camera footage of the hallway for that hour. In two minutes, the vid feed was on the wallscreen, and Janey ran the through it first at 4x speed to pinpoint the grey blur, then slower to find the duration of blur's appearance. She grabbed the two seconds she found. "I have more for you to work with," Janey said. Valdez watched her play the two seconds at a super slow pace.

"Let me see what I can do," he said, and he waved over the board to send to his holos and sat down to get to work. For someone with no enhancements, Valdez was sure handy with his tech.

"What about the names from the scrap you were running down?" Janey asked.

"I'll wave you what I found," he said without looking up at her. "Just as I thought, these men were Bakaj's business rivals. Not much on them in the public realm."

"I'll cross-check these names with the current L'Étoile guest list. Maybe we'll land a person of interest that way," Janey said. In a minute, the results came back null. None of them were guests at the on L'Étoile. Great.

She stared at the still image of the human-shaped

smoke. While she couldn't make out any distinct features, if she did some geometry, knowing the height of the ceiling, the angle of the camera, the height of the door, she could determine how tall this smoke-covered person was. She did the math.

"I narrowed the height down to five feet seven," she said.

"Great," Valdez said, distracted.

She gave him space to work and examined the stills and vids again, reviewed Doc's findings, and then reviewed the footage of the crime scene. Nothing new stood out.

Finally, five minutes later, he punched a fist in the air. "I sharpened the image. Here." He sent his rendered image to the murder board and it took up two feet square. "Gotcha!"

"Thanks, nice job." Janey studied the enhanced shadowy image of a man's floating face. No body. The man had a fleshy, bulbous nose and a straight edge mustache goatee combo, all above the faint outlines of his neck and shoulders. The eyes were dark, empty sockets. "How could you render the details of the goatee and not the eyes?"

"Because of the way the light refracts off the old-model face mask," Valdez said. "The cloaking is good but not foolproof. The rest of the suit must be top-of-the-line."

"Maybe he's on a budget," Janey said.

"He would have gone undetected, except for your eagle eyes."

"True, then he may be well-funded," Janey said. "Now we need to determine: staff or a guest."

"That's your department"

"Yep. I'll cross-check the facial characteristics with

height, give or take an inch." Janey set the parameters for the hotel guest and staff databases, then ran the search. It would take a while to search everyone on board. Evidence pointed to a man, but they could be looking for a woman in disguise. Next, she set the database to run a headcount and make sure every guest and staff member were accounted for and were where they normally were. She also ran the shadowy image through her own personal database via ocular implant. It stored everyone she'd ever encountered.

While she poured herself another cup of coffee and savored it, her personal database connected via a quantum encrypted data flow to Rhea, where she stored her daily backups. No way could she actually keep everything in her head.

Now she had to wait. Maybe Soren had results from his DNA analysis. She commed him. "Anything on the DNA for me yet?"

"Yeah." His voice broke, and he cleared his throat.

"Did I wake you?"

"No, I'm fine. Only a cat nap. Hold on. Checking." Soren's comm went quiet, and then there was some faint swearing in a language that she didn't understand but sounded Nordic.

"You okay over there?" Janey said.

"Yeah, my shin didn't see the cart there."

"Careful, cowboy," Janey said with a chuckle. "Don't hurt yourself for science."

"Ha ha. Nothing yet. DNA results usually don't take this long. Let me check a few things and I'll get back to you."

"Thanks, Soren. We're counting on you. Clock's ticking."

"I know. I got this. Soren out."

Janey wanted to stretch out on the long conference table or maybe the rug and take a cat nap herself while she waited for test results and database searches. As Valdez said, time didn't stand still for investigators.

She turned to him. "Valdez, what do we have? And what's missing?"

"We don't know who specifically, and we don't know why."

"But we know when and by what. Around 11:21 p.m. and via Ghost, this lethal dose of Felicitan and high-grade cannabis. Tell me about the drugs used to kill Bakaj. You've seen this MO before, haven't you?"

He looked haunted "Yes, too many times."

"But used in murders, like this? Oh!" Janey slapped the table. "Why didn't I think of this before? Will you run this through the Sol UP crime database for other murders committed the same way?"

"Right. Of course. I should have thought of that too." He frowned at his holo and waved in the commands, his vitals showing elevated heart rate and respiration.

"What's wrong?" she asked.

He shoved away from the table, stomped to the window screen at the far end of the room, and stared at the distant field of stars. She stood beside him and let her shoulder touch his. He didn't move away.

When he started speaking at a low volume, his voice cracked. "I come from a rough area, at the edge of a corporate ag town. A fly-over speck of a city in the middle of the corn belt the world has forgotten—that has forgotten itself. The main industry, shooting up on Felicitan. My parents, that's all they did. I had to steal to feed my sister and me. Drugs were free. Food wasn't. Neither was housing or healthcare." He shook his head. "One day I came home to find Mom and Dad OD-ed on Ghost, the latest rage. At least that's what the med tech told me later."

"I am so sorry. How old were you?"

"Sixteen and mostly living on friends' couches." His vitals dropped to cool, as if he was freezing his innards. He slowed his breathing to next to nothing.

Janey inched closer, so more of her body heat could spread to his.

"They did it to themselves. With Bakaj's Felicitan." Valdez's breathing was shallow.

"And the cannabis?" She inched closer and took his hand. He squeezed it.

"High grade. Grown in the Kenten Southland. I haven't pinned down where Ghost was created, only heard unsubstantiated rumors that it was one of Bakaj's companies." Valdez stepped away from their warmth, let go off her hand, and turned his back on the stars. "Need to check on the searches." He clamped his jaw tight, headed back to the table and sat, not looking at her, and disappeared back into his work.

Her comm beeped. It was Soren. Finally.

"I have your DNA results from the button. But it's weird," Soren said.

"Weird how?"

"Three kinds of human DNA. Three people, not counting Bakaj. Sending now."

"That is weird. Thanks, Soren. Can you come to the conference room and explain the results?"

"Yah, sure. I'll be there in a sec. Soren out."

The murder board beeped with the incoming data: the DNA idents. Janey set up another cross-check of the DNA idents against all staff and guests on L'Étoile.

The DNA search results popped up. That was fast. Ah, because there were no matches to anyone on the station, staff or guest. Another dead end. Janey growled. How could that be? What was going on? A partial print that couldn't trace, and DNA that led nowhere. Was the suspect purposely looping them into a fruitless cat-tail chase?

Soren arrived and examined the board. "No matches? I need to check my work again."

"I'm sure you've double-checked them," Janey said.

"Twice!" Soren said.

"Could someone mask their DNA with another person's DNA?" Valdez asked.

"Not easily." Soren scratched his head, making his spiky hair stand up even more. "But there are factors that could affect people's DNA. Organ transplants, illegal enhancements, or cloning."

"Bakaj might have had his replacement organs grown inside another body," Janey said. "Could the host's DNA have mixed with Bakaj's? If so, then maybe that was his DNA on the safe in the paraffin. Oh, were you able to trace that?"

"I couldn't trace the paraffin—it's too generic," Soren said. "It is possible in some cases for organ host DNA to mingle with the recipient's."

"That could account for one of the unidentified DNA codes," Valdez said. "What about the other two? Maybe our suspect has switched out his organs too."

"Possibly. There's also the high-cost lab cloning of organs. That'd be an awful lot of trouble to go to for murder and theft." Soren blew out a breath.

"Maybe we're looking for a guest then. Someone of means," Janey said. "The organ cloning or transplant could have happened years ago and still be producing foreign DNA, right?"

"I have heard cases like that in the literature," Soren said.

"Where does that leave us?" Valdez asked. "The DNA is a bust in terms of a clue unless we have something to compare it to."

"It's a longshot, but run the unidentified DNA through the Sol criminal databases. If we get a hit—" Janey shrugged. "You tracked Bakaj here. Someone else could have too."

"True. It'd give us something to run down. On it," Valdez said. He waved in the commands and sat back. "So, how's it going on your searches?"

Janey waved aside the working search and called up a map of the station—all fifteen levels. She called up the biotrackers for everybody aboard. The map was lit up like a holly tree, red and green dots all over. Red for the staff and green for the guests—red in staff quarters and work areas, and green mostly in the casino, lobby, spa, guest suites, and upper recreation areas.

She then ran the biotracker dots for the hour leading up to the presumed time of death, 11:21 p.m. Red and green dots flowed a little or a lot, but only two green dots passed in front of Bakaj's door. She zoomed in to them. They were two guests who were on the same floor, in suite 45, and they were in their suite by 11 p.m. They might have heard something, but no reports had come in. And Lane had verified that.

She did a few knee bends, a few toe-raises, shook out her limbs, and checked the time. 2 a.m. "There are a few irregularities… Valdez, you're registered as a guest even though you're on the staff side. There are two other staff in guest suites."

"I'm sure that's not so unusual," Valdez asked.

"Not for these two staff members." Janey shrugged.

"Sleeping with guests?"

"Yes. Like anywhere, there's going to be hookups. Every time we've investigated, the parties always say it's consensual and non-remunerative," Janey said. Fraternization with the guests was frowned upon but not a firing offense.

"Okay, what else? Anything out of the ordinary?" Valdez examined the station map. "No guests where they shouldn't be?

"One. There's a guest in the kitchen." Janey tapped the board. "The chef doesn't want anyone down there, except kitchen staff."

"Well, she let Bakaj in there."

"True. The guest is a woman, Liz Read. So she doesn't fit our profile. I'd like to check her out anyway." Janey called up her profile. No picture, only a check-in date three days previous and paid up for four more days. She ran Liz Read's biotracker backward to the time of the murder. Her tracker shut off for an hour starting at 11 p.m.

"That's suspicious," Valdez said.

"You bet. And I can't dig any further into her records without cause. I need to talk to her."

"Shall we?" Valdez headed for the door.

"Absolutely. I need to talk to Chef Gina too about her dinner and meeting with Bakaj." Janey glanced at the murder board. The height match and facial recognition search was almost finished. "One sec." She waved in the commands to have the search results sent to her comm.

Valdez went with her. The door snicked open, and they stepped into the corridor.

"We're not dressed for the front of the house," she said and brushed his curly hair off his forehead.

"Our casual look should do. It's only 2 a.m. Who'd be

up? It's prime time for the diehards. But, jeans and jackets work for mavericks and the rich next-gen kids, which we could pass for if we're obnoxious enough." Valdez rubbed his hands through his hair so that his brown curls stuck out every which way. He swaggered, exaggerating his walk, and hiccupped a few times.

Janey undid a button on her shirt, shook out her hair from the elastic she always had it in when she worked, and pretended to chew gum. She skipped ahead of Valdez for good measure and loosened her gait.

She looked over her shoulder at him. "Stop staring at my butt."

"But it's such a nice one." He waggled his eyebrows at her.

As Janey crossed the quiet, near-empty front lobby, her comm pinged with the data dump. She stopped to study the list—the male staff members who met the height requirements and basic face shape from their grainy image and had no solid alibi for the time of the murder. Finally, a suspects list.

TWENTY-TWO

"What do you got?" Valdez asked.

"Leads from the facial rec." Janey did a little shimmy dance. Excitement jumped in her chest.

"Yes!" He pumped a fist in the air. "We're gonna have fun tonight!" He said that in a slurred voice. Ah, so he wanted to play the tipsy persona.

She nodded. "Hold on, babe. I got to send a wave back."

She recognized three of the seven men of the engineering, maintenance, and housekeeping staff on the list, including Richard Bander who'd served them tea in Bakaj's suite early that evening; Dewey Weiss, who was one of the engineers working on her office; and Sasha Boone in maintenance who'd helped her with her clothes maker fittings.

She waved over her comm to send the request to her on-call team—Shawhan, Lane, and Kou—to question each of them about their whereabouts around 11:21 p.m. They were to question the suspects one at a time and report back as soon as possible.

Then she linked her arm with Valdez, flipped her hair, and finished crossing the lobby into the casino. People played the noisy gambling machines, and a few poker tables had players and dealers. Janey didn't know the bartender, a slender woman with elaborate red braids on the top of her head and freckles highlighting her cheeks. Two guests huddled together at the bar, limbs draped over limbs.

As they came even with SkyBar, Valdez touched her arm, stilling her. He put his arm across her shoulders and opened his mouth to speak. But she jumped with her plan of action first.

"You get to the kitchen through the bar. Like we did earlier today," Janey said. "I'll take the swinging doors. But wait for my signal before you breach."

"What signal?"

"You'll see." She smirked, waved at him over her shoulder, and strode toward the far end of the casino, passing an empty restaurant.

Most of the high roller tables were vacant too, except for one near the enormous wallscreen. That must be incredible, playing high-stakes poker at the edge of space. What a way to spend one's free time. Not what she'd do with her extra money. Not that she had any.

She headed for the swinging door to the kitchen. It wasn't being guarded by anyone. That was odd.

As she approached the door, a big guy in black camos got there before she did. Hamish Fujimori was his name, according to her ocular screen. She showed him a small holo screen with her badge. "Station Security Investigator Janey McCallister. I need to get into the kitchen."

"I can't let you in," Hamish said, recognition in his gaze, arms across his wide chest. "Chef's orders."

"I don't have time to argue with you, Fujimori. Sorry about this." She kneed him in the groin.

He yelled in pain, and she pushed him over and rushed into the kitchen.

She hoped Valdez got the signal.

Janey jostled the swinging doors and dashed into the kitchen. She passed an empty supply room and quickly came to a counter. No one was there. In fact, as she headed deeper into the kitchen, she didn't see anyone. Not until she got to the big stoves. Wrapped in a long white apron and a short white cap covering her hair, one person was at the grill, frying up some eggs with grilled onions and oregano-and-rosemary spiced potatoes from the delicious smell of it. Janey stepped closer. The cook glanced up. It was Mai Chen.

"Janey, what are you doing here?"

"Are you the only one here?" Janey peered around, farther into the kitchen.

Mai Chen shook her head. "I think there's a prep meeting in Chef's office. An early order came in. I drew the short straw."

"Do you know who is in there?"

"Besides Chef?" She shrugged. "No. I've just been in the kitchen." She smiled. "Want anything?"

Janey waved her off and headed for the chef's office.

Mai Chen didn't warn her away. She wasn't protective of Gina the way the other kitchen staff had been earlier in the day. Thank the stars.

Janey didn't encounter anyone else on the way to the office. The door was shut. It wasn't an electric door but one with a door handle. She tried the handle. It wasn't locked, so she pushed her way in.

"Hey!" Chef Gina yelled. "You can't just barge in here."

"I can," Janey said. "I'm investigating a murder, and I need to speak to you about your conversation with Dima Bakaj earlier tonight."

The other person in the office turned around. It was Eliza Jamon, also known as Beliza Ramon, who Janey had spotted mingling with guests during the show the previous night. Tonight she dressed in a silk, black pantsuit with a dropping V-neck, a necklace of diamonds at her neck. Her Latina high cheeks looked more prominent than before, and heavy kohl accentuated her dark almond eyes. Bright red lipstick coated her lips.

"And I need to speak with you, Eliza, or should I say Liz Read."

"We are in the middle of a meeting, Investigator." Standing in front of her table, Chef Gina put her hands on her hips. In sleek black slacks, she wore a cream-colored angora sweater, with diamonds sewn into the sloping collar, revealing a bare shoulder. "Wait, a murder? Who?"

"Dima Bakaj."

"No!" Gina paled. Tears came to her eyes. It was hard to fake such a reaction of shock.

"What did you talk about tonight?"

Gina sniffed, but she didn't wipe at the tears on her cheeks. "Business. Investment. He wanted to help me expand."

"Is that all?"

"Yes. When? Did he suffer?"

"No, it was quick. It was tonight. Around 11:30 p.m."

Gina turned her back to Janey and leaned heavily on the table. Gina was taller than the five-foot-seven-inch person they were looking for. The tall chef was probably six feet without heels. Still—even though they were most likely looking for a man as their chief suspect, it was good to keep an open mind.

Janey then checked Beliza's staff record on her ocular screen. She was the right height. Plus, she showed up on biotracking as a guest tonight, as Liz Read. Yesterday she'd been registered as Eliza Jamon and she'd come up in the staff elevator with Janey under the name Beliza Ramon. Suspicious. The goatee could have been a disguise.

She spread her feet a little wider, ready for anything, and looked Beliza in the eye. "Come with me. I need to ask you a few questions. Now."

"No," Gina said.

"It's all right, Gina." Beliza stood. "I'll be right back." She turned to Janey. "Right?"

"Come with me, please." Janey waved for Beliza to step ahead of her.

"You have no right—" Gina said and reached for Janey. "I—"

Beliza shook her head at Gina and waved her off.

"I do." Janey followed closely behind Beliza, out of the office and through the kitchen. Valdez met her at the door to the bar's storage room and eyed Beliza coolly.

"Where are you taking me?" Beliza said, her voice even, her heart rate slow. This was a cool one.

"To an interview room. We need to ask you some questions," Janey said. "In private."

She took the staff door to the security wing and led Beliza to the interview room. Janey palmed the door entry holo, and the door clicked open. The room had a table and four chairs, two already set up at the table, cream-colored walls, and no windows.

"Do you want some coffee?" Valdez asked. "I want some."

Beliza shook her head. "Water, please. No ice."

"I'll take one," Janey said and turned to Beliza. "Please sit."

Valdez nodded and left the room.

Beliza sat with grace and folded her hands in front of her. "What is this about?"

Opposite Beliza, Janey leaned on the back of her chair. "Where were you at 11:20 p.m.?"

"I know you can track us. Why don't you tell me?"

"Well, Beliza, you seem to be a special case." Janey sat down and crossed her arms. "You came up with me on the staff side, and then you show up in our system as Eliza Jamon last night and Liz Read tonight. Which is it?"

Beliza crossed her arms and leaned back, relaxed, not concerned. "Do I need legal representation?"

"Depends. What are you up to?"

"Nothing." Beliza's vitals spiked slightly, and her pupils dilated a little.

"Who are you really?"

Beliza peered at her impassively, but her heart rate notched up another ten percent.

"Fine. We'll find out soon enough. The man who was just with me is a Special Investigator for the Sol. We'll get to the bottom of this."

There was a tap on the door, and Janey got up to open it.

Valdez carried two coffee mugs and a full water glass on a tray. "At your service."

Janey served the water to Beliza and grabbed a coffee mug. She inhaled the fragrant brew and sipped, lifting an eyebrow at Valdez. He shook his head slightly and gave her a small shrug. He eyed his wrist comm and glanced back at her.

Translation: Not much on Beliza—she was probably not their suspect.

On the table screen, Janey called up the data Valdez had compiled while he was out of the room.

Beliza took a sip of water.

Valdez leaned against the wall, arms crossed, and nodded at her. Her interview.

Janey studied the data. Beliza Ramon was her real name, and she was actually related to the chef, Gina Gutierrez. Second cousins.

Janey eyed Beliza. "Gina is your cousin."

Beliza sighed. "Mr. Schoeneman can't know that I'm her cousin."

"Why?"

She held the glass and stared at it. "He frowns on bringing family on board."

"You two are only distantly related."

"Enough to create a red flag in the application process."

"Why not arrive as a guest?" Janey sat back.

"I wanted to work with Gina. She was going to train me personally."

"I thought you were a project manager for the engineering department and in charge of supplies management."

"I am. But cooking is my passion."

Janey frowned at Beliza's profile, which posted nothing about cuisine training. "I still need an alibi for the time in question. And I need to confirm your DNA."

"Go ahead." Beliza pushed the half-empty glass toward Janey.

Janey entered a command into the table keyboard and scanned the glass where it stood. She sent the data to compare with the list Valdez had compiled.

"Your alibi." Janey prompted.

"Around 11:30 p.m.?"

"11:20 p.m."

Beliza stared at the ceiling. Her eyes glazed over and she stilled. Her heart rate and blood pressure elevated, her cheeks flushed, and she made strong eye contact with Janey. "Gina can vouch for me."

Janey glanced at the table screen. She'd set it to pick up olfactory particulates. Beliza's pheromones had spiked. Pheromones were often associated with sex.

"You two aren't really cousins, are you? You're lovers."

Beliza eyed the table and drew a random pattern in the water condensation. After a long moment, she finally whispered, "We're cousins only by marriage."

"You two were together at 11:20 p.m. last night."

Beliza sighed. "I'm sure your records will show that if you look at my ident under Liz Read." Her heart rate slowed and leveled out, as if revealing the truth calmed her down. Janey had seen that many times before with suspects.

Janey stood. "You're free to go."

"I'm not in trouble for faking idents?" Beliza glanced at Valdez and then her.

"I only handle special Sol-wide cases," Valdez said.

"As long as you don't start any fights or commit a crime, I won't come after you," Janey said. "Since you passed the health and wealth checks as a guest, and the Luxembourg headquarters has no problems, then I have no problems with you."

"Thank you. And the relationship?" Beliza stood. "Please—"

"I won't say anything to Schoeneman."

"Please say nothing to anyone. Our—it's so fragile.

She has to wine and dine so many men for her work. Investors, you know. She wants them to think she's available to them. And our thing is—" Beliza blushed. "New."

Janey nodded. "Private."

"You understand." Beliza headed to the door and then turned to Janey. "Did someone really murder Mr. Bakaj? That's horrible."

"It is." She firmed her lips and mimed zipping them. "I need you to stay quiet about our interview. It's an ongoing investigation, and we don't want to spook the guests."

"Even Gina?"

"Tell her to keep her mouth shut."

"Oh, she's very good at that." Beliza nodded to her and left the interview room.

Who else did they have to consider? She crossed to the table screen and studied the list of seven male staffers. Shawhan, Lane, and Kou had cleared all but one name, Richard Bander from housekeeping. The man who'd served tea the night before Bakaj died. The man she and Valdez had run into in the lobby on their way to the spa. He wasn't where he was supposed to be according to his biotrackers—his quarters—and no one near his quarters or the mess had seen him.

TWENTY-THREE

Janey took a gulp of the cooling coffee and studied Richard's employee record.

"Fill me in, McCallister," Valdez said.

"All the staff suspects have been cleared with check alibis, except for Richard Bander. He's not in his quarters, and no one knows where he is. His biotracker said he was in his quarters—"

"Ah, the old fake-out," Valdez said.

"Thought you said you didn't know how to trick the biotracker system."

"I don't if you're only using one identity."

"You think he's switched idents? How?"

"First, tell me more about him."

Janey summarized what was in Richard's employee file. "He's been on the station for ten weeks with no incidents and has worked in housekeeping and lobby service for high-end hotels for over two decades. He's forty-nine years old, from a small private-sector town on the Eastern Seaboard, and he received basic military training before working hotels."

"Let's go see for ourselves," Valdez said.

"Agreed. Staff junction three, level two." Down the corridor and opposite the security offices.

"We're going hunting," Valdez said.

"Indeed."

Maybe Richard was their guy. Maybe not. But why? What would motivate someone like him to kill someone like Bakaj?

They left the interview room and headed to the staff quarters.

"I ran his name through the criminal database," Valdez said.

"And?" Janey was glad the corridor was empty this early hour of the morning.

"And nothing. What do we have on him?" Valdez frowned.

"Only that he matches the height and face shape profile and has no alibi, and we can't find him," Janey replied. And that he gave her the creeps. But that wasn't enough to mention. She didn't know why Richard made her skin crawl.

Quincy commed her just as they approached Richard's quarters.

"Go ahead, Quincy," Janey said.

"Chief Milano wanted me to let you know that Schoeneman will dock soon—ETA thirty minutes—and air lock seventeen was just activated, unauthorized. Identity not in the system."

"Shit," Janey said. Was that Richard doing a runner? Why would someone take a space walk and think that would get them away from security? "Thanks, Quincy. Send the on-call team to the air lock. We're nearest that air lock. I'm going after…whoever is out there."

"Lead on," Valdez said.

Janey jogged, then ran, and Valdez matched her stride for stride down the grey corridor.

At the air lock door, Janey palmed the door, but it didn't open. It made an error beep, an annoying three-tone minor chord, more like a cat in pain than a machine indicating a malfunction.

"I got this," Valdez said. "I know some overrides." He fiddled with his wrist comm and his holo screen. Twenty long seconds later, the door slid open.

"Some other time, you'll have to tell me how you did that." She sprinted past him and grimaced at the familiar space suits lined up against the wall on hooks. One was missing. Their guy was out there.

Her comm buzzed against her wrist. Janey tapped her wrist comm to open the channel. "Quincy, what?"

"Heads up. Chief Milano is on his way to your location. Back up too."

"Thanks, Quincy. McCallister out."

Janey blew out a breath. Oh, Venus hells. Space walking. Her least favorite thing. This time it was after an alleged criminal and not some training maneuver.

She'd been top of her class in everything, except for the space walk. She'd barely passed the test after her third try.

It was good enough for the Space Wing Command. It was good enough for her, she reminded herself. Had to be.

She took stock of her weapons. She didn't have her standard issue weapon, only her small laser-sighted pistol in her boot holster, and there was a harpoon and all-purpose knife attached to the suit. The weapons locker was back in the security section on the other side of L'Étoile.

She removed her pistol from her boot and slipped it

into a pouch on the space suit. Ignoring Valdez, she stripped down to her skivvies—a long-sleeved thermal and short-pants underwear—and donned the space suit.

She was just getting dressed, she reminded herself. *Breathe, girl.*

The space suit was a multi-layer one-piece. The inner layer was a skin-tight insulating layer, like a wet suit. That layer was inside a state-of-the-art puffier ensemble, like snow gear, and it was made of near-indestructible carbon fiber nanofabrics. This gear would keep her body at room temperature in the frigid vacuum of space and protect her from the sun's harmful rays, as they were outside of Earth's protective atmosphere. She admired the engineering and ignored how her heart rate picked up as she slipped her legs in, then her arms, before finally closing up the front layers, zipper, snaps, hooks, and magnets.

These suits were a marvel of engineering, she reminded herself. Geniuses designed them, and heroes tested them ad nauseam. Space Wing believed in these suits. So did private corporate, asteroid miners, space adventures and ordinary Sol citizens. The suit durability was rated triple-A, and she was sure Schoeneman had spared no expense in keeping the suits in top working performance.

"Janey—you okay? Sorry, I can't come with. I only have emergency basic training for space suits, not authorized for combat training. I'm more useful here."

"Okay, fine." She finished securing the front. The suit was designed so one person could get into it without help, but Valdez made a spinning motion with his hand.

"Turn around," he said. She did, and he checked the slim oxygen and propellant tanks on her back. "Turn back." She did, and he checked her front hooks and belts and knelt to check her boots. The boots would zip her back to the air lock, handy jets on gyroscopes, though you couldn't tell by looking at them. They looked like ordinary thick utility boots. Bander had the same gear. She wouldn't be able to out-tech him. She'd have to rely on her inner resources. Who wanted to win more badly, her fight instructors said. And that required a cool head. Her heart was racing, her irrational fear wanted her to curl up into the fetal position and yank a blanket over her head.

Valdez must have noticed her fear, because he said in a soft voice, "Janey, you could wait until he comes back or shows up at the hangar or elsewhere. Or at least wait for Milano."

"He's out there. I'm not waiting for back up. What if Bander has a ship out there behind one of the recycler scows?" The robot recyclers operated just outside of high Earth orbit in the so-called graveyard orbit, where corporates sent their dead and dying satellites they could no longer resuscitate.

"Wait, Janey. Please. Back up will be here soon," Valdez said. "Nothing shows up on sensors that there is someone out there. Just because a suit is missing and the air lock opened—it could just be a fake lead to throw us off."

"Doubt it. The air locks are triple redundant and off the main electrical grid. Besides, we can't take that risk," Janey said and slipped in the earpiece and checked the suit's fluid tubing.

Never space walk alone, her instructor had told her—had told all of them in training. But this was an exception. She could do this. She had to do this. She breathed out, then in. Her heart rate was still up. She could live with that.

He gave her a stern look and handed her the helmet. "Comms are connected."

She slipped on the tight-fitting headgear that would connect her with the rest of the crew and twisted it for the click in place. Then she ran a soundcheck.

Valdez gave her a thumbs-up and waved open his holo screen. "Levels look good. Green. Nominal." He scrubbed his face, fatigue in his eyes. He'd been up for as long as she had. "I'm here for you."

"Thanks." On her ocular implant, her oxygen and fuel levels looked fine, too. Janey blinked at him and swallowed past the dry mouth. The pit of her stomach felt heavy.

Breathe through it.

Valdez peered at her with a frown. "I'm here if you need me." He didn't say anything about her deep breaths.

"One last thing," Janey commed Quincy.

"Sir."

"Make sure the nearby air locks and escape pods are guarded. Wake up the day shift early if you have to," Jane said and commed off.

She gave Valdez a thumbs-up and headed for the air lock door. She punched in her security code to the door pad and it slid open. It felt like her heart would leap out of her chest, but her actual heart rate hadn't shifted, still only slightly elevated. She stepped over the ankle-high riser wall into the small round room, large enough for four people. The door whooshed shut behind her. She was here, alone. Foolish. But time was ticking down. Bander could reach the hanger and the Sol jet there or float off to a rescue craft hidden in the space junk and recycler debris field.

In front of her was one more door. She only had to wait ten seconds for the small room to depressurize.

She yawned to counteract the tightness in her head, and her ears popped. Her chest felt tight. Breathe through the tightness, she coached herself.

The air lock slid open without a sound.

Black.

Stars, cold and white.

Nothingness, her mind whispered to her.

"Janey, you good in there?" Valdez's deep voice rumbled in her earpiece. "Your vitals show a jump in heart rate and respiration, blood pressure too."

"Yes, fine." She knew he was telling the truth, but it was hard to comprehend with the buzzing in her ears.

Well, here goes nothing.

Shut up, a stern inner voice said. The voice of her instructors.

You can do this, a softer voice chimed in her head. That was Mom, always encouraging, always there for her when it counted the most.

She could do this. Janey bent her knees and sprang toward the exit. In half a breath, she floated slow-motion in the zero-G of space outside L'Étoile. Its rounded silver hull extended out in either direction. It was huge, and she was an ant floating beside a behemoth.

Where was Richard? She couldn't look around—the face mask gave her a limited angle of sight. She grabbed the handle beside the air lock exit and swung for the ladder that was anchored nearby.

There was a buzzing in her ears. It was only the effect of the energy shield buffer. That was all. *Right.*

Breathe through the buzzing. She did it in training.

An indeterminable time later, she gripped the ladder rung.

"Hand over hand, Janey. You can do this." Valdez's voice came over the comm. He could see her on vid. No doubt he could see her heart rate shoot up another notch.

Janey ignored her vitals scrolling red on one side of her helmet screen and climbed up to the F panel ladder on the curved silver space station hull.

There he was, near a jet opening, fifty feet away from her on the G panel, walking slowly away. He'd turned on his magnetized boots. The Sol jet was docked in the hangar beyond that. Schoeneman's jet would be there soon, too, if it wasn't already.

What was Bander planning? Was he going to enter the hanger from the outside and maybe hijack the jet? He was an idiot if he thought he'd get away with it.

"Valdez, I see him. Alert the hangar and Sol agents he could be headed their way. Patch me through to the other suit." Janey felt her heart rate accelerate another notch.

It's all part of the chase, she reminded herself. Nothing to be freaked out about.

"Got it. Use the left-hand controls, finger to thumb, to comm him."

"Right." She knew that. "Listen in, okay?" Janey blew out a breath.

"Of course. Comm channels open here and to your security team. Quincy patched us through," Valdez's voice was steady, calming. "I'm not going anywhere."

Janey gulped and took a sip from the fluid tube. Nutrient-rich fluids flooded her body—an energy kick. She clicked the comm to the other suit. "Richard, hey. Wait up, man."

No answer.

"Richard, it is Richard Bander, yes? It's Investigator McCallister. Stop."

"Who?"

"Richard, I'm station security."

Richard kept moving away from her toward the hangar.

Janey waited a beat for her heart rate to slow. It didn't. She dove in. "I have to take you in, Richard. We can do it easily, or we can do the hard way."

"Go to hell."

TWENTY-FOUR

"I SEE YOU DON'T TAKE ME SERIOUSLY." JANEY'S breathing was way too loud in her ears. No matter. She had a job to do. "Richard, we only want to talk to you."

No answer. She tried again.

"Whatever you're running from, you won't get far."

No answer from Richard.

Janey bent her knees and jumped, putting all her force into it. She kept her gaze on the curve of the station's exterior surface and came down hard on one foot. She then bent her knee to push off and land on the other foot—the zero-G version of walking. Jarring vibrations shot up her leg and on up her spine. The boots were magnetized to the outer surface of the silvery space station.

She was on the day side, and soon the sun would make an appearance. For now, the focused beam from her helmet sparkled off the space station, so bright. The white light bounced off the silvery surface and reflected off her suit, coated with nano-mirrors. She dimmed her visor screen so the glare wouldn't notch up the low-grade headache blooming at her temples.

With each step, she focused on the tug and pull of her magnetized boots connecting and disconnecting with the hull. Her leg muscles burned as she tried to go faster. Anything to stay connected to her body awareness.

Richard leaped, too, putting him one risky jump away from the edge of the enormously wide opening to the enormous hangar. One more leap into open space and he'd float down into the hangar. Not an easy move, but doable. But a stupid one and dangerous. Station security would swarm him, not to mention Sol Police. What was his game plan?

He stopped near the precipice. What was he waiting for?

A red light flashed on her ocular screen. She opened the warning blip and swore. A tiny craft, no bigger than a personal vehicle, zoomed toward them. A beat-up recycler scow from the looks of the dents and patchwork of steel soldered together. Richard's pickup.

She had to stop him from reaching the scow. She opened the comm channel to him again.

"Richard Bander. This is Investigator McCallister, L'Étoile Station Security. You are under arrest for the murder of Dima Bakaj."

Richard stopped and turned toward her, his face visor full of reflections from the black of space, stars but mostly black. She'd been ignoring the black, but she couldn't ignore it now. She couldn't slow down the racing of her heart.

"The man was no better than a common thief. He needed to be stopped before he ruined everything." Richard's voice was gravelly, bitter, and full of anger.

"So you admit killing him." Janey kept her eyes on the man, grateful he wasn't moving, and she bent her knees and took bigger leaps. He pushed off from the edge of the hanger and toward the higher levels of the station and away from her. She followed, had to gain on him, one footfall after the other. She would not let him get away. Her muscles burned. "You know you just confessed, right?"

"So what? You'll never catch me." He unhitched his harpoon and a gun and aimed them at her.

Crap. She was only two leaps away. He had a clear shot with either weapon. She had no cover. Unless she charged him. No, that wouldn't work.

"Janey, get out of there," Valdez said, his voice taut, urgent. "Back-up is suited up and approaching from the opposite direction, but they're too far away."

Her head buzzed, and her heart clobbered in her chest. Her vision narrowed.

"Janey, jump!" Valdez said.

"What?"

"Jump. Demagnetize your boots and jump."

Richard pointed his harpoon outward toward the approaching craft. She understood now. He'd shoot at the craft. The pilot would send out a maghook to catch the metal harpoon. He'd shoot the gun at her as he escaped. Valdez was right. She had to time it right, throttle up the boots and lunge after him.

No, she couldn't. Sweat broke out on her forehead and over her whole body. She shivered.

Dammit, McCallister. This was it. She couldn't let the killer escape.

The recycler scow was slowing on its approach, three hundred feet distant from the hull. Any closer and it'd be zapped by the station's defenses. Whoever was piloting knew their defense systems. It was now or never or Richard would escape.

"Valdez, I need your help."

"You got it. What do you need?"

"Throttle up my jet boots past the safe zone. My suit will block me if I try."

"When?"

"Now!" Janey turned off the magnetic pull of the boots and pulled the pistol out of the pouch. "Freeze!" she shouted and propelled herself toward Richard.

He didn't even glance at her, so focused was he on the scow above him, above them.

She slammed into his body and grabbed one of his front hooks. The gun got knocked out of her sticky grip by the impact. There it was, floating barrel over grip into the dark, away from her and the station. Hells. At least it was also away from Richard.

The impact also knocked the harpoon out of Richard's grip, but he still had his gun. He grabbed one of her front hooks, their bodies sandwiched together. She had no room to maneuver. Valdez had cut the boot rockets and re-magnetized her boots. She was stuck in place, hanging on to Richard with one hand, no gun in the other. She was breathing hard. Her vision narrowed. Something like an elephant pressed on her chest. Panic attack.

Richard swung an arm up, gun in hand.

She had to get it together. She blocked his upward swing, but the gun went off a few inches from her, and the force snapped her head against the back of her helmet. The smoke from the blast billowed around her and blanketed her faceplate. Too much. She couldn't breathe.

"Janey, gun! Wake up!"

Shit. She'd blacked out for a millisecond. Red was flashing in her faceplate. *Warning. Warning.* Her suit was losing pressure and oxygen. The bullet must have grazed her suit and nicked one of the vital lines under the layers of carbon fiber nanomaterial.

"Engage auto-repair," Janey panted as Richard brought his arm back up, the gun pointed at her faceplate. Again.

"Let go of me!" Janey yelled and batted his arm away, again. The gun went off above their heads, the gun smoke cloud thankfully not in her face this time. She had to distract him. She released her hold on Richard's suit and pounded on the back of his hand gripping one of the front hooks on her chest. "Let go!"

He finally released her and floated backward. He hadn't re-magnetized his boots.

How was she going to get that gun away and take him in? Think. She'd practiced these scenarios in training, but her mind was blank. Maybe she could ram him, get him off-balance, get help… there was nothing wrong in getting help, using her team. They were on their way.

Janey grabbed her knife and jetted toward him, boot rockets throttled as high as possible. "Valdez, more power!" He gave it to her, and she rammed Richard, jabbing her knife through the thick bulk of his suit toward his ribs. She felt the soft thud in her center mass and knocked him off his perch. Linked together by her knife in his suit, they went tumbling into the black, away from the safe, silvery exterior of L'Étoile. They were free-floating in the nothingness.

Shit, shit, shit. What the hells?

A scream lodged in her throat. Janey closed her eyes against the spinning starfield and the lights flashing on her helmet's readout, clashing with her ocular implant's data.

Valdez came over the comm, his voice high and tight. "Not good, McCallister."

"Hey! Get off me!" Richard yelled. "What are you doing, lady? You're going to get us both killed." He aimed his gun at her again. He didn't seem to notice he'd been stabbed. Maybe his suit was auto repairing.

Her screen readout beeped red. Had she been hit? "Auto repair," she commanded to her suit again. Her voice wavered in panic. Her suit didn't respond with a characteristic beep to her command.

"Valdez! Activate manual repair!" Janey said, bile rising in her throat. Someone needed to reel them back in and now.

"It's not working," Valdez said. "Your suit's leaking. You have maybe five minutes of oxygen. You have to trigger the manual repair directly."

Janey groaned and opened her eyes. All she saw was black and stars far away, tumbling over and over.

She panted. Spots danced in her eyes. She had to keep it together.

"Janey, you need to repair your suit yourself," Valdez said.

She moaned. Double Venus hells. She tightened her grip on the knife in Richard's side. "I got him." Her heart sprinted for anywhere but here. The station spun in her center view. No, that was her and Richard spinning.

"Drop it," Shawhan's voice came into the shared comm channel, calm and measured. "We have a laser sight on you, Bander. You'll be incinerated in under a second."

"We also have weapons hot on your rescue vehicle," Lane said.

"Boss, you okay?" Kou said. The gang was all here.

"Go, team," Janey said. Yay. Her heart rate was still too high, but she could smile through the panic.

Richard released his gun, and it floated away from them.

She needed that weapon. She could do this.

Janey gave the boots some juice. Dragging Richard with her, she caught up to the weapon and grappled it into her pouch. He wriggled, apparently not as injured as Janey thought. Her shoulder muscles strained to hold on to him.

"Boss, the junker is leaving," Kou said.

"Not our jurisdiction." With her free hand, she felt along her belt. She depressed the button needed, and her suit's auto-repair kicked in with a whoosh and ding in her earpiece. Adrenaline washed through her, leaving her shaky. She gulped and peeked at her helmet screen.

"Good, McCallister. You're back to green. Nominal."

But it wasn't. The readout of her vitals appeared as gibberish. "Screen is wonky. Code, not words. What's happening, Valdez?" Her voice shook. Her brain wasn't working right. No ideas were flowing. Not good.

"You're doing fine," Valdez said. "Use your boot rockets to propel you back to the air lock."

"We got you, boss," Shawhan said. "We have your back."

TWENTY-FIVE

THE AIR LOCK DOOR OPENED, AND JANEY floated in, gripping the knife still in Richard. He'd been yelling obscenities for the last five minutes, but Janey had muted his comm on her end. She practically sagged panting against the wall, her legs rubbery.

The last few minutes were a blur, just holding it together, focused on the air lock portal. The round room re-pressurized. Janey waited until the door slid open to the anteroom and handed off Richard to two day shift security agents, knife and all. He still seemed unaffected. The two agents, Mandlenkosi Dube and Natalia Goldberg, marched Richard between them toward the other side of the air lock to get him out of his suit under guard.

Valdez was waiting for her. He tapped on the glass of her helmet and mimed taking it off. She nodded and let him help her. She didn't need to be so independent. She needed help, even from him. A smidge of pressure released from her chest at the thought.

He pulled off her gloves and lifted off her canisters.

These suits were designed for one person to get into but usually needed at least one other person to get out of.

"You okay?" he said softly, standing close to her, gazing at her, looking concerned.

"Killer headache. Forgot about that part." She grimaced and pulled the tabs and hooks on her top half. "I'll be fine." But she leaned against the wall. Air was hard to come by.

"Hey, Janey, you need help getting out of the suit?"

"No, I can do it." Her voice sounded tinny to her ears. She shivered and smiled weakly. "I mean, yes, thanks."

He put a hand on her shoulder to steady her as she pushed from the wall.

"Stay here in case I fall over." Janey clamped him on the shoulder. His strength felt real, felt good. "Thanks."

"Post-opp adrenaline crash," he said and stayed as she managed the other snaps and connectors.

She was about to strip the whole skin-tight suit off, when across the room, Richard exploded in a whirl of kicks and punches. Taken by surprise, Dube and Goldberg were down in a flash.

Without thinking, Janey acted.

"Freeze," Janey said, his gun pointed to his head—her gun was still tumbling in the black.

Richard glanced at her, defiance in his gaze, and he sprinted for the door, not at all affected by the knife wound. The door swooshed open before he got there. He somehow managed to unlock it from one foot away. She didn't know anyone who could do that.

Janey sighted lower and shot, and Richard crumpled to the floor, yowling.

"You shot me!" He grabbed his shin.

"Surprise. You'll live," Janey said. "It's a through and through."

The bullet had embedded in the thick wall.

Valdez lifted Richard off the floor and cuffed him. "Doing your job for you, agents."

"He surprised us," Goldberg said, rubbing her chin where Richard had clocked her.

Dube hustled over with the first aid kit, cut off Richard's pants, and wrapped his lower leg. Even with a limp. Richard had thwacked him in the groin.

Janey stripped off the rest of the space suit and donned her jeans, sweater, and coat as quickly as she could.

"Let's go," she said and motioned for Valdez to lead Richard into the corridor.

"Hey!" Richard yelled. "I need a hospital! This is a human rights violation."

"You were attempting to flee arrest. So, no, it isn't," Valdez said. "Besides, it's only bleeding a little."

Richard glanced at Valdez. "Who the hell are you?"

Janey jumped in before Valdez could speak. "We'll properly introduce ourselves when we all get settled. Or not." She turned to Goldberg. "Have medical meet us in the Interrogation Room Two."

"Yes, sir."

"And take his suit in as evidence," Janey said. "Get Soren on it."

Goldberg nodded and got to work.

"Let's go," she said to Valdez and waved him ahead.

In the observation room, fifteen minutes later, she and Valdez sipped coffee and watched through the one-way transparent partition as Richard squirmed and rubbed the bandage wrapping his calf with his foot. Medical had found the smallest of nicks in his side. The self-repair unit of his space suit had worked superbly to cushion her stab wound.

"Shall we go in and relieve him of his boredom?" Valdez said, eyeing the one-way transparent partition.

Time to discover Richard's motive and who he really was. He wasn't only a standard career-class hospitality worker, not with his fighting and space-walking skills.

"It's about bloody time!" Richard shouted at her when they entered the interrogation room. He rattled his cuffs, linking him to a hook in the center of the table.

Janey sat and tapped the table twice. A screen illuminated before them, filling almost the entire table of six feet wide and four feet across. Soren had worked fast and gotten what they needed off the suit Richard had worn.

She rearranged the images on the table and started in. "With your DNA from your suit, we found you." She tapped a grainy image of a younger Richard from about ten years ago and enlarged it in the center. "We know you're a part of a Russian separatist cell, the underground, and you go by the name of Mikhail Lebedev."

Richard, or Mikhail, said nothing.

The image showed a grainy mug shot, text typed in Cyrillic beside it, and data scrolling across the bottom of the page. "The Russian GRU has a dossier on you and an outstanding warrant for multiple crimes including theft, bank robbery, and data theft." The Russian Empire Secret Intelligence Unit. Janey sat back.

He shrugged. "It is nothing."

"Since you've already confessed to the murder of Dima Bakaj, this"—she waved between them—"is more of a formality. When we're done here, the Sol police will take you into custody. I hear the lunar penal colony is pleasant this time of year."

Richard grimaced. "You're not taking me anywhere. So I confessed. So what? You have no evidence to link me to the crime."

"We'll have it soon," Janey said. "Why did you do it? Revenge? Somebody put you up to it?"

The door swooshed open, and Schoeneman barged in. Richard paled.

Janey stood. "Sir, I'm in the middle of my interrogation."

Valdez's vitals dropped to cool and hiding mode, reminding Janey of the baseline of a lizard.

"I need to speak to your suspect, Investigator. Now. Clear the room and cut the feeds!" Schoeneman barked.

TWENTY-SIX

JANEY OPENED HER MOUTH TO PROTEST BUT caught Valdez's eye. He shook his head slightly at her. She shut her mouth, tapped the table screen to make it go dark, and left the room, Valdez right behind her. She strode to the viewing room and stood in front of the one-way pane.

"You're not going to turn off the recording?" Valdez said quietly, his shoulder touching hers.

She shrugged. "I don't manage that equipment."

Schoeneman stood across the table from Richard. Janey couldn't see the casino owner's expression, but her ocular implant could read his vitals fine. They were calm —too calm.

"He does vitals suppression like you," Janey said.

"I knew there was a reason I didn't like him." Valdez frowned at Schoeneman through the pane.

Richard was sweating, and his vitals were racing, as if he was running from a predator.

"Do you happen to know who runs the penal colony on the moon?" Schoeneman said conversationally.

Richard shook his head.

"I do." Schoeneman headed for the door and then turned to address Richard. "If you want halfway decent treatment there, you'd best cooperate with the investigators." He shrugged and made a chopping motion with his hand. Death. "Or else."

Richard flinched.

Then Schoeneman left the room and from the sound of his footfalls, he strode away from them.

That was it? That was all he interrupted her interrogation for?

Janey eyed Valdez. "Did he just intimidate and threaten my suspect? Now, why would he do that?"

"Why, yes, I believe he did. As to why..." Valdez frowned and said bitterly, "The rich and powerful aren't like regular folk."

"No, they're not." She scrubbed her face. "Schoeneman is not a man to be crossed."

"You didn't know that?" Valdez said wryly.

"Rumors only. Never met the man until now. He always keeps his face in the shadows, except to those he wants to intimidate." Janey watched Richard through the glass, who was rattling his wrists against his cuffs. "I think Richard's trying to figure out a way out of those."

"He doesn't know that they're old fashioned low-tech devices." Valdez chuckled. "That metal is soldered to the table."

"Did you see in his Russian records that he's an engineer, specializing in nanotech and biomechanics?"

"Yes, I saw that. Doesn't explain his martial arts moves in the anteroom and toughness in the field, though. Basic training doesn't prepare you that much." Valdez flipped open his holo-screen. "Let me see if my contacts with the Russian separatists have gotten back to me about Richard Bander or Mikhail Lebedev and can shed some light on his background."

"Mikhail Lebedev is also probably not his real name," Janey mused. "I'm going back in. You coming?"

Valdez pursed his lips at his device, then finally looked up at her. "No news yet. Yep, I'm with you."

He was with her, all night working. She quirked a small smile at him and brushed passed him and exited the viewing room.

"You know you want me," Valdez called after her.

"Not the time, Valdez." She palmed into Interrogation.

Richard glared at her and rattled the cuffs against the ring. "What do you want?"

"Why did you kill Bakaj?" Janey sat and tapped to make the table screen come to life again. Richard's scruffy mug shot filled the screen. "I could always turn you in to the Russian Empire. They've been hunting you for ten years."

Richard rattled his arms in the cuffs. "No. No way, man. Their gulags—he said— he said…" Richard calmed. "He said he'd take care of me."

"Who did?" Janey asked.

"The man who was just here." Richard tipped his head to his shoulder, trying to reach his ear. "I got an itch. Can you—?"

"No." No way she would get close to him. He'd probably pull a move. She didn't want to give him a chance to attack her. "Tell me why you killed Dima Bakaj."

"We couldn't let his secrets out." Maybe he'd been looking for the information stored on the gem, only Valdez beat him to it.

"What secrets?"

"About the cure."

"To what?"

"Felicitan, Ghost, what do you think?"

"Why you?"

Richard sat back, a smug look on his face. "Why not me? I'm good."

"Not that good. We caught you, didn't we? You're working for someone. Who?" Janey sat.

Richard eyed the right ceiling corners, as if looking for cameras. The cameras were there, but they were tiny, too small to see for those with normal vision. He examined the other side of the ceiling. "This room bugged?"

Janey slapped the table. "Who? Who hired you to kill Dima Bakaj?"

Her comm beeped a priority alert from Shawhan. She tapped it, and the message opened on the table. Vials of the Felicitan drug and high-grade cannabis had been found in Richard's room, both labeled from one of Bakaj's labs. Richard had made his own mix of Ghost. There were vials of blood in his mini-fridge, and there was also evidence of paraffin and bio-organic plastic residue on the food crafter. Janey guessed Richard had used the paraffin as a carry agent on his gloves, laced with the DNA in those vials. The bio-organic plastic residue could be used to make cloaking material. Soren would confirm her guesses.

"Where did you get the ingredients for Ghost?" she asked Richard.

He scratched at a smudge on the table.

"Here's how it will go," Janey said. "We'll turn you into the Russian Empire, and they'll send you to the ice gulags. There's no coming back from that place."

"You can't do that. I'll die there."

She wanted the one truly responsible for Bakaj's murder, not a foot soldier, but no one knew who actually ran the Russian separatists. Lieutenants popped up, generals even, but every time they were captured or killed, another one would take its place. A multi-headed hydra.

All this time, Valdez had said nothing. He now pushed off from the wall and stood beside Janey. She peered at him. He lifted a brow in a question, and she nodded. Let him take a run at Richard. They'd get what they wanted, either way. They were a team.

"You stole something from Bakaj. Why?" Valdez asked.

"Shouldn't the question be 'where is it?'" Richard rattled his cuffs.

"We'll find it," Valdez said.

Richard shrugged. "It was in the safe. I thought it would be valuable."

"So, you don't know what's in it."

Richard frowned, then look puzzled.

She glanced up at Valdez. "That would be a 'no.'"

Valdez nodded thoughtfully and stepped back to lean in the corner.

"I just have one question, Richard," Janey said.

"Just one?"

"Don't look so smug. You're going away for the rest of your life."

Richard shrugged and spoke. "I have been working a long time before anyone caught me. You're the first. It's new."

"I'm flattered. I think," Janey said quietly. "Who do you work for?"

Richard shook his head. "If I tell you, I'll be killed."

"We can protect you. Make a halfway decent existence for you." She stared him down. "Who do you work for?

Cooperation, remember? You heard what the man said, earlier."

His eyes widened. He got her reference to the moment Schoeneman had threatened him. He shook his head and tightened his lips.

"Richard." She let the warning drip from her voice.

"I only know one name." He wouldn't look at her.

"Go ahead."

He stared at the table and whispered, "Phoenix."

TWENTY-SEVEN

"WHO IS PHOENIX?" COULD THE CHEF, GINA Gutierrez, be this Phoenix? Her restaurant was Red Phoenix. But Janey had no evidence connecting the chef to any illegal activities, not yet anyway. Never mind that the chef was a pompous, entitled haughty woman. Janey's personal feelings were not evidence.

"I swear, lady, I don't know."

"That's Investigator McCallister to you."

"Investigator McCallister, I never met him."

"Him. You sure?" she asked.

"Or her. I don't know," Richard said. "I only knew my cell. My group."

"Where?"

"Vladivostok."

Russia.

"When?"

"Over ten years ago."

"So you've been a sleeper agent since then in the Eastern Seaboard?"

"Something like that."

"Explain."

Richard slouched, looking small, defeated. "I was sent on small jobs. Petty theft. I was never caught. I think they wanted to keep me on my toes."

"Who was your contact?"

"He's dead now."

"Who was it? We need to know."

"I only knew my contact as Pedro. He lived in Newark when I was in Livingston."

"Last name."

"Ivanovich." Richard stared at the table.

Valdez sucked in a breath. "I found the connection to Phoenix."

"Ivanovich?" She glanced at him.

"No, Spelto Ceriseo—one of the names on Bakaj's list," Valdez said. "Enough to follow the thread." He sounded excited, like a bloodhound on the hunt.

Her comm beeped. It was another message from Shawhan. They found the little black book hidden in Richard's quarters, wrapped in cloaking material at the bottom of a pile of dirty clothes. She acknowledged receipt.

She grinned not a kind grin at Richard. "We have the black book found in your quarters, wrapped in the cloaking material you wore to commit murder."

Richard sat back in his chair, slumped his shoulders. "I should have left sooner." He shifted in his seat and rattled his cuffs against the center hook. "Do I really need these on?" But his words had no heat. He knew he was beaten.

Janey gave him a look, and he stilled.

"Why didn't you leave sooner?"

"My ride. She was late," he said glumly. "Never rely on others. All these years solo…"

There was a knock at the door.

"Those will be my guys," Valdez said.

"Do you have enough to take him in?" she asked.

"We do," he said.

Janey unlocked the door and two guards entered, huge burly guys, each twice as wide as Richard.

"He's all yours," Janey said to Valdez. Her chest tightened. He was leaving. Doing his job—as she was. It would be strange to solve cases without him. He'd gotten under her skin in only two days, okay, almost three. They made a good team. Maybe she could get used to this interagency teamwork.

"Can you unlock the center loop?" Valdez asked.

Janey pressed a button under the table and fished the tiny steel key from a drawer that slid out. She undid the lock holding Richard's cuffs to the table hook. Low tech was necessary in times like these. Too many tech-enhanced suspects had gotten out of cuffs in her experience.

Without a word, the two big guards shackled Richard and led him out the door. Valdez followed them out but glanced at her, part excited, part apologetic before continuing down the hallway and out of sight.

Janey stood in the empty investigation room. Valdez hadn't even said good-bye.

TWENTY-EIGHT

Janey shut down the table and room recordings.

"Status, McCallister." It was Chief Milano. He hadn't shown up at the air lock as Quincy had told her. He'd probably been monitoring from his office or the bullpen.

"I'll have your report in one hour." Janey strode out of the interrogation room and headed to the other side of the service level to her quarters.

"Thirty minutes, Investigator."

"Sir, I've been up for over twenty-four hours. I'd like to—"

"Thirty-minutes, McCallister. Send it, then report in person." His voice was stern.

"Yes, sir." Janey commed off.

She had to stop pushing the rules. Milano wouldn't bend to her needs. What was she thinking? She was looking out for herself because no one else would. But she got it. Schoeneman was probably breathing down Milano's neck. And she didn't need for her boss to find a reason to fire her. After the shaking probationary period, she'd done good work. So what if it wasn't always at Milano's tight timetable?

Janey dictated the report as she headed for her quarters and took the world's fastest shower. She dressed and checked the time. She had five minutes to proof her work, and then she waved send. By the time she was at the chief's door, she was composed, professional, ready.

She left his office two minutes later. The man had barely looked up from his screen as he read her report before he sent her away.

At least he didn't say anything bad, like "you're fired." No, she'd closed two cases for them—and fast.

She needed sustenance, and not the fabricated stuff she could get in her room. So she headed for the conference room. Kim was brewing a fresh pot of coffee. Its rich aroma filled the room, a hint of cinnamon wafting in the air. The murder board was still up, full of notes, data, the timeline. She'd need to take that down, make sure it got archived. Time to move into her new office anyway.

"Ah, there you are, hero of the day," Kim said and bustled toward her. "Let me give you a hug."

Janey let her. Kim stepped back and examined her. "What's wrong?"

Janey shrugged. "Nothing your amazing coffee and Mai Chen's pastries won't cure."

Janey served herself and sat at the end of the table where she gazed out the window and admired the live feed of how dawn pinkened Earth's curved horizon. It was less scary now after her walkabout earlier, but not by much.

Kim plopped down with her full, steamy mug and a cinnamon twist still radiating heat. Janey's own cream-filled donut waited at her elbow.

"Spill." Kim sipped and gazed at her from over the top of her mug.

Janey glanced at the faint stars and sighed. "The case is over. Both of them. Standard end-of-case blues."

"Go get some rest. There will be plenty of time for a pity party later. I need to report to the admin desk. My shift starts in—ten minutes." Kim gave her a stern look. "And you've been up for over a day. Bed for you."

"Yes, ma'am." Janey headed for the door.

"Hey, Janey?"

Janey turned around. "Mmm?"

"Can I have your special donut?"

Janey chuckled. "Of course." She waved over her shoulder and stepped into the grey corridor. Time to check in with Mom, who'd be getting up soon, then shut-eye. She was officially off work for the next seventy-two hours.

Milano commed her. She blew out a breath of exasperation. "Yes, Chief?"

"Good job, McCallister. Meant to say that earlier."

"Thank you, Chief."

She had her job, a boss who recognized her work, and she had made a few new friends. Not bad for her first month in her new occupation as a lead investigator on a space station hotel-casino for the extremely rich. Her new home for the next four years.

She made it to her quarters without falling over.

"You have a message, Janey," Rhea said. Her personal AI had a soothing voice.

"From Mom?"

"No, he says he's the hottie you've been lusting after all day."

Janey stripped down to her skivvies and fell into bed. "Play it."

"Sorry I had to leave like that. I owe you a dinner," Valdez said. "I'd send you a sexy vid, but I'm on the jet with these yahoos." His team yelled protests in the background. "Janey, see you soon, querida. And don't forget to send me the gem when you're done with it." His warm voice rumbled low and steady, like how he'd guided her through the space walk earlier. He was steady, and he was warm, and he'd been vulnerable with her.

"That's it?" Janey asked.

"Yes, would you like to send a reply?"

"Sure." She smirked. She knew exactly what she would say. She wasn't all work and no play after all.

———

WOULD YOU PLEASE HELP OTHER READERS discover and enjoy Janey's adventures by leaving a review on Goodreads or wherever you love buying books?

Then read on for a sneak peek of *Lured By Light*, Book 2 in the Janey McCallister Mystery series, where Janey cracks open the world of high-priced escorts and human trafficking.

LURED BY LIGHT EXCERPT

CHAPTER ONE

JANEY McCALLISTER, LEAD CRIMINAL investigator at Bijoux de L'Étoile, the planet's most luxurious space station hotel-casino, sipped the vermouth she'd been nursing the last hour and pondered the stars in the SkyBar screen viewer.

She was off duty and using the time to worry about her mother. Mom's new experimental treatment was holding, but for how long? Her thoughts kept drifting to *him*, then she shut them down.

From where she sat, the view was outstanding. The last guest to use the screen viewer had left it at high magnification centered on the luminous star Rigel—the big beautiful one at the foot of the Orion constellation.

The Orion constellation was actually a nebula—a nursery where stars were born. The most brilliant star in the constellation, Rigel shone achingly bright in the rainbow-speckled starfield, its stark and perfect beauty calling to her. There was no atmosphere between her and it to mar its brilliance. A perk of being in high-Earth orbit, in the fanciest, most exclusive space station turned famous hotel-casino.

Scientists said there was a massive black hole at the center of the Orion Nebula where all matter near it had disappeared.

Just like her love life.

Normally at 10 p.m., she'd be in her quarters, getting ready for bed, chatting with Orlando, flirting while he was on his lunch break in New York, but he'd dropped out of touch about two weeks previous. So there wasn't any point in hanging out in her teeny space waiting on him.

What the Venus hells had happened?

She thought they'd had a pretty good thing going—vid calls nearly every day for two months, sharing stories about their workday—it was almost like he was there with her. He'd made her laugh. He listened to her. She'd liked that about him.

They'd met on a case on L'Étoile. An intense, rocky beginning, but then they connected. And how! Like two stars colliding and making something new. Then he was gone, and she didn't know what this new thing was or had been.

Was he okay? Or was he just being a jerk, playing her like she'd thought when they first met? Even though he'd come clean. It'd been for the case, he said. Yet there were layers she didn't know about Orlando Valdez, Sol Unified Planets undercover cop.

Why was she pining after him? She had her friends. She had her mom. She had her interesting job that kept her on her toes. She had the amazing starfield views. If he wasn't reaching out to her, he wasn't worth her time or energy.

The stars held no answers.

Didn't matter. Her life was here at Bijoux de L'Étoile, hotel-casino space station, the premiere experience for those chasing the latest glamorous thrill. And she was paid—and paid well—to preserve the guests' safety, jewels, and reputations. So that's what she'd focus on.

"Take my mind off pointless black holes," she said to Faizah, the bartender on shift. "Let's talk Kim's surprise party. Help me plan it." Janey was dressed in her casual-chic off-duty outfit—stylish jeans, a jacket, and a sea blue silky blouse—preferring those to the jewels, gown, and the heels she wore when she was on the job watching for card sharks and pickpockets.

Kim Iona's birthday was in two days, and Janey wanted to give her friend something to smile about. She'd seemed down lately but wouldn't tell her what was up.

Kim Iona was the security staff office manager. Ten weeks ago she'd helped Janey out with a challenging murder case. That was when she'd met and clashed with Orlando.

Faizah smiled and gestured for her to hold one moment while she served another guest at the other end of the bar. The elegant older woman wore diamond studs in her ears, and if Janey wasn't mistaken, tiny diamonds even adorned the woman's silver hair, which was done up in a coiffed, fancy bun. Her neck was adorned with a diamond choker. Her jewels must be worth at least the value of a major corporation zone. Such wealth could be helping those who needed it, not adorning some rich maven on a pleasure stay at one of the most exclusive casinos in Earth's orbit. Then again, maybe the woman donated twice that amount to helping people in need. Janey tried not to judge.

The woman grabbed her cocktail and, at a quick pace,

she crossed the bustling casino floor and headed toward the viewing area, where guests clustered to watch the acrobats in their nightly zero-G show. In her off-the-shoulder silver shimmery evening gown, fit for a ball-room, the woman sat gracefully in a grouping of couches facing the floor-to-ceiling window and applauded dancers in jetpacks and sequined slim-fitting space suits. In the background, the starscape sparkled through the thick viewscreen windows.

Just another evening living it up in outer space.

Faizah came back to Janey's end of the bar, a laugh in her voice. "You're here to bug me because I didn't reply to your comm?"

Janey swiveled back to her friend, who tried to hide her mirth behind a lifted elegant eyebrow.

"You know it." Janey gave her a mock-stern eye and tugged on her leather jacket collar. "I want to get this party planned by tomorrow night, so not last-minute. Never know what I might be dealing with." Odd cases pulled her away when she was on-call.

"Relax a little, *Shigetu*." *Beautiful* in Oromo, the predominant dialect in Ethiopia. "You could be dealing with a *who!*" Faizah winked and twirled one of her rainbow ribbons entwined in her braids. A tall Ethiopian beauty, Faizah was dressed as a flamboyant hippie tonight with her faux-leather fringed jacket and ribbons.

"None of that." Janey's heart fluttered. "Haven't heard from him in over two weeks. Thought we had good vid-pal thing going." Constant contact for eight weeks, almost every night since he left. That was a relationship. Right?

"Of course, I'll help you with the party. You've been brooding here for an hour. Why don't you call *him*?"

"Did. No answer. Not even a way to leave a message."

Janey lifted the glass of clear liquid to Rigel and its nearby supposed black hole. "Here's to my non-existent love life. Not sure why I bother."

"He could be working…"

"I know." Janey finished her drink, sighed. "He could have at least told me he was going undercover. What if …"

"You want another?" Faizah asked sympathetically.

"Want? No. Need? Maybe. But no, that's enough of a nightcap. I have an early start tomorrow." As usual. She stifled a yawn and stared up at Rigel.

Maybe she didn't know him as well as she did. Maybe they weren't colliding stars after all, just one big black hole.

She rattled her empty drink, ice cubes clinking. Rehashing how he ghosted her wasn't going to help.

Faizah headed back down the bar to serve more patrons. The casino was busy as usual at 10 p.m., but it was close to her bedtime. She wanted to be up for a 7 a.m. vid call with Mom, so she could check in on how the latest doctor's visit went. Then she had to be ready for her 8 a.m. team briefing to get her security team up and running for the day. Except for that murder a couple of months ago, they handled mostly petty theft, cheating at cards and the other casino games, and sorting out staff altercations. She yawned again.

Faizah came back down to her side of the bar. "*Shigetu* —investigations, you're great at, but parties are my domain. Let me plan the party. I'll let Kim know, and we're good to go."

"Don't tell Kim. It's supposed to be a surprise party."

Faizah frowned and rinsed a glass. "Stop with the surprise party angle. Kim hates them."

"But she handles surprises at work so well," Janey said.

"Which is why she doesn't need any in her private life."

"Makes sense. So what shall we do?"

"How about a picnic in the arboretum?" Faizah asked.

"A potluck! Kim loves my mom's cherry pie recipe."

"Perfect! You round up the friends and menu, and I'll clear it with Madge. I was going to check out the teff starters she set up for me."

"Does that mean you'll bring your yummy bayenetu?" Faizah's vegetarian ampler plate on injera bread was delish.

"Absolutely!" Then Faizah headed to the thirsty guests clamoring for refills and to the waitstaff bringing orders over from the raucous gambling tables, crowded three people deep.

Janey sipped the last drops of her watery drink and surveyed the busy casino from SkyBar one last time. The swirl of movement around the huge room was like eddies and waves and currents, as random and complex as any natural phenomenon. Men in tuxes or long jackets and women in elegant gowns or chic pantsuits drank as they gambled, laughing and chattering.

She said good-night to Faizah and stood up to go. Just then, from deeper in the casino, a young woman in a short, rainbow-sequined, barely-anything-there dress dashed past the bar. Fear had tightened the young woman's mouth, her olive skin splotched red. Her short brown hair flopped in her bloodshot eyes as she pushed through the crowd, saying something Janey couldn't hear above the huge room's clangor.

She made barely a ripple in the boisterous, game-playing crowd, but Janey noticed her. She was trained to notice anything out of the ordinary.

She sucked in a breath at the uncanny resemblance to her best friend, Christine, who'd been dead six years now.

Time to find out why the young woman was in such a hurry and so distressed.

Janey rushed to intercept the woman's trajectory toward the casino exit.

Janey strode through the crowd while her ocular implant did a facial rec and fed her the woman's name and hotel registration: Amelia Gain. Her check-in date was seven days ago, her hotel registration and premium room service paid for by a Kave Holdings, a coffee corporation. She looked young, probably no more than twenty-three, but corporate often sent their staff to L'Étoile as a corporate perk or for bonus vacations.

Amelia's heart rate accelerated, and her breathing shortened—all details Janey registered in a flash on her ocular implant in her right eye, which scrolled data continuously across the top of her visual field.

Janey was two arm lengths behind her, then one. Close enough to hear what the young woman was saying under her breath.

"Oh my god, no! No more. I can't...He can't...I won't..." Amelia's words burst out between sobs.

Near the slot machines at the casino entrance, Janey reached out to touch Amelia's shoulder to slow her progress and get her attention. "Can I help you?"

Amelia flinched from Janey's outstretched hand and shook her head. Tears streaked her cheeks. "No!" Her strident voice carried above the hum and buzz of slot machines.

Casino guests glanced in their direction, shock and even disapproval on some of their faces.

"I'm security." She showed Amelia the holo of her badge, flashing up from her wrist communicator. "What's going on?"

Amelia shook like a leaf in a strong gale and stared at her, as if not comprehending. She glanced over her shoulder, back toward the bar, the poker tables, and the restaurant. Her gaze darted up toward the mezzanine level, where the hotel had private and secure meeting rooms.

Janey didn't see any movement out of the ordinary. No one was on the stairs between the mezzanine and the casino floor.

"Is someone coming after you?" Janey tried again.

Amelia's lips quivered. It was like Christine was pleading with her. Janey blinked. No, it was Amelia pleading with her eyes. In the next moment, apparently no longer able to hold herself up, the young woman collapsed in Janey's arms, babbling hysterically. Janey caught the words, "Hate him. No more. I can't take it anymore. Got to getaway. Got to."

Janey wrapped an arm around the girl's slender shoulders, helped her stand, and hustled her past the noisy, bright slot machines and into the elegant hotel lobby. She was thankful that the lobby was at that moment mostly empty. At the welcome desk, Peter Redstone, one of the hotel managers, was on duty. Concerned, he glanced at her.

Janey mouthed, "Back door."

Peter nodded and pressed a button under his counter. A door cracked open in front of Janey. It led directly to a service elevator that would take them three levels down to the security wing. Saved time.

In the almost four months Janey had been on the station, she'd found all the short cuts and secret passages she could use. The station maps for the guests didn't show these secret passages, and neither did the station maps for new employees.

Helpful in a pinch, like this one. She wanted to slip away from the front of the house as quickly as possible, in case this woman was in danger. Even if she wasn't, Janey would get to the bottom of this—whatever was happening here. She always did.

"This way," she said, leading Amelia into the secret passage and onto the elevator. Amelia didn't resist.

A few minutes later, Janey guided the young woman out of the elevator and down the grey corridors of the security wing. Amelia's sobs slowed a little. Her bioreadings were a bit wonky, fluctuating on Janey's readout screen faster than most people's. Understandable given the girl's circumstances.

Gazing about at the grey corridor walls that curved toward what was for her a distant unknown, Amelia seemed to come out of her upset and wriggled out of Janey's arms. "Let go of me! Where-where are you taking me?"

Janey lifted her hands, palms out. "It's okay. I won't hurt you. I'm Janey, and I'm with station security. Remember?" Janey flashed her badge via her wrist holo screen again.

Amelia peered at her with wide eyes, an unusual violet, her pupils dilated. Could she be on a synth? Drugs flowed freely on L'Étoile.

"Security? Then you-you can help me, right?" Amelia covered her mouth, holding back a sob. "I just-just had to get out of there! He-he...no more. I can't take it anymore." Janey's readings for the young woman flickered for a moment on her readout screen and then showed a slowing and more normal heart rate.

"I can help you, if you're in danger." Janey slipped out of her sheep-wool lined leather jacket and wrapped it over the girl's bare shoulders.

Amelia shivered and drew the jacket closer around her. Janey wrapped an arm around Amelia's shoulders again. "Come on. I'm taking you to a safe place, so we can talk and sort this out. And we'll warm you up."

"Where?"

"To the conference room a few doors down."

"Who's we?"

"Just me and a friend, my colleague." Janey led Amelia to the conference room around the next curve and palmed open the door. It snicked open with barely a whisper.

"You'll be safe here. It's the security staff wing." Janey led the girl to a cushiony chair at the wide table, near the coffee maker.

Amelia sat and stared at the view, another wide expanse of stars. Someone had left the viewer at high magnification on Saturn. Probably Kim. She knew Janey loved Saturn. All those rings and moons.

Janey sat beside Amelia and asked, "Do you have someplace safe to go?"

Amelia just shivered and rocked in her seat. A soothing gesture.

"Water? Coffee? Tea? Something to eat?" Janey popped up and busied herself with getting a glass of water for the young woman.

No response from Amelia. Shock could be setting in or a high melting off.

Into her wrist comm, Janey waved to medical

requesting a full workup for a possible rape victim. She needed to cover all bases.

"I could use some coffee too," Janey said quietly. It looked like it would be a long night.

She'd been helpless when Christine went missing. She'd been untrained and hadn't seen any of the signs to indicate her best friend wanted out of their wonderful life. She'd been powerless to do anything to help Christine.

She wasn't powerless anymore.

She had the full weight of her investigative team, the authority of being lead investigator. She'd prevent anything worse from happening to this young woman.

The best thing she'd done for Christine was to find her body when the police couldn't. It'd broken her heart. There was no way in Venus hell she'd ignore the signs let any bad befall this girl in front of her.

———

READY TO RESERVE YOUR COPY OF *LURED BY LIGHT*? Click here to preorder wherever you love to buy books: https://author.bethbarany.com/lured-by-light/

ACKNOWLEDGMENTS

So many people helped me create the book you have before you. A huge thank you to all of you! It takes a village to create the world that lives in this book. Special thanks to:

To my Early Reader and Beta Reader teams, including Ashley Hedden, Beth Perry, Bob Morton, Briana Burgess, Carol Malone, Catriona Bain, Danielle Jones, Dodie Coe, Harland Monroe, Hayley Guertin, Hugh Tipping, Joyce Tang, Kay Lalone, Ken Rahmoeller, Keri Kruspe, Lea Kirk, Marilyn Lugner, Mary Van Everbroeck, Meisha Mull, Mellissa Green, Mylène Priam, PJ Ferguson, Sally Stackhouse, Sarah Monroe, Shelly Small, Tess Rider, Tinthia Clemant, Trent Gaylord.

To my Patreon supporters: Chloe Adler, Elayne Griffith, Janet Patterson, Lisa Boragine.

To my students for giving me feedback during our One Hundred-Word critiques classes.

To my first cover designer, the awesome Elayne Griffith, who helped me refine the cover concept and shape the book titles.

To my amazing, diligent, and patient critique partners, Patricia Simpson and Kay Keppler.

To my mastermind group, Leanne Regalla and Bonnie Johnston, for their moral support and cover feedback.

To my Blurb Babes, Lea Kirk and Tess Rider, for never ever tiring of refining my book blurbs.

To my proofreader, Paul Martin of Paul Martin Editorial.

To Dr. Peter Swan, International Space Elevator Consortium, who helped me with backstory on StarEl.

A huge second thank you to Bonnie Johnston for her belief in me, amazing brainstorming sessions, and incredible unflagging support.

And a universe-sized thanks to my dear husband and fellow creative nebula, Ezra Barany, for all the re-reads, edits, and more edits, and geeking out on science right alongside me.

ABOUT THE AUTHOR

Award winning author, Beth Barany writes in several genres including young adult adventure fantasy, paranormal romance, and science fiction mysteries. Inspired by living abroad in France and Quebec, she loves creating magical tales of romance, mystery, and adventure that empower women and girls to be the heroes of their own lives.

For fun, Beth enjoys walking her neighborhood, gardening on her patio, and watching movies and traveling with her husband, author Ezra Barany. They live in Oakland, California with a piano, their cats, and too many books to count.

Sign up here for news on new releases and other goodies: http://bethb.net/itbbk.